Julio Toro San Martin

Among the
Dark
Places
of the Earth
and other stories

JOURNALSTONE
YOUR LINK TO ARTIST TALENT

ISBN: 978-1-68510-045-2 (sc)
ISBN: 978-1-68510-046-9 (ebook)
Library of Congress Catalog Number: 2022939739

First printing edition: July 15, 2022
Published by JournalStone Publishing in the United States of America.
Cover Design: Don Noble
Edited by Sean Leonard
Proofreading and Cover/Interior Layout by Scarlett R. Algee

JournalStone Publishing
3205 Sassafras Trail
Carbondale, Illinois 62901

JournalStone books may be ordered through booksellers or by contacting:
JournalStone | www.journalstone.com

Dedicated to all my family and friends. "Now faith, hope, and love remain—these three things—and the greatest of these is love."
—1 Corinthians 13:13

Contents

AMONG THE
DARK
PLACES
OF THE EARTH
and other stories

R

Excerpts from a small diary:

Entry 1
I cannot control this any longer. R. says to look at his navel. He says there is an eye. I look, and I see there is. It even blinks.

***

Entry 2
For what he lacks, he has acquired an extra thing.

***

Entry 3
The eye astonishes me when I look at it. It follows me when I move. I ask R. if he does this. He says no, that it moves of its own volition. I don't like this. R. is terribly frightened. When I run my hand down his belly I can feel another protuberance. I think a nose is coming, also. The eye looks at me. I don't like it. It has an evil look to it. There is an intelligence behind it, but I don't think it is either of man...or of beast.

***

Entry 4
R. yells at me to get rid of this demon growing inside of him!

***

Entry 5
We went to sing today. R. sang as usual with the voice of an angel. R. kept his hands mostly on his belly, like a pregnant woman. I

laugh to think of it...but, I don't want to take the comparison too seriously. It isn't normal.

***

Entry 6

The new priest inquired about R. today. He notices a slight growth on my friend's belly. He wanted to know, he said, a bit embarrassed to ask, I think, since he said it like this, "Is it ... I mean ... is it possible for you fellows to get pregnant?" I laughed, and said of course not. He laughed and said he just asked since he wasn't used to being around people like us. I told him R. was just overindulging in food, that it was nothing.

***

Entry 7

The Black Bishop said it wasn't necessary for R. to show up at the church choir any longer. He said I could if I wanted to, and could also attend to my classes at the conservatory. In our private rooms, at the end of the city, he visited us and said to R., "It comes perfect through you, who are neither complete man, woman, nor child."

***

Entry 8

R. asked me to tell him again how it was for me when it happened. He has morbid curiosities now. I told him how I sang as a child in our little parish. How much also my grandfather enjoyed my singing, asking me to sing for him whenever I could. I told him of my father's death, and how my uncle decided it would be best if I was castrated, that with my singing I would have a beautiful career, that the voice of the angels would sing through me and never leave me. An operation was planned. I was rather old when it happened so I have some use of my member. R. is especially fascinated with this, and a little sad. When it was done to him, he was completely emasculated.

***

Entry 9

I try to keep R. away. I have had success, and have many visitors now. The Maestro di Cappella said that in no time I will be singing in the Opera House. A Lady from Firenze visited me recently for a private audience. I entertained her in my room as best I knew. Before this, R. came into our shared living space and made a spectacle of himself. I don't know what is wrong with him. He grows forgetful. He passed us and returned to his room, just as abruptly, keeping the head that is growing out of his belly, hidden. The Lady laughed, and asked, "Musico, why does he hide that melon under his shirt?"

***

Entry 10

I fed R's second head today. It snarls. At night it whispers blasphemies. There is a strange look of amusement, mystery and evil written on its face.

***

Entry 11

He stays in his room, weeping, and lying supine. I ask to see him. He tells me to stay away. Last night, I entered his room secretly. I opened the door, and saw him silhouetted against the light from the full moon outside his window. He had no shirt on. I saw that hideous head, snarling from his belly. And also, now, two long bony arms sticking out of his stomach flesh. A new body is emerging out of my friend. He smells like a charnel house.

***

Entry 12

The Bishop has returned from the Black Pilgrimage. They have taken my friend away. I was told I can visit him if I want.

***

Entry 13

I returned today. I have been busy. My fame spreads. But I must see my friend with whom I was initiated at a young age into the sect. When this ordeal is over we will all have great fortune, but I regret that R. took this course. I do not think he was prepared. But truly, can anyone really be prepared for such an experience contrary to all natural law? Were we prepared when castration was done on us? And is this procedure not worse?

Before letting me see R., the hunchbacked porter asked me to make the black sign, and then read to me some pertinent words from the Scrolls of Pith:

There is a place where black things crawl, and no sane mind dare taste of its madness, for there evil has made its home and things not good to look at stare at other worlds with eyes of greed. Fortunate, or perhaps unfortunate, are they who manage to cross, for a little while, its dread Lord into their domains to taste freedom from his realm, for this he grants great wishes. But first, the sacrifice must be made of one worthy for the fire.

He then unlocked the metal door, and let me look at R. Oh, horror of horrors! I nearly faint to write it. *What did I see?* My eyes burned with tears! It crawled around like a spider. The lower body and legs were those of my friend ... but his upper half was separated into two separate torsos, heads, and sets of arms!

One torso is R's, while the other torso is our lord's. This new upper body had grown to rival R's own! Two torsos! A head on each torso! Each torso with its own two arms! The snarling head laughed, while R's made no noise, but was obviously in the most horrible of griefs. The thing was bent down hideously from its back, and the legs and arms touched the floor. This thing moved around like a contorted centipede. In the darkness the two heads looked like hanging mandibles. The hunchback laughed, and with a gleam in his eye, said, "There is another him that is within him, rising. It is our lord. Do not feel sorry for him, but for yourself. The sacrifice must be by fire."

***

Entry 14

I have seen R. again. He is fading into our lord, Mastema. Where once the lord was emerging out of R, R. is now disappearing into the lord. R. is only a head now on Mastema's belly. The body he spewed forth swallows him into itself. Like water into water. They are switching places. R. does not talk, only gibbers.

***

Entry 15

I can only see R's eye staring out of Mastema's navel. It is moist, and teary. To where has my friend disappeared? What must it be like in that foul place, whence the demon came, and to which R. goes?

***

Entry 16

R. is totally gone. Now there is only the Dark Lord.

***

Entry 17

Great news! I will finally sing at the Opera House! No more private concerts in great houses. All of Italy will know me. Today, when the Maestro told me, we dined on the most sumptuous of meals. Afterwards, I sang and played the harpsichord to great applause. I hear the Prince himself will write the piece I am to perform!

***

Excerpt from Travels through England, Italy and Greece, Volume 1, by Jean-Pierre Lafosse:

Of these, Mastramore was one. He was a tall, thin castrato, long-faced and clumsy, as these creatures often are, whose crowning achievement at an opera I have not forgotten even after all these years. The hunchback I sat beside was particularly struck by him, and irked me with his incessant chirping of, "Look, look! The sacrifice must be by fire! By fire it must be!" But as for the capon, such a voice he had! *Par les dieux!* Such strength, skill, and virtuosity! Such ethereality, as if Orpheus was come, or an angel had fallen from paradise! His long, graceless arms, ungainly walk, and pronounced jaw were completely offset by this!

Then, from the stage, arose a man dressed as a shaggy-haired, goat-footed, black thing, which sat on a throne like an ancient pharaoh, or Anubis. I was repulsed, as were most of the audience members in the stalls and boxes. As Mastramore sang, and the creature arose, there descended mechanical spheres, which I took to represent planets. The elaborate stage machinery then descended one of those spheres, into which the eunuch entered, and was locked. It then rose, and burst into flames. I thought this was some misfortune, as did most of the audience, when we heard the man scream and flail, but we all were calmed when the orchestra continued playing. The beast on the throne laughed with a hollow timbre from hell, as the hunchback cried, "The sacrifice has been accepted!" Then the spectacle continued without the castrato. It was the most atrocious of works, and yet I hear that those involved in its performance have gone on to great things. It was called, I think, "The Festival of Moloch." Mastramore has disappeared from history, and I can find no further information about him.

The Seeder from the Stars

Always, the High Priestess communed with her Lady, Inanna.

We lived in the great temple ziggurat, and out of all her servants and retainers, I alone can boast that I was the closest to her, in her detached affections.

My Mistress was the En-Priestess of the Moon God, Nanna, but his daughter, Inanna, was the deity most dear to her heart.

I served her in the high place, closest to the stars, charting the heavens and their revolutions. I saw from above the great city, clearly—the vast buildings, houses, orchards, and agricultural lands. My name is Smenkhkare.

Always, she'd say strange things to frighten me, and that I didn't understand.

I knew she was possessed of the divine, and that I, a mere commoner, could never know of such things. But I was proud to be the friend of such a mighty princess, and to serve her, body and soul, in the Temple of Ur.

Because my Mistress was a member of the Royal House of Akkad, and En-Priestess of the Moon, her decrees were unquestioned. She handed out many secret prohibitions, such as: never to peer behind the curtains of the Holiest Room.

The years rolled unnoticed in the Temple of Nanna, in the now far city of Ur, and great were those early times. Great was the drink of youth we enjoyed. Great, especially, were the hymns of my Mistress, Enheduanna.

If I praise her too much, it's because I can do no else, and if I speak of myself but little, it's because I am not important.

* * *

Ishme arrived from the ruined city-state of Kazalla, from west of the Euphrates River, in the seventh year of my Mistress' En-Ship, without father or mother, and orphaned to the world. He'd been found amid toppled blocks of burnt mud, clothed in filthy rags, and eating dirt and crawling bugs. I was assigned to tutor him in the duties of the temple, but early on, he showed promise of greater things. Secret rumours spread that one day Ishme would outgrow the temple, and leave to be a great administrator.

Because I was the boy's principal teacher, he was moved to call me 'Father'.

I was pleased with this.

* * *

My Mistress took an early interest in the boy also. She taught him much of her secret wisdom, but of the hidden thing of darkness that was whispered to live behind the curtains, in the Room of Nanna, she remained quiet.

When sometimes, because of the rashness of his youth, he'd say something untoward towards the noblewoman, I'd scold him severely.

"Do you think of him as our son, perhaps, Smenkhkare?" she'd insinuate and laugh.

Oh, never let it be imputed to me that I, Smenkhkare, ever harboured any sacrilegious thought towards the Holy One of Nanna!

One day, as the three of us walked the lonely corridors of the dark temple together, a crazed man approached and attacked my Mistress with a sword.

Ishme jumped in front of her. Quickly, the rest of the temple household, having heard our commotion, arrived and subdued the man.

* * *

All night my Mistress knelt by the bedside of Ishme, praying her beautiful poems under the stars. Her poems had power to soothe the gods, had power to change their wills, or could summon screeching Ereshkigal from the nether hells. But this day, the high gods remained silent.

I knelt beside her. I looked at her eyes and saw, for the first time—the second would be many years later—that they were watery. I reached out and touched her shoulder, covered by her woolen robe. I touched her just this once, and she didn't stop me.

"Why did the boy do such a thing? I could have protected myself," I heard her say. We both wept together.

Then she arose and left the room.

* * *

Hours later, after the temple physicians told me the boy's health was worsening, I went to look for my Mistress, and found her behind the curtains.

Strange now were her songs, strange yet beautiful, sung in a language I didn't understand, and that disturbed me deeply. I let her finish.

When she emerged, I looked at one of her hands, and saw she carried something. I could not make it out.

Entering the boy's room, she ordered everyone out, except for myself.

Then she placed the thing in Ishme's wound.

I heard the boy cough.

I looked and saw the boy's wound was healed. The child looked at us, perplexed. Then he turned to Enheduanna, opened his arms, and hugged her tightly.

* * *

Shortly after my Mistress' assassination attempt, great anticipation engulfed the temple. Sargon, her father, was coming to Ur. From atop the stony girths of the temple, Ishme and I watched, engrossed, as the Great King with his hundreds of military men, carrying weapons of flaring bronze and sturdy bows, marched in ordered phalanx into the celebratory city. Later in the day, a small band of mercenary men arrived, and encamped on the outskirts of Ur.

We knew they were hostile towards my Mistress, and her father.

He conferred with his daughter and counselors in the temple, instead of in the customary palace of the ancient kings of Ur.

"The whole of the city-states of Sumer," I recall the Great King saying, "are not pleased being ruled by just one city. They want their autonomy back.

"It isn't safe here anymore."

"I have sung to the gods," my Mistress said, while braiding a lock of hair dispassionately, "and will sing again. They are always pleased with my offerings."

"It isn't only the gods that keep you safe, daughter, but also the sharp edge of my battle-axe. When I go to the distant north, what great army will stop the rest of the Sumerians, as now Uruk and Lagash do, from rising against you? Your death and dethronement from the High Place of Nanna would be a great blow to my ambitions. Come with me and be safe."

My Mistress laughed fearlessly, and showed those terrible eyes, while saying, "My Lady, Inanna, loves me as she loved you long ago, when you were taken from a basket and placed as the Cup-bearer to the King of Kish. She helped you usurp that dreamer, Ur-Zababa, and now helps you in this empire that you create for Akkad. But she helps me also. She's given me a pet. With this pet I'll strike such fear into the traitors' hearts that they will cower like defenseless babes, and dare not rise against me."

"Do this, then," Sargon said, with a ferocious look. "Show this beast, tonight. But if, by tomorrow morning," he warned, "the forces of our enemies are still encamped, I'll flay them alive, and then you'll come with me to the far north, where already great hosts of my armies march."

He left immediately. We were left speechless at what we'd heard pass between them.

* * *

A mist-enshrouded evening came.

That night, as the High Priestess sang her songs in the Inner Sanctum, Ishme and I went to one of the higher places of the storied temple. It was especially dark that night, and the strong fog, which was heavier in some places, and sparser in others, made visibility a jest. Yet, still, we tried to see what we could across the teeming land. From our vantage point we could barely make out, dim in the foggy distance, the vast, sprawling, campfires of the enemy.

Ishme, who at eight years old barely reached my waist, held my hand with a full and nervous anticipation.

Suddenly, a slow wind began to pick up, gnawingly cold, and in its rising crescendo, through the darkness and the fog, we felt the rudiments of something huge awakening high above. Ishme pointed deliriously up. We heard a loud scream and saw, vaguely, a black presence, broad-winged above us, in the night sky. The wind blew terribly, and the scream grew louder, and a rising panic began to overpower my senses. Ishme hugged my legs in fright.

Now, totally terrified, I grabbed the boy in my arms and rushed quickly into the safe womb of the temple. From inside, I could hear the frenetic shrieks grow dimmer as it flew away, and then, after a small interval of silence, began the desperately mad screams of the encamped men.

In the clear morning Ishme and I returned to the spot where we'd stood that night, and noticed the enemy was gone. Ishme pulled at my tunic, and pointed excitedly at the spot, and yelled. I could tell the boy was proud.

Later that day, I went into the city to gather news. What I learned, I gathered from several citizens in beer halls, who were intimate with some of Sargon's spies. These spies, it was rumoured, later went mad, and the king put them to death.

I learned that once the creature, with thunder-loud shrieks, had appeared over the enemy, they hastily sought to arm themselves for war. In this confusion, overtaken by this nightmare wraith, the men saw, from the bedeviled skies, spores of luminous matter fall. These spores, wherever they fell, grew astronomically fast, into frenzied monstrosities of chaotic life. All that was heard was a babble of screams from beasts and dying men, and then, as if for the climax of some grand cacophony of sounds, the Seeder from the Stars itself dipped into the pith of those unfortunate men, wildly tearing and ravening with abandon.

Sargon left that very day, to continue his conquests in the far north. When he left, I could tell he was deathly afraid and in great awe of his daughter.

* * *

Lazily the years unwound afterwards. Ishme continued to improve in favour, and it was certain one day he would leave to become a well-respected Ensis of the empire. I trembled to think of this, for after all, was he not ours?

During this time, I began to be plagued with inexplicable dreams of an archaic Nile; that long, meandering river being the place from which I'd originally come. In my dreams, I was no longer

Smenkhkare, but another, who couriered secret messages, and who fought alongside King Scorpion to subdue the red, sceptered crown of Lower Egypt. I lived, and relived, this troubled man's life, yet if he ever existed, it would have been centuries before my time.

I also began to notice a gradual change come over Ishme's behaviour. He became detached, less welcome in his affections. At first, I thought this was because he was becoming a man. In time, however, this episode passed.

When the day arrived for him to leave the temple and continue as an administrative assistant, he told me to follow him to the Holiest Room of Nanna.

Already the stub of manhood was thick on his face. I remember him looking at me, and saying, "I'll never leave to be a governor of this empire. I'll never serve it in that capacity."

His refusal was incomprehensible to me. I knew the old ghost that troubled him before was now resurfacing. I decided to confront him. I said, "Ishme, Sargon didn't mean to hurt you when he killed your parents and caused your people to suffer, when he razed your old city of Kazalla to the ground. It was done as policy. He wanted to unify, and they refused. It is the way of this world. Did not his daughter, with Sargon's blessing, take you in? And see, today, you leave to be a great man in his empire. You cannot hate him, or more especially, she who is like your mother?"

Ishme looked at me with the eyes of a son; they softened. But suddenly, another thought struck him, and they hardened to stone. He said, "It isn't so simple. It isn't so simple, Smenkhkare."

I tried to reason with him, "If there is something else bothering you, Ishme, tell me. I will help."

"I can't!" he yelled at me. "You love her too much!"

"It is so," I answered. "I am loyal to Akkad and always will be."

"If you love me, come with me behind the curtains of Nanna. Let us see what lies behind them."

The boy was now extremely agitated, and spoke madness. I refused to entertain his wish.

He said, "What lies behind the curtains, Smenkhkare? Haven't you ever wondered? Let me pass!"

Then he made a great effort to pass the curtains. I grasped him, and would not let him go. As we fought, he yelled angrily, "She and her father—they are murderers and usurpers! She is a sorceress, a witch, and a devil! Can't you see, Smenkhkare? She is a devil!"

Hearing his insinuations, I grew furious, and threw him hard to the floor.

It's then that I said what I now most regret in life. It would be the last lie I ever told the boy. It was then that I angrily told him that I would never speak to him again.

He rushed from the room.

We desperately searched for Ishme, first throughout the temple, and then throughout the entire city, and empire. He didn't want to be found. We could only hope our beloved boy was safe.

* * *

My own and Enheduanna's thoughts never strayed far from memories of Ishme. In time, we heard from a potter in Nippur that he'd gone to the Zagros Mountains, many years before. We shuddered when he told us. Tales of distant travelers, and traders in lapis lazuli, and other treasures, spoke of the far-off Zagros Mountains, and of a mist-enshrouded kingdom on ghastly peaks, overseen by what was only whispered of, as 'the Monstrosity on the Throne': a king of evil learning, who worshiped gods of strange names. The tales were vague, however, and never an exact route was divulged in these rumours. We prayed Ishme had not found it.

As for me, my unwanted dreams continued and became more baffling and bizarre. I dreamt I was a man leading a group of ragged humans out of Africa; a fisherman in a village on a frosty continent; a king in Serannian; a pauper in Girsu; the coiled serpent that talked with dimly-remembered Gilgamesh; a lute musician in the glorious palace of Olathoë, in doom-laden Lomar.

One day, the princess came to me with the libation baskets and wearing her Crown of En-Ship, from under which I noticed long strands of grey hair falling, almost obscured by the rich black, around a face still young and pretty. She looked at me sadly and said, "Why do you never age, Smenkhkare? Were you too chosen for your role, as I was, by the gods? A duty you cannot shirk?"

I didn't know what she meant. I was only Smenkhkare, and when I died, I would be nothing.

She smiled and continued, after a pause, "We are all offspring of it, Smenkhkare. Some of us are more closely linked to it." She then looked at me with a look of new recognition, which made me shiver. "It came from the emptiness of space and brought its secrets with it, a terrible and distant God, unlike the fickle and stern gods of Earth. Earth's gods, who have forgotten the touch of cold stars, and love high mountains, seas and virgin forests, who dance on misty mountaintops, they forbid us to come to them, and yet, at times, will come and kiss us tenderly in our sleep. It is gone now, the Seeder from the Stars. I haven't seen it in many years, and my Lady, Inanna, who wears the Laws of Civilization tied around her waist, does not acknowledge or speak of it anymore."

She finished, and left to continue her work.

With the passage of time Sargon died, a mortal death, and passed into legend. The Kingship of Sargon then devolved to his heirs: first, Rimush, then Manishtushu, and then the so-called God-King, Naram-Sin.

*　*　*

During the reign of Naram-Sin, the nephew of Enheduanna, shattering revolts broke out throughout the whole of the civilized lands of Sumer and Akkad. Shortly before this, I'd been warned in hushed tones by my Mistress that the gods of Sumer and Akkad were in strife, and preparing for battle. I was terrified, and shook in awe of this coming apocalypse.

It began when Lugal-Anne, vassal King of Ur, turned against us. Having no respect for the semi-divine being my Mistress now was, he cast her Crown of En-Ship off, bid her commit suicide, and then smashed the holy and adored things of the temple. On a day when fire began falling from the sky, we fled with the temple household and our meager possessions, and wept on the hills, tearing our hair, and scratching our eyes in grief.

During a blinding storm on the road to Uruk, I experienced my first vision of Earth's gods. I saw mysterious Lady Tiamat, towering in the clouds, engendering disorder and flames, and coaxing Lotan, the vile serpentine dragon of many heads, from the sea to hinder our escape, with hell-winds upthrown by his foul, membranous wings.

Weather-beaten, tired, and near collapse, we managed to make our escape to Uruk, and find exile in the temple of An.

Soon, messengers arrived, and said a great army was marching from the Zagros Mountains. Where the army stepped, they informed us, the mes, the very Laws that governed in order our cosmos, dissolved. Darkness heaved, and took on distorting, palpable form. Once it crossed the Tigris River, Lugal-Anne was seen to join them.

My Mistress, hearing this, was worried.

She'd put up curtains in the Sacred Room of An and, upon hearing the news, she immediately rushed behind them to pray for the mes, that our order might not completely break.

I remember dimly the elaborate words she spoke, but my weak, scribal hands will still attempt to transcribe, albeit poorly, the magnificence I heard. She prayed, "Lady Inanna, hear me, you whose shield is the moon and whose star is Venus. You, whose least simple command cannonades like a streak of gold across the fervent atmosphere. I kneel before you to pray for the mes of this sphere, and their continuance, for the harmony, alignment, and form they bring. Without them, what will become of the strong, well-built cities? Cities of architectural symmetry and splendour, great altitudinous towers, and sylvan gardens, founded under Order and the Laws of Civilization, by the black-haired people so many years ago. People of art and music, workers in words, in metals and gold. These are your people, who built mighty ships, and when the ships sailed out, they returned with cargo, laden from remote, mystical lands, for your greater pleasure. Do not let the good people perish, or does my Lady now favour strife over love, darkness over light, unworked rock, chaos, lawlessness, enmity, and discordant sounds? Is this what you want, my Lady? Shall I also break what you brought with your ordering presence?"

She sang all night and, emerging in the morning, she stood before me, disheveled and tired-eyed. Moving towards me, she slowly said, "Smenkhkare, it's Ishme who is coming."

* * *

Chaos reigned at that time.

The King of the Four Quarters of the Earth, Naram-Sin, couldn't protect us, since he was embroiled in deadly battle with Iphur-Kisi of Kish.

The King of Uruk, Amar-Girida, went to Enheduanna, to supplicate her to sing her beautiful hymns to the gods, to help Uruk, and fight Lugal-Anne, and the dread King from the Mountains, Ishme, whom all men called the 'Creature'. He begged her to summon the Seeder, as she'd once done.

"It's impossible," she said.

***

From a high place I saw the advance of Lugal-Anne and Ishme's army. In their march, tremors hit the earth, buildings shook, and the sky became dark, bilious and smoky. The army came in spastic motion, coiling and pulsing out of existence. I recall hearing an old priest, holding a bronze sword, yell at the sight, "Now, at the end of all things, let none seek to stop me as I break free from the Lords of Creation!" Then, running into the temple, he killed himself. Many followed his example. Prescient with defeat and fear, King Amar-Girida let their armies enter the city.

"You are weak, and you bring this on us," the King said. "I will now fight alongside Ur and Kish."

The city was spared, but we weren't. Lugal-Anne wouldn't stop until he'd destroyed the En-Priestess and her nephew.

Once the black armies entered, soldiers loyal to my Mistress fought to protect the Temple of An, which was also our fortress. Against the combined might of Ur, Uruk, and the shadow kingdom, however, they were no match. The enemy advanced easily.

Screams of dying men assailed our ears from all corners, amplified a thousand-fold throughout the enclosed corridors. I carried on me a sword to protect my Mistress. When I entered the Room of An she looked at me strangely. "It is back, Smenkhkare," she said. "The Seeder is back." And then she walked behind the curtains.

As this happened, a soldier hurriedly broke into the room. He implored us to flee. He said the Creature was coming. Realizing his pleadings were useless, he resolved to stay with us, to the bitter end.

We stood a few paces from the entrance. Unholy noises of dying men continued to sound the depths of our despair. I stared at the opening, into the dark hallway. Seconds passed, agonizingly slow. Confused war-cries bellowed, and I felt every fibre, nerve, and tissue in my body, ache. The blackness of the open entrance took on the illusion of a solid tableau, the more I looked at it, and then, out of the blackness, a darker outline began to emerge.

As I saw a cyclopean shape grab the soldier, I was blinded by the man's viscera and blood, meat and limbs, which sprayed the room. My hand grasped the hilt of my sword tightly, as if to break it, but before I could make a mad, desperate swing, I was on the floor, weaponless.

The air itself heaved and swayed to and fro, like a beast in the room. The soldier was a grotesquery of pieces, and I a hopeless wretch, lying before the towering arc of Ishme.

He stood a monumental shape, hooded, and in a long cloak of black, a cloak which seemed to embody more negation, an absence of all light, rather than colour. It twined and slithered around the contours of his body, and from its bottom, where legs should have been, instead swirled and twisted outwards massively pink, tentacular limbs, coiling and writhing purposely, like heavy pythons. Under the darkness of his hood, I discerned—oh, but how can I explain to you the sadness and horrified wonder I experienced when I saw those large, grey, abnormal lips, and engorged, abscessed tongue, or the small, blinkless, couchant yellow eyes? Hands, swollen and cracked like crevices of grey stone, or the foulness of his smell, which was as if worms were inside, gnawing on his innards?

Carrying a ponderous sword, he proceeded to walk, or glide, fluidly, towards the curtains, his awkward and distended robe flowing, and his tentacles leading and searching. As he did this, the hulking shape said, in a voice hoarse and deep, yet, in a manner of articulation recognizably like Ishme's, "Do not try to stop me, Smenkhkare. I know who and what you are, even if you don't."

When he was near the curtains, Enheduanna stepped out and stood defiantly in front of him. "Do not do this thing," she warned.

Like a wounded animal, Ishme gave a sudden, long-winded moan; then, lowering his face, he eased it towards hers. He passed it in her view, so she could scrutinize it. Upset, I saw her contract, and then compose herself. Staring at her, he asked, "Am I hideous to you? Is your work hideous to you?"

Perplexed and saddened, she answered, "What do you mean, Ishme?"

He gave another bellow, and yelled angrily, "It's because of what you put in me! You should have let me die, rather than live and suffer this shame!" Then, looking at me, he said, "When I ran away, Smenkhkare, hidden in Nippur, I began to change. A hideous thing, I remained hidden. Ashamed, scorned of men, I fled to the Zagros Mountains, and there met a man, who explained to me secret lore passed down from ancient times. He divined that my transformation, because I possessed a part of it, was caused by the Seeder. I killed the man, and began my kingdom on the mountains."

He turned towards my Mistress. "What lies behind the curtains? If my first cure came from there, then whatever is there can cure me again; isn't it so? I must see the beast. Then I'll be a man again."

He pushed my Mistress, and she struggled to hold him back, saying, "No, Ishme, it can't be trusted!"

Breaking free of her grasp, he entered the room and, in distress, she followed him.

All this while, I'd tried to help, but I couldn't. I was paralyzed. I trembled with fear for them both. I exerted and worked myself into a frenzy to move, but it was as if my body were a foreign entity, and I an unbodied mite trapped within. I lay on the floor and, after they passed behind the curtains, I willed myself even more desperately to move, but to no avail.

"Do not go there, Ishme!" I heard her yell.

He thundered, "Get away from me, sorceress! Move! It's your fault all that's happened to me!"

"No, Ishme—do not say that! How could I have known?"

Fumbling noises I heard, a loud bang, and then a body fall. After which, Ishme hollered triumphantly, "There you are! What manner of thing are you? I only want to be human! Speak to me! I'll make you with my sword!"

Commotion followed after, and I heard a great noise. A blinding light pierced the curtains. The temple rumbled. I felt a strong wind, and then, only Ishme's voice, growing dimmer and dimmer, roaring, "By Yog-Saduk, the Keeper of the Gates, and Aniburu, the Fearsome Planet, I order you to help me!"

A silence ensued, and I started weeping uncontrollably. I couldn't imagine what had happened behind the curtains. Then my Mistress appeared, bloody and with tears in her eyes, and lowly whispered, "A fissure cracked through space. I saw the cavernous void. Ishme is no more. It has taken him." Then she collapsed.

***

My chronicle ends here and, even though there is more I could say, with Ishme's passing, the story is finished. My Mistress was eventually restored to her temple in Ur and, at long last, she joined Inanna and the gods in Heaven. When she changed and her eyes became like spindles of flaming fires, and her form in expanse as huge as gigantic cedar trees, I heard her voice filling earth and sky, saying,

"Do not fear, Smenkhkare. If there is fear, it's only in you. I'll go and look for Ishme, and if he still lives, I'll come and tell you—but the spaces beyond are much vaster than I had imagined."

Once she left, I never saw her again. By my reckoning, that was over seven hundred years ago.

Whenever I tell my story, men call me mad and a liar, saying no man from Kemet on the Nile can serve in a foreign land, but they don't know that I wasn't always known as 'Smenkhkare,' for I've had many different names, and sometimes I confuse them. For I know now more of my mystery. Every one hundred years, I must go to steamy swamps, and shed my skin. I make strange, sibilant sounds and, once the process is finished, I emerge a new creature.

I remember in dreams the ancient Lady once saying, "We are all a part of it." I've come to believe I am more so. The mystery of my beginnings I still search out, though I've partly convinced myself that I am one of the unwilling eyes of the Seeder from the Stars.

I've left Crete and, after centuries of other lives, I'm finally returning to the Land of Two Rivers. Sumer and Akkad are dust and gone, and I travel as a merchant to Babylon. I'll bury this papyrus scroll. If, in the aeons to come, I don't forget, I'll dig it up again, when the time is right, and remember.

I'll remember Ishme, poor Ishme, and the God-Woman, and what mysteries happened, what mysteries I lived and what mysteries lay behind the forbidden curtains. What really happened? I believe only two on earth have ever known—and one is surely dead.

Interview Excerpted from a Blog Site Dedicated to Supernatural Investigations

KP: Good. We're settled, I guess we can get on with the meat of the matter. You've said before, and correct me if I'm wrong about this, that you originally just stumbled onto the phenomenon?

CT: Yes, that's correct. No need for a correction. Like my brain sores, it just found me.

KP: Brain sores? There we go again with the peculiarities of the disease, as some would call it. It's really quite similar to other effects I've heard, and read, about. You are aware of the woman in Peru, who says she has a little head in her head that tells her what to say, and what to do? I find this fascinating.

CT: I'm aware of her, as I'm aware of others. But we're different, in that I'm the only one who isn't severely incapacitated, in some sense. I was extremely lucky.

KP: That's the thing, isn't it? How you stumbled on this, and miraculously survived. I think it's time we really got to the heart of this. That's what my listeners will be most fascinated by. You've said it started with YouTube?

CT: Yes, though I still can't believe most of it. It's just so far out. Well, a few days before I went on YouTube, actually. It's weird, extremely weird, weird in the 'there's a face with an elephant's trunk-type thing floating over South America' weird.

KP: Interesting. Good that you mentioned that. I'm going to cut in and remind my listeners that such a phenomenon was reported. Apocalyptic stuff, indeed. Good stuff!

CT: Like I was saying...where was I? Okay, I'd been reading the latest news on the internet, I think from the Associated Press website, when I noticed a link to a separate news article about protests in Chile. On the picture, attached to the link, you saw students holding up signs and, sure enough, when I went to the webpage, it was about student protests occurring in that country. This was back in August of 2011. There was a lot of this stuff going on back then. Remember the Arab Spring protests, and the Occupy Movement?

KP: Right. Can you just let the readers know where Chile is located exactly? Perhaps it might be unfamiliar to most of my readers.

CT: It's a country in South America, bordering Argentina, Bolivia and Peru. Antarctica is at its southern end. Pinochet was from there, if anyone remembers who Pinochet was? Well, anyways, this isn't the main point of my story, so I'll just skim over this fast.

KP: Gotcha.

CT: These student protests were about educational matters, and were pretty intense. Cops were called out and everything. A few days later, due to boredom, I went on YouTube, to see if there were any videos showing this. Sure enough, there were. After a while of browsing I clicked on a link that said 'Camilla.' This video I quickly realized had nothing to do with the previous subject. This is where everything really started to happen.

KP: Right. This was the Hastur and Camilla video that was posted briefly.

CT: It was. By someone named HasturSinNombre, which, translated means HasturWithoutName. Now, when I clicked the video I was completely fascinated with what I saw. It was like the Anonymous hacker group's videos of that time, which showed current events in a sensational matter, and featured either a gowned guy or gal (you couldn't tell which, what with that mask from the movie *V for Vendetta* being worn, and the fake, masculine voice used).

KP: You mean the Guy Fawkes mask?

CT: Exactly. Except this mask wasn't real. Wasn't human. Well, I shouldn't say that it wasn't real...the problem was that it looked too real. Think of something by H. R. Giger, Zdzislaw Beksinski, or any of those other horror art masters that show you creatures from other worlds, faceless things, or things with faces that we wouldn't recognize as faces, except brought to life. I don't know what the mask was really supposed to represent. It seemed to have an elephant's trunk, and feelers, or tubes, and was possessed of either metal, or flesh. The figure wore tatters, and what I definitely discerned was something like a crown atop its head. It was perhaps a tattered king figure of some kind. Well, this was my first impression, remember? But it was arresting. And it spoke in beautiful Spanish poetry, of stars and constellations, impossible loves, and faraway places, and of course, also, of current events and the mundane horror of things, as they currently were. Its poetry seemed to promise other, faraway things, and I was captivated, as I've stated, and will keep stating, for emphasis. Then it spoke of Camilla, and this being it spoke about was not of this sphere, or galaxy. The video finished with the figure promising to make more videos based on El Rey de Amarillo and El Signo Amarillo.

KP: The King in Yellow and the Yellow Sign. Go more into that. Tell us more about what that is.

CT: Okay, I'll tell it this way. I watched the video over and over again, and the next day I was elated to realize that a new video was posted. The figure now spoke of Cassilda, and Camilla, and the Lake of Hali. Again, I was transfixed. What were these beautiful things spoken about by a figure that inspired such horror? Days passed until a new video was posted. This time the figure promised that in one week, a full performance of a Spanish translation of the play *The King in Yellow* was going to be posted on YouTube. It promised that we would never be the same again after watching it. The figure promised us Carcosa, where we would always dream. Intoxicated, I immediately set out to research the play. It turns out the play was originally written in France, and though never performed, was rumored to cause madness in whoever read it. No one remembers it now, and it went out of fashion, like the absinthe that was popular in the Bohemian quarters, at the end of the 19th century. Perhaps we shouldn't be surprised, since thousands of crazes from days gone by are no longer remembered, and thousands of books have been written, and printed, which no one remembers nowadays. However, it received sufficient underground notoriety in its day, to be translated and printed into other languages. You're lucky if you can find a time-worn copy for sale on eBay, and I hear they sell for quite the high price.

KP: And who exactly is the King in Yellow?

CT: That's the million dollar question, isn't it? Some have tied him with Hastur, and other demons from books of esoteric lore, such as are found in the *Necronomicon*, or the *Unaussprechlichen Kulten*. Is the King in Yellow related to Cthulhu? I don't know. I have a lot of amnesia about the subject.

KP: Interesting. Would you advise anyone to track down the play?

CT: To sound clichéd, not if they value their sanity. The play is very dangerous to read, or see performed. It can summon things from the Outside that I am now convinced are evil. These things, you have to understand, are incredibly more powerful than humans, and are old, very, very old. And Carcosa is near...but isn't really near. Close by Aldebaran, and the Hyades. And by our sun. There's strange physics involved that only now science is beginning to understand. Perhaps someday we will be able to travel to Carcosa, by a tunnel of some kind. Hali and Alar and Carcosa might be hell, though.

KP: Great stuff! Can you go on now with your story? Tell us, tell us about your encounter.

CT: Okay, well, a week passed and during that time I couldn't think about anything else but the play. I lived with my girlfriend and she was getting worried. She said I should see a shrink. I work as a fork-lift driver, and my workmates were worried about me, too. Well, somehow I managed to survive the week, and then the day of the performance came. I went on YouTube, and sure enough, it was posted. Had just been posted, really. I locked myself in the room, with only a lamplight on. My girlfriend was in the living room, asleep. And I saw the play. Saw Camilla, and Cassilda, and the Lake of Hali. It was beautiful. I almost fainted with fright when the Stranger appeared. There were things going on, things that are hard to explain now. The black stars were too real, and the Pallid Mask, I swear, I thought I could touch it. Then the Second Act began. The one that supposedly drives men into such fear, that they go insane. Something in my head said: These are all symbols, symbols of deep truths, about everything, knowledge so advanced and nerve-wracking that once you understand but a small fraction, your mind will be fractured, and you will not be human anymore, but something else, something from dim Carcosa. And I saw the figure from the previous YouTube posts, and I can tell you—it indeed wore a mask. Because now the mask opened...and what I saw...I won't...I can't describe...and at the same time, the world outside got darker...and from behind me, from the darkness, and from my side-view, I noticed a...a shadow something...a dark thing...lurking towards me...and it reached out to me...then I screamed, and fell off my chair! And that saved me, I think. I didn't watch anymore, and passed out.

KP: You've talked about brain sores. What happened next?

CT: My girlfriend awoke me in the morning, by banging on the door. When I checked the video I saw that it was no longer available. I wasn't the same person. Not for awhile. You can't be, not after you've experienced these things. But life goes on. Nothing else about *The King in Yellow* has been posted, well, except imitations. Then, a few weeks later, I started getting headaches. Headaches...like cold sores under my skull. One time...I swear, I saw a piece of my brain slide out of my nose, and get lost in the apartment.

KP: You've heard about the man in Uruguay who claims that, once in awhile, he opens up, and a full grown man steps out of him, and walks away, and then he closes up again? Investigators say this was caused because of the same phenomenon. Can you shed any light on what these strange occurrences are, that are happening to so many people?

CT: Only that they're strange. I can't explain any of it. It's all insane. I have only one theory. I think these people are like me. I think they're the ones who didn't watch the full Second Act of the play. I can't even begin to speculate about what happened to the ones who watched the whole thing. Maybe they're in Carcosa?

KP: It's a better theory than what the skeptics say. That this is all nonsense. Would you mind describing more about the contents of the play for us?

CT: No. Not now. I'm a bit rattled. Maybe later.

KP: Okay, I don't want to keep you anymore. You've said enough. I understand how hard this must have been for you. I only want to ask you one more question: How many people do you think watched the final video?

CT: I can't guess. A lot, maybe.

KP: Thanks. Keep in touch.

CT: I think the Imperial Dynasty is on earth. I think they're coming through. I think Carcosa is here, just hidden. I think the Yellow King rules, as he rules on Aldebaran, Demhe, and Yhtill. Beware of the Yellow Sign.

KP: We've run out of time. Thanks again.

The Green World

Like warm breath that's exhaled and evaporates in winter was Annie's life. She came and was gone. But what an amount of happiness, and eternity, was held in that time! How can I describe to someone who hasn't felt the intensity of true, unselfish love, and hasn't met her, how I felt? Like a lightning bolt that flashes across a dark sky was Annie's love and mine. Rapid, bright, violent, ominous, and brief.

We would often escape into the woods, my studies now forgotten, for Annie was a worshipper of Nature. She was also classical and heathen. She would describe to me what she saw, of centaurs and satyrs and other magical creatures, and maybe it was the fastness of our love or the intertwining of our souls, but in time, I grew to see those supernatural things too.

Ah, those moments of happiness and of pleasures! All that was, or will ever be, of imagination, were our private magic kingdoms! We swam with naiads and ran with dryads! All sorts of fabulous creatures were our friends! The reeds made music for us as we passed! A thousand living things were our choirs! All nature, and fabulous beasts of myth, danced with us at times, and Annie led the dance!

Ah, happiness upon happiness, and joys past joys, and yet, sadly taken! Those long and sun-lit days gave way to dark and horrid winters, lived and living still! The green world was gone.

Soon, the ugly hold of death touched my life. I saw its slow ravages as tuberculosis spread throughout her body. She grew emaciated and weaker, as treatment followed treatment, until one day, all hope was gone. Near the end, all day and night I sat by her bedside, and my Annie rarely moved, numbed with too much pain and morphine. I saw her rheumy eyes, blank with the realization her life was over.

It was a cold evening on a Tuesday, when most of the leaves had fallen from the trees, that Annie stirred from the delirium that engulfed her, and feebly whispered, "Nature was my goddess, and to her I dedicated my succulent hours. She was my world and mistress, and something I could understand—but she wasn't good to me. Our love was the only precious thing. Promise me, Arthur, that I'll live a little in your memory, after I'm gone, and after the green world's vanished with my passing, and then forget me, and go and do those things I couldn't hope to do, or ever will. Spring follows winter; the green world will be resurrected, as I won't."

She died and I buried her on a Thursday.

* * *

I was without hope.

One day, I ran outside the mansion into the cold world of trees, desperate in my sorrow and my anger, and as I sobbed with my head between my elbows to the ground, I looked up and saw a tall being, swathed in blinding light. It was him, now come to me—the God of the Woods, the son of our goddess, Nature! Atop his head of short, curly hair grew two grotesque and massive antlers! Behind him were the trees, and the world grown green again, where his light touched. I saw him bend his gaze to my right, and stretch his arm, and point, and turn his heavily-antlered head with ease, and a slow repose, in that direction. In that spot was a vision of my withered Annie, hollowed-cheeked, and decomposing in her tomb. Then looking at Annie and pointing, the god said, "I will plant thee, and will labour to make thee full of growing." Then looking at me, he said, "You two will love again. Get thee the Book of Eibon."

Then he vanished.

* * *

Oh, how the words spoken by the god haunted me afterwards! What meaning did they convey?

Long I searched for the meaning in the god's words, until one day, high atop a wind-swept, Pyrenean mountain, I found the meaning and the book. The deathless Bogomil priest who gave it to me, issued this stern warning, which I've always remembered: "The joys of the gods are not the joys of men, and how a god thinks is not the way a man thinks. Inscrutable are their ways. Often, I have seen them dancing on the clouds, but to what music, I have not heard. Often, I have also seen them come in thunder. The gods of Eibon are the green gods of earth, as are the gods of the sky also, as there are other gods you have not known. Fortunate is the man the gods have touched, when a man's will, and a god's will, is one."

Then he spoke no more.

* * *

One day, I stood before her mausoleum, outside my ancestral mansion, and began the incantations that would bring my Annie back to me. I chanted in the language of Occitania, the *langue d'oc*. My copy of the Book of Eibon was a translation, into this language, from another language now lost to time, as ancient as Hyperborea and the dead Lemuria. I chanted to wild, savage, unholy, forgotten elder gods, gods older than Jupiter, or Ngenechen.

The Horned God of the woods appeared to me as I chanted, and by nightfall, he disappeared, only to be replaced by sinister shapes far in the trees. These shapes, I knew, were the soul-stuff of the trees emerging from their ancient shells. These shapes disappeared into the open mausoleum, and by daybreak, now totally exhausted though I was, I noticed something begin to emerge from within the dark recesses of the idyllic tomb.

A horror I felt when I first saw it—that thing that once was her, my loved Annie! And still I feel it! It's an abomination! *That thing that shouldn't live!*

How quickly my love had turned to hatred and fear! I also felt, from deep within me, resurface my long-repressed Christian sympathies, which made war against this demonic aberration. That the dead should live before their appointed time is unnatural, a blasphemy, and a sin against God and Nature!

Out of the tomb emerged a shambling, upright thing, neither complete woman, nor tree, but an unfinished fusion of the two! It was as if some deranged mind had smashed together, in chaos, a decomposed human and a tree, and the resultant malformation lived! In one eye that I could discern on it, I read either agony, shock or terror! *It was unholy*, I yelled! It moved awkwardly towards me, and its unpleasant gait aroused in me feelings of revulsion, to behold its mockery of the human form. I felt like retching! A branch which I took to be an arm, perhaps, it strenuously moved to point towards me and, as it did this, I ran. From behind, I heard a word spoken in an inhuman lisp, and it was my name, it was "Arthur."

* * *

The thing didn't go away. I convinced myself it wasn't really Annie. I couldn't bear to look upon it.

Day and night I heard it in the woods, walking alone and hidden, yelling my name, "Arthur!"

The yell would come at uneven times, with different moods, but still I wouldn't go to the thing. I would stand by the windows for hours on end, in a panicked trance, staring at the woods, and listening to that inhuman and nightmarish voice.

By the sixth day, my servants became sufficiently unnerved that they begged to be discharged. I couldn't do anything but acquiesce to their demands. I would have gone, too, and left this horror-stricken place, if not for the fear that I might lose my ancestral mansion forever if I left this place alone to the ghoul, and the unhallowed hells from whence it came. I was also responsible for the thing, since I'd summoned it.

I was now alone with it.

* * *

Days and weeks passed, and the creature became bolder in its cries from the dark. No minute passed that I didn't hear its squeamish cries that echoed terribly in the barren countryside.

"Arthur! Arthur! Why don't you come to me?"

Hysteria engulfed my world, and I wished for nothing more but that the hellish thing would stop its blasted screams from the dark.

"Arthur! It's because of you that I am here! You owe me your help!"

I didn't sleep. My days were an icy terror. Sickness engulfed me, like a blanket of night. Still, the monstrosity cried to me.

"Arthur! Can't you remember our love? Help me!"

I cursed the time that she and I spent together. I cursed the Green God of the Woods for bringing this malady upon me. I cursed the Dark Gods of Eibon, and the diseased book of their creeds. But most of all, I feared. I feared so much that I marvel that my body didn't collapse in a monstrous breakdown. I feared even more, when I began to suspect that she wasn't alone in the woods. I began to develop sense impressions, which I can't describe now, that with her in those blasphemous woods was a thing more hideous, and inhuman, than she was. And still, her cries persisted.

"Arthur! By all that's good in Man, help me!"

And then, one day, the screaming ceased. I don't know what was more terrible: the screams, or the unnatural silence which now surrounded the countryside. Days, days passed, and the silence remained, so that I began to think the thing was gone.

Then, one terrible night, as I lay in one of my disturbed slumbers on my bed, I heard a voice whisper in my ear, and say, "Arthur."

It was the voice of the thing, in my home! Beside my bed! I convulsed to know my walls were no protection, or barrier, between the evil and me! I summoned my strength, and sat up to confront the thing—but it was gone! It was then that I heard a fumbling thing, walking down the steps to my room, and traversing my ground floor, and exiting through the main door. I fainted from horror for the first time in my life.

* * *

Through the next few days, I witnessed a dismal transmutation in the woods, which would begin at sundown, and last till sunrise. A light shone in the darkness, from deep within the forest. I sensed that the trees were moving. Every morning, I noticed that the woods did not look the same. The horror when I realized, also, that every morning the woods were closer to the mansion!

I resolved, then and there, to end this madness forever. Fear or no fear, I would confront the thing. If in the maelstrom I was destroyed, so be it. Better to die in a confrontation soon, I thought, than to let this monster reach my mansion with its haunted trees, and die anyway.

One afternoon, I entered the woods, and passed the trees which were my besiegers. I quieted my fears, for I was resolved. I fancied the trees were giant sentinels, which could move at any moment. With me I carried my knives, and a rifle. Poor weapons with which to combat the unnatural, but I was a desperate man, and near the end of my wits. The hounds I owned wouldn't follow me into the woods, and my best hunting horse foamed at the mouth every time I brought it near the border of the two worlds.

I walked deep into the forest of dead silence and bunched-branches and leaves. If silence has a sound, it is the sound of horror.

I looked warily upon those faerie-haunted trees, which I imagined looked upon me with eyes of malice, and thoughts of hurt.

My direction took me where I supposed the strange lights I saw at night originated. Soon, I came upon an almost insurmountable wall of trees. This obstacle looked to me like a defensive wall, no doubt housing the aberrant command of my besiegers. I was near the source. There wasn't need, however, to scale the wall and find out. At that moment, a voice both familiar and unfamiliar began to address me from the other side of the wall of gathered trees.

* * *

"Arthur, so finally, you have come."

It was her voice, but now with a tone of calmness, and strength, which unsettled my nerves.

"I know, Arthur, that you don't love me anymore, but I still love you, and if to have you by my side, though without love, is to be my fate, so be it. I can weather eternity. Can you, Arthur? I was afraid once, but not anymore. It has granted my revenge.

"You never stayed by the tomb long enough, my love. You ran away, and never looked back. You never stayed long enough to see the thing that emerged from the tomb, behind me.

"And it wants you."

* * *

With her words ended, the trees opened up, and made a gateway to what I can only surmise was another world, a world of infernal chaos, and darkness, and light that stings, and coming from it, towards the gateway, I knew, was the Lord of it.

I ran from the aperture, and fled into the safety of the trees. I didn't look back. I could hear the thing behind me and, through the din of its advance, the laughter of my Annie.

In terror, I fled through branches and undergrowth. The trees seemed to close around me, but somehow, I managed to make my way through them. I took no set path, yet always made my way towards where I thought my home was. My instincts were correct. Soon, I saw the blessed paradise of my mansion. I passed the threshold of the trees into the clearing of my grounds. I was safe from the threat of trees.

Then, root-like tendrils grasped my legs. They flung like projectiles from the ground. From behind me, these root-like tendrils grasped my arms. In all directions I looked, I saw octopod arms, like roots, sway before me. They all converged on me. They immobilized me, and picked me up. They turned me around. I was held as a puppet on a string. They turned me around, and made me look on *it*!

I could not close my eyes. I stared in fascination and horror. The bulk of it! The insanity of it! Nothing compared to it! No animal, or twisted imagining I knew, had ever conceived of it!

The tendrils were an outgrowth of it. And the tendrils were the only sane things on it!

I passed before it, as the tendrils took me. It was then that I saw Annie sway towards me, held by one of those demonic arms. She was still laughing.

I called her name, as we swayed side-to-side, and past each other.

"Kiss me," she said.

I saw her clearly, now. She was my Annie. Only her flesh was different. It was a flesh of bark.

The tendrils made us face each other, and then I kissed her. The harsh lips eviscerated my lips.

She laughed, and said, "Don't worry my love; soon, you will not bleed."

I noticed a trembling in this Dark God of Eibon. Its being shook. It came together, and elongated. I yelled at my Annie that I was sorry. The process continued.

The thing stretched itself high into the sky. It set itself firmly on the ground. Its shape took on the form of a tree. Then bark appeared on it.

In panic, I realized what was happening. I tried to break free! The tendrils that held me forced my head towards Annie's. I was pushed to kiss her! They held me tight in that position, so that my lips bled even more profusely. With my eyes I could see clearly into my Annie's eyes. They were ecstatic!

I felt my flesh harden and crack. We were both pushed towards the body of the thing. We three became one. The last sight I had was of staring into Annie's wide, monstrous eyes, until bark covered the white-and-blue yolk of my own.

* * *

Since then, I've known what eternity is. Love eludes me. I am forever in bondage, and attached to these creatures.

If you should ever find yourself on a dark path, and you come across a tree, which has on its trunk the haggard outline of two lovers in a kiss, don't be deceived by the outward show and beauty of the thing.

Inside is Hell.

Walk past.

The Reverie of Space

In darkness, in the mantling of the night,
When Earth is calm and troubling noises cease,
I turn with wonder-looking eyes, to please
My dulled senses from the day's untranquil sight;
And first gaze upon heavens lesser light:
The moon, whose beams far into space, she shines;
Next to the farther planets, whose bright lines
I trace in a trajectory of might;
And over all holds the dominion of the stars,
Numberless, in endless infinities of space,
Old, perhaps their very being is a place,
Untouched, of which we may not breach the bars;
And farther still lie worlds on worlds to chase,
And unknown caverns of eternity to trace!

Extraction

Through vast stellar space, the Extraction Company crew travelled beyond their people's safe cosmic horizon, the centre and spiral arms of galaxies wheeling and spinning past them. Unfathomable energies propelled the fleet forward, and in normal space-time they were nothing but an aggregate of co-ordinates and numbers, seen only in the minds of their cosmic theorists and scientists back home. This was because, at this moment, they were nothing but phantom voyagers, as close as they'll ever come to being like the Immaterials.

Soon, one-by-one, the massive convoy of ships would leave the interdimensionality of hyperspace, burst into real time and solidity and slower time speeds, capped by the near speed of light, and then their work would begin.

We're coming, the Captain thought, *get ready*!

Beside him sat his Lieutenant Captain, a thin, lanky grey humanoid with skin like the dangling wrappings of a mummy, and a head like a five pointed star. When they'd first been introduced, Captain Sal Greta had thought he was an alien, until the creature told him he was from Earth. His phenotype, when they weren't traversing outer space, the Captain learnt, loved basting under a hot sun on Earth's seas. The Captain himself had only ancestral connections to Earth, and so it was forgivable for him not to know this little detail. The Captain was born and raised on Earth 142.

"Nearing time to jump hyperspace," the Lieutenant Captain said.

"Have all attack ships ready."

Breaking into normal space-time, the fleet found itself alone, with only three moons for companions.

"Just as the Generals predicted, sir. Not a ship in sight. Should we command the fighter ships in."

"Do so. Also, Brik, order for immediate construction operations to begin."

Looking out the command window, Sal Greta saw infinite space stretch out before him. He also saw tiny pinpoints of stars, a far distant sun, and then the real gem of these quadrants—*A104X*.

He couldn't actually see it, though he knew it was there, by observing the three moons which rotated around an empty spot. An empty spot which was planet A104X.

A planet invisible to sight and trapped, embedded, hidden in folds of space.

Sal Greta smiled as he remembered when his superiors had asked him if he was up to the challenge of going fishing for a world. He was, and was now about to build the massive fishing rod that would pull the thing out.

The planets, the negative solids, the Immaterials, like this orb, were the diamonds of his people. With it they lived, died, and maintained the survival of their civilization. The ship Sal Greta commanded was itself powered by an Immaterial, its cosmic energies harnessed by the Dyson sphere, or shell, built around the negative planet. The shell was Sal Greta's ship, named Earth 142.

"Should we go to the briefing now, sir?" asked Brik.

"No, you go on alone. I leave you in charge. I'm going to sleep. Wake me when the Construct's finished."

"Are you sure?"

"Yes. Wake me when it's time for extraction. What could possibly go wrong now?"

* * *

When he awoke Sal Greta felt a cold sucker on his face. Grabbing at it, he realized the top was a hand. He inferred the sucker was a palm and began to panic. He knocked the hand away as he sat up quickly on his stasis unit.

"It's just me," he heard Brik say. His second-in-command then turned away from him, and walked towards a holographic unit, on which were projections of starfish.

"Why were you touching my face?" the Captain asked, as he became acutely aware of the darkness of his quarters and the strange silence that permeated it. "I take it it's time for extraction?"

"No," Brik answered, while looking intently at the projections, "that began some time ago. I'm afraid you've been asleep for quite some time, Captain."

Puzzled, Sal Greta slowly moved one of his hands towards his side-weapon. Brik paid no attention to him, but merely kept studying the starfish. Had thousands of years ago Brik's ancestors been only starfish? Sal Greta tried to remember.

"Why wasn't I woken up when extraction began?" he asked sternly. He then slowly sat up on his stasis unit and quietly removed his weapon.

"Interesting specimens," Brik said, "but *Mother* must know all about it." He then looked at the Captain and, smiling, rushed headlong towards the wall closest to him and, stretching out his six arms, curiously began to melt into the wall. *Brik's species could not do this.* Alarmed and sure his Lieutenant Captain was about to completely disappear into the wall, Sal Greta opened fire, but this didn't stop Brik.

"If you wish to see where the rest of your people are, come and follow me down towards the planet, Captain," Sal Greta heard Brik say. Instantly, he realized the voice was impossibly coming from outside.

He rushed towards his quarter's windows, in time to see the thing that had once been his second-in-command and his friend falling eerily towards the half-extracted planet below, like a bed sheet blowing in the wind.

* * *

Outside, with his exo-skeleton suit on, Sal Greta held on firmly to one of the millions of steel girders that ran along the length of the Construct. He was alone in the immense emptiness of space. Atop, high up, he could see his people's Immaterial and his greatly diminished ship, its ribs only, since most of its material had been removed to supply the body for the Construct. His people had been doing this for aeons, as had all the other 579 Dyson sphere worlds of the Extraction Company. It was this way of living which separated them from almost all the other alien and terre civilizations, and also Earth's great empire itself. They were a civilization of hunter-gatherers, and the beasts they hunted throughout the cosmos were the Immaterials.

Sal Greta blasted off the Construct intermittently, flying a few feet before landing and holding onto the girders. He slowly made his way along the Construct, which at this moment was, with

JULIO TORO SAN MARTIN

inconceivable energies, extracting the black planet below him from its hiding hole in space. The Construct surrounded the planet like a great ring. As he advanced he felt like a tiny mite on a cosmic merry-go-round.

Cautiously he made his way to one of the few shaft elevators that stretched all the way down, to about 20% of the distance to the Immaterial, and which culminated in an observatory. From it he would blast down to the planet, thereby conserving fuel.

* * *

When first he'd left his quarters, Sal Greta had run to the Dyson sphere's main command bridge, and had checked to see if he was in fact the only person left on his world. The computer told him what he feared and suspected—that this was indeed the case. He also learned that the ship-world was on low power, and that most of its energy was concentrated on running the Construct.

Remembering what Brik had said to him, he'd run a thorough diagnostic on the emerging planet below, and had seen that Brik had not lied to him when he'd told him where his people were. Yet, why were they there, and how were they alive? Never before had he encountered an Immaterial capable of harboring life, especially during the planet-wracking process of extraction, which threw out the equivalent energy of a flaring sun. At first he didn't believe, but all systems said the life-forms were there—hundreds of thousands of them.

While he was checking and rechecking the readings, the monitors had come on, and he'd seen the barely discernible image of his world's Supreme Commander, Oseia.

"Captain Sal Greta, is that you?"

After some hesitation, he'd answered in the affirmative.

"Good. There's much interference and I haven't the time to explain completely. Come down, immediately. Once we'd finished the Construct we all came down. Somehow, you were overlooked. I can't explain everything now, but don't worry, soon everything will be made known to you. Come quickly. There's a paradise here, Captain. You can't imagine it. Come down. That's an order."

When her image had faded, he'd run codes on the main computer, and had been heartened to discover that someone had sent a distress bot into hyperspace and to the Generals. Eventually an emergency fleet from the 579 worlds of the Extraction Company would arrive.

However, it could take from a few months to up to two years for the fleet to arrive. Despite the message most definitely being a trap, he needed to know if his people were safe now. And if they needed help, he needed to offer it now. Suicide mission or not, he would go to the planet below, and reconnoiter the situation. It was his duty as the main officer in charge of this extraction.

And so he'd suited up with his most durable and toughest exo-skeleton, since all ships aboard Earth 142 were gone, and had blasted down, even if it was to a trap.

**

For Sal Greta looking at the process of extraction never got old. He stood on the open cargo platform of the lowest rung of the observatory. He heard only a low rumbling that vanished away into silence. Between open space, machinery, the process, the stars and infinity, he had never felt so alone.

He knew it wasn't only the shade of his viewing screen, nor the toughness of his exo-skeleton suit, made to withstand from a distance the extreme buffetings and poundings, heat and energy of extraction, but something else, something in this slice of space, something willful perhaps, or perhaps some law of physics, some as yet undiscovered power, that kept him safe.

He could see the beauty of the harnessed power and miracle below him. He could see the ring of the Construct as it vanished in a circle, fading in the distance, and below him, on one side, a black planet emerging; on the other, empty black space.

It was a planet being pulled from extreme curvatures of space, from where its nearly inconceivable density, pent-up energy and weight, and the laws of nature, had embedded it so deeply into reality, that reality had curved over it like a black marble pushed hard into a soft pillow, becoming hidden from view. This was the working hypothesis of his people's scientists.

Sal Greta fixed on his view screen where the thousands of his people were located; then, setting his thrusters in the proper direction, powered up and blasted off the open observatory towards the Immaterial.

***

Oseia had said the planet was a paradise, but as yet he could detect nothing of a paradisiacal nature on it. It was black just like any other Immaterial, except once past a certain limit, all signs of extraction disappeared. It just looked like dead rock.

His sensors picked up the distress signal from the fighter ship of his Chief Tactical Officer. He recalibrated trajectory and headed in her direction.

***

His propulsion blasters were powering down, his sensors were reading no massive energies or heat, incredible this close to extraction, when he heard it.

As he neared the planet, he heard a slowly rising crescendo of noise that slowly turned into one great concerted wail, like the death of a species, the death of a world, a scream of madness.

Simultaneously with it, he shut down his auditory mechs, to stop the noise from pummeling his ear drums, and switched his helmet screen to comp view to swathe the planet below him. In less than seconds, in an over-all view, he saw great patches of lighted dots, of groups and swarms of people, disappearing, until in mere seconds, all lights went dead.

"Shit! Shit! Fuck!" he yelled.

***

He landed softly on flat rock, and saw all before him acres of exo-skeleton suits, derelict ships and empty clothing, lying motionless, like one vast boneyard of detritus.

The planet was dark, the only lights coming from the stars and the faint sight of extraction in the sky above, coruscating like a high-up aurora borealis. The Construct was barely noticeable here from this distance, though an alien moon in the sky, separate from the sectors original three, pronounced itself as Immaterial 142. His Chief Tactical Officer's ship was nearby, still sending its distress signal.

Numb and emotionless, he sat down and rested.

***

Suddenly, his automatic auditory warning system came on alert. His bio-detector told him there was another life-form near him, by the fighter ship. Sal Greta looked in that direction, and saw one of the exo-skeleton suits trying to get up. He knew who it was.

"Lorna! Lorna!" he yelled, as he tried to shake the sunken form into life.

He could clearly see through his Chief Tactical Officer's view glass, and what he saw upset him greatly. She possessed the face of a thing that seemed to have melted, and had then recombined again, though not completely in the same way it had formerly been, or should be. There was no trace of her former beauty. Pangs of long-gone memories, and of lost love, began to surface in his being. Love and anger were at war in his chest, though there was more of pity in it. Now was not the time for such feelings, he thought. There was no place for humanity here. Not at this time. Not in this place.

"Captain," she barely whispered, while in pain, through vocal cords that now were not hers.

"Don't speak."

"Sal, we were deceived. You were asleep for so long. So much happened." She tugged at him desperately, with what, he could not bring himself to imagine, beneath her armor.

"Just lie there, officer. Do the med mechs aboard the ship work?"

"Don't. Listen. Why do you think in times past the Immaterials were never noticed? Because they weren't there. They were placed recently, as cosmic time goes."

"What? By whom?" he asked frantically, but she could no longer answer him. Her face, perhaps her whole body, he couldn't tell, broke down into something like porridge, and then set itself again, but this time into something less human. She couldn't speak; her rudimentary mouth barely allowed her to breathe. There were no more eyes on her.

She stopped struggling.

Sal Greta got up and, pointing his arm weapon at her view glass, fired.

"Good night, my sweet princess, may flights of angels sing you to your rest."

***

Something behind him began to seep towards him. Something old and yet young. A thick liquid like black mire, that undulated under the stars as it came. Like cold lava it stopped behind him, and then and there began to grow and expand into a living entity, as cellulose skin covered it. Spirals became etched on it, its tissue coarsened and became prickly, it turned grey, and then the head and flat piscine face of Brik appeared.

As Sal Greta looked at the dead waste before him, Brik said, "Beautiful, isn't it."

Sal Greta did not bother turning around. Did not even show surprise, but merely whispered, "Why?"

"When minds are the same they share the same points of reference, the same biology and mental make-up. In a story told by someone with the same mind as you, you understand what suspense, fear, darkness, love are, because your minds are the same. But what if your minds aren't the same? What if your minds don't share any points in common? The words would be merely gibberish. The story— incomprehensible. Our story is incomprehensible to you."

The surface rock below Sal Greta's feet now became as slush, and all around him in the blackness of the planet the exo-skeleton suits began to move, and the discarded clothing began to fill up with bodies. The mire was reconstituting itself into his people.

"Come, sisters!" Brick yelled.

He looked down and saw Lorna breathing again.

He sensed the black liquid trying to blend in and pass through his armor.

The planet began to shake.

"What is happening?" Sal Greta asked, angered.

"Mother is finally fully awakening and we, her children, rejoice in it. Across your universe her sisters are also awakening. Look up!"

He looked up and saw his home suddenly and violently explode, sending fiery debris and a white light hurtling through space. What was left, like the after-birth of a cracked egg, was a planet-sized white spider-thing, suspended and twitching in space.

"It's now time for final extraction," Brik said.

*　*　*

The Captain jumped quickly to one side, as one of Brik's six arms tried to violently grab him. He turned, and fired a lethal blast at his former Lieutenant Captain. The creature fell back and disintegrated in fire and smoke. Luckily he had saved enough energy for one massive blast.

He then dashed towards the ship's doors. They opened, recognizing the identity of the Captain. Yet as he tried to step in, two hands held on to his shoulders. They pulled him back. He fell, and the attacker fell on top of him. The assailant didn't have an exo-skeleton suit on, so Sal Greta could see the man's face. It was a soulless, dead face, with large eyes, black as night. Except for the mask-like resemblance, there was nothing human about it.

Using all his strength, Sal Greta managed to shove the shape off himself. Then quickly getting up, he kicked the man hard on the side of the head. The man went limp.

Once inside the ship, he quickly removed the exo-skeleton suit with the mire seeping into it and threw it outside.

He rapidly closed the doors and began to panic when he felt the ship tilt and begin to sink into the planet.

He threw himself at the controls and, firing the thrusters, lifted the ship off the muck. Great lumps of ooze fell from the ship as it sliced into the sky.

On monitors he read the life signals of his people again. He heard from the comm a recognizable voice.

"Sal," Lorna said. "Sal, come back. You don't understand." After a few seconds of silence she continued, "We had many great adventures together across the galaxies, didn't we? I love you."

He turned off the comm.

* * *

He maneuvered close to the twitching monstrosity in the gulfs of space.

As he powered up the fighter ship's attack weaponry, his concentration was forcefully jerked to one side, to the Immaterial instead. He gasped as the black planet horrifyingly came to full life and began to constrict, and then try to wiggle its way out of the space it was embedded in. Space-time dilated violently as the planet, like an insect trying to free itself out of a cocoon, thrashed in two different dimensions of reality. It tried to heave itself out.

Unexpectedly many tentacular appendages popped out of the embedded space, their moon-sized widths whip-lashing brutally into his dimension. Their sudden action sending energy like a disturbance, like a cosmic tidal wave, rippling destructively out in all directions.

Just as this pulse of energy crashed into Sal Greta's ship and sent it reeling uncontrollably, he'd fired his weaponry, and missed the spider-thing. Then his ship went dead, drained of all energy except for that running his life-support systems. This was impossible. He'd had enough power to last at least 52 days. Now he was dead in space, without the ability of motion, and at the mercy of those inscrutable things.

Helplessly he watched as a wormhole opened near his vicinity and the planet, now a strange black tentacular beast, with many eyes and mouths, flew squid-like into hyperspace, followed by its thousands of children.

The devil-kin, resembling smaller versions of their parent, filled the hell spaces around him.

He saw as Lorna flew past his ship's window and, looking unemotionally at him with her black eyes, dived like a sea-thing into the void.

Defeated, he lowered, then raised his eyes, only to see Brik staring back at him from the other side of the window, smiling.

"Mother, and her fellow centillions and more of sisters, have awakened throughout the universe," Brik said, his voice breaching the hull of the fighter ship. "Grandmother is headed to the galactic centre of your terre civilization. It will be one of many stops. Her visits will reform all life-forms, even those unknown to you, and those greater than you, throughout the cosmos. Don't think that any help will come. The 579 Dyson sphere worlds are no more."

Brik left, and Sal Greta saw as the last of his people disappeared into the wormhole, like schools of fish.

As it closed, he felt the impression of something grand, malign, and galaxies wide, pass and brush by him, from that other dimension of hyperspace.

That must be the grandmother, he thought.

***

Days later, with the fighter ship's life-support systems nearly depleted, Sal Greta resigned himself to his, and his human civilization's, possible destruction. If they were to be destroyed, so be it. They'd had their time, and that brief time, however short, was better than nothing. They'd lived and breathed, and even if the universe should forget them, it couldn't erase that fact. What had it all meant? That humankind had existed—that's all the meaning he needed it to have.

Curiously he watched as the former Immaterial planet that once powered his home Dyson sphere, began to tilt, so that he finally got a good view of the creature's underside.

Once, years before, when he, Lorna and Brik, had been young, they'd travelled to a small watery planet on a diplomatic mission. This was after the first missions of their salad days and before their involvement, and decorated heroics, in the Yzqill Wars.

On this planet, young cadets who'd wished to rise to the next tier of their careers had to go out on ships and hunt on vast seas a monstrous, carnivorous whale-like creature called a Jirmak.

The elders of the planet decided that if the three interlopers wanted to be listened to, they too would have to hunt a Jirmak and prove themselves.

For 73 days the three of them hunted through wild seas the thing.

Then, on the last day, while sinking into the ocean after their ship had capsized, Sal Greta caught a glimpse of the belly of the great fish. As it turned to face him, he'd seen rows upon rows of terribly sharp teeth, as much as perhaps thirty or more, within its huge mouth. Beasts as large as plesiosaurs and megalodons were staked upon them. Parts of bitten off lands and buildings were in that mouth. The mouth was ripped and raw.

The moon-sized mouth he now saw rapidly and voraciously coming towards him was more terrible than that sight.

Yet now, as then, bravely he stood.

The Sleeper on the Throne

Xulthal, the Fearsome Planet, was situated by the dim shade and senescence of a dying sun, in the time of the star-forging races known as the Atudiani Collective, Masters of All-Space.

Anathema was the rocky orb to the Atudiani in the dim reaches of space, and many cursed themselves bitterly when, by accident, their long ships found themselves within a light year of its noxious fumes. Then they would halt suddenly their ships, and plow deep their metaphorical oars, opening their brake ports to let escape in trailing mists their anchoring exhausts. Most unfortunate was that person then, who, after mooring and after libations were spilled into the dark aether, because of tradition and rites of strange sortilages, was chosen as sacrifice to the God Lord of Xulthal, who sits and grins on his colossal throne of black gneiss. Unhappy were the eyes of those who countless times witnessed their star-pitching vessels leave, and terrible the mien of they who knew themselves marooned and abandoned forever on this, the penultimate boundary marker and farthest delimitation of the known universe.

And so, heavy with the weight of years on them, did those abandoned, in sad aeons, await in hopeless hope word from the empty skies of rescue. As each generation of star-cartographers kept watch, little by little was forgotten all knowledge of space, and was lost the lust of voyaging into elder gulfs. Civilisations rose and fell, and the watch-towers slowly crumbled into decay, until each new tale brought forth from beyond by the recently abandoned was met with incredulity and laughter.

Always, throughout this degenerative passage, the foul eidolon sat, eternal-wise, dreaming and grinning.

***

Great with cheers and pennants rode forth the 450 soldiers of the High Emperor, Galahir, from his decadent city by the Iglios

Mountains, in the seventh cycle of the Empire of the Crushing Hand, on Xulthal. With him rode the necromancer, Vesenthal, and the infamous barbarian from the mists of Calahar, Udian Andkar.

Pale shone the sun on the massive colonnades of the far city behind, when the army stopped, and the necromancer turned to his toad-like master and said, "Galahir, High Emperor, your cruel yoke straddles the land as is fit for one of your station, but I fear even these scores of gimmaled men may be no match for the Dark Lord, upon whose true empire we tread. Your empire is this corner of Xulthal, but his empire is the full circumference of this baleful and ribbed world. Behold: Yon far Iglios Mountains, of vast, nebulous peaks, are but the turrets of his walled fortress. Even should your men overpass his craggy citadel, what then? What if the Sleeper should awaken? Evil auguries warn that someday, our All-Master shall ope his Stygian eyes, when the powerful spells that keep this Old One buried, wither and dissolve into a mist. Doom is prophesied for Xulthal then, when the stars are right. What if this venture is precursor to that foresaid day? Rather would I listen to him when he communicates to us in dreams, than hear one word of his spoken to us from his actual lips. Rather would I marvel at that miles-long, baffling, incomprehensible jester of grinning stone by the mountain, than behold his true quickening horror. It is not too late and I counsel we return."

Galahir threw an angry look at his bug-eyed vizier, while flicking his tongue. Removing one hand from his fat paunch, he placed it hotly atop the gilded hilt of his Friezun sword. Then, gently stroking it, he said, "For long years you have mocked at my indolence, necromancer. Now, when a deed of valour may be done, you shrink away in cowardice. Go back and sit upon my purple couches, and drink from the high viands your yellow mouth often scorned to touch. I will go on. When I return in glory, be sure to know your head will be the first to roll." Finishing, he turned towards the haughty barbarian by his side, and asked sarcastically, "And you—do you also wish to stop?"

Udian Andkar's eyes narrowed into two black marbles as he spat and said, with cold ferocity, "The sons of Calahar were born to plunder. Rue the hour you say, fat king, 'Halt! We must return!' Lest I turn on that hour and slit your throat."

Pleased with the barbarian's answer, Galahir laughed heartily.

"I fear we will witness many prodigies from here to our fate," Vesenthal added.

"I welcome it," the barbarian said. Then taking firm the reins of his eight-legged warbeast, he shot first into the wastes.

* * *

On the fifth day, with gleaming armours and hard hauberks, the company, arrayed in royal blazonries, hilted blades wrought of pearl, battle axes, crested helms, pikes, and heavy maces, rode war-rigged beasts full speed onto the long-dead road that would lead them closer to the jutting mountains. To left and right of them stretched in unfathomable distances the silent mountain ranges and ahead loomed the tall peaks that legend said housed the Old God.

Legend also said the foul idol of the stars had fallen from black worlds beyond the sane universe and, at its plunge, had cast upon itself huge mountains with its multifoliate snaky arms and built itself a subterrene kingdom, full of the outer laws from whence it had come.

The descendants of the marooned whispered this around broad campfires and dwelt on it when they travelled, canopied with golden helms, to far lands. None knew whether these myths were true or not, since these events were rumoured to have occurred in the long years before the advent of any tongue to speak of it. They could only wonder at the rude and ancient shape of doting gneiss carved on the side of the mountain, representing it, and marvel at its unknown provenance from the perspective of eternity. Many averred it had been deathly old even when the first dwellers had come.

Whenever Galahir thought of the legends, he grimaced with disgust, and laughed inwardly at his fellow countrymen's ignorance and superstition. He knew the secret, that what dreamed behind the mountains was not, in truth, a god, and deserved no worship or veneration. It was, instead, an evil entity from beyond the skies that dreamed only to return thence again and resume its once-cosmic debaucheries.

Vesenthal had told him this secret, for Vesenthal was old and the last so far marooned on this planet, nearly two millennia ago. The necromancer had helped his ancestors build their mighty empire. They had esteemed his powers, but, most importantly, they had believed his stories of the outer dark, as now Galahir did.

When the High Emperor was young, he would often loaf, a flaccid toadman on soft divans, and ruminate on the false god of the glaciated peaks. Of all the First Emperor's progeny, he was the lowliest and basest and most industrious to vice. Not a noble thought he had, but indulged instead in all voluptuousness and every carnal sin of the flesh and mind, until, one day, total madness engulfed him.

In this madness, he decided to blot out the vast image from the mountain. Slowly, he grew to hate it, since he could suffer no other power higher than himself to live.

* * *

Past molten rivers of flames the columned coursers marched, and ever up volcanic rocks the broken path took them. Crooked and scattered ghoul-like trees that grew sometimes on this dismal world, bleak and wild, they passed, until a great, trembling earthquake hampered them.

Mighty warbeasts fell. Stalwart men and thick, robust shields and scabbards hit the rocky ground. Some animals frightened into a frenzy rushed into rivers of raging fires and were lost, as beast and man burned and screamed in hopeless mania.

"By the great dark that at all times surrounds us!" the barbarian yelled. "Keep tight your reins and stand your ground! It is said in Calahar that ground-shakes are but the batting of an eyelash the Old One makes in his slumber! I scorn to be afraid of so small a thing! Keep to your senses!"

Bringing themselves to order again, after Udian Andkar's loud command, and seeing no further auspicious prodigy emerging, the army, after Galahir's order, began once more their hellish ascent.

After awhile, Vesenthal turned angrily towards the barbarian and whispered, "When the time is right, kill him, as we have agreed. Then the throne of the Crushing Hand will be yours. Only then shall we return alive from this madman's quest. Few will weep for him; believe me. Do not shrink away from this great enterprise that I have placed before your feet. With you, the empire shall once more be feared and not be laughed at by our enemies."

"I will kill him even if the God Lord of Xulthal stood to defend him, old one."

"Let us hope we never make it close enough to find out."

* * *

As the ancient and dying sun shone pale on the rock floors, from which fissures mawed and great heaving tentacles and serpentine appendages issued, the barbarian found himself hewing and hacking furiously. The army was now by the first low foothills of the Iglios

Mountains. Already, many dangers had they passed and many men had been lost.

As the battle raged outside, Vesenthal chanted alone in a shadowed cave. His hood was off, revealing his shiny carapace and insectoid eyes and mandibles, common to those life-forms of his former planet, Socchid. His long locust arms were curved as in prayer. He chanted over a strange, obelisk-shaped metal.

He had found it, buried for millennia, in the southern deserts. When he saw it, he knew the thing for what it was: a teleportation mechanism, built by some mad unfortunate soul out of nearly impossible-to-find materials and long-forgotten technology. He knew that only the right words would activate it. Over the years, he had said every word, in every language, out of the thousands known to him from the Atudiani Collective, uselessly. He had never been able to make it work. More than likely, neither had its original creator. Nothing on this planet seemed to work when it involved escape. Even all the former civilizations, as far as he knew, seemed to have mysteriously crumbled once their people had reached the rudimentary knowledge to begin to dream of charting accurately their knowable cosmos.

Now he chanted furiously and thoughtlessly to escape the battle and, hopefully, this world altogether.

Looking outside the cave, he saw how the huge slimy appendages grabbed, encircled, and crushed or crashed against the strange scum-flesh of Galahir's army. The creatures, the god-forsaken races, the descendants of the discards and refuse of a thousand and more far-flung planets, fought bravely and desperately to withstand this latest onslaught, they were sure, from their All-Master. Mindless saurian warbeasts, the strongest and fastest known to the Crushing Hand, rammed or tottered by the dancing tendrils, as vegetable and biological life slithered or crawled, jumped, flew, ran away, or rushed headlong into the melee. Blades slashed, shields clanged, and weirder noises sounded from things that needed no exterior weapons to fight. Here and there, in places Vesenthal could not tell apart in the darkness, the shambling races and slugging things fleeing from the snakish attackers.

Then hell-born laughter assailed his ears as he saw the barbarian, smeared in gore, enter carrying a vast, twitching tentacle. In his other hand he carried the bloody squamous head of the toad-like emperor, Galahir. Great terror was writ on the head's face. Still, its round eyes rolled, and its emerald mouth moved unwittingly in nervous tics, gurgling gibberish commands from its mangled voice-box.

Throwing the head at Vesenthal, the barbarian yelled, "I have changed my mind, necromancer! We shall continue to the God Lord's lair! I shall rule the Crushing Hand and also be thought its greatest emperor, when I bring back news of the slumbering Old One's defeat! The woman! The woman will explain more!"

"What woman?" the necromancer shouted back, puzzled. Yet, almost as soon as he finished his question, from behind the barbarian, Vesenthal saw a womanish shape begin to materialise. As she floated towards him, slithering, he was shocked to realise the mist-shaped thing developed fangs and, also, sinister and hypnotising yellow, reptilian eyes.

***

"I came from sky-flung towers," the serpent woman, who was named Aesika, said from her abbey by the mountains. Near her, around a table, set with common food and drink in wooden utensils, sat the barbarian, resting his head on a huge clenched fist, and also near her sat the necromancer, deep in thought. "Still, I dream of those towers," she continued, "reared by my serpent people on that young earth, on a continent now dead hundreds of millions of years ago. Now it has fractured, and pieces of that once-mighty continent float slowly on deep waters around the planet—a planet now ruled by a creature called 'Man,' a creature that did not even exist, whose ancestors had not yet crawled from the muck, when my people first looked and took to the stars. I helped rear those Babelian towers in the youth of my world. I knew their first architects, and now I am trapped here, as you are, while aeons have passed at home, and in the universe at large. The Dark Lord of the Stars has given me the gift of immortality, to merely weep like a caged, eternal bird, while he slumbers days and years away. I am tired. I want to fly. I want to leave. I ask again: Will you help me?"

Vesenthal, the addressee, looked at her hard, as if searching for signs of any trickery on her face, and then replied, "The God Lord of Xulthal is powerful. Even now, he watches us from his dark halls, and knows everything we do. I do not know why he has not deigned to come against us, but I do not wish to find out, and neither do I crave to feel his wrath."

"He sleeps and dreams, insectoid, as I have also slept and dreamt at times these uncountable years. He found me while I dreamt, and brought me here. I travelled through vortices of time and gates it is not proper to speak of, to be his slave, for then he was amused by us lesser life-forms. However, I know he has forgotten us—I am certain! For aeons, his thoughts have been elsewhere in the universe. Like specks of dust we are to this mighty being. When, in truth, is the last time in living memory that anyone has had commerce with him? Those creatures you have fought are not him, but his worshippers that fell to this planet before you. He has forgotten us. Let us escape while we can, and are able to get close to him to work our magic. You may never have this chance again, necromancer. What do you say?"

He looked at her more closely. Realising that she was telling the truth, that this might indeed be his last chance to leave the unholy planet, he answered, "Let us go, then."

* * *

From beneath four dead and lustreless moons, the necromancer and the barbarian saw the beasts, which the reptile woman had summoned, land. The beasts would transport them over the Iglios Mountains. Only the three of them would travel—the rest of the army now being unnecessary.

The beasts landed by thrawn and black trees. Two big, ice-pale and transparent verminous things, like maggots or inchoate nightcrawlers, they were, with long, gangly wings and two bird-like legs. From their nauseous mouths, below their prostomiums, dripped slime and came unsettling croaking noises.

Once airborne, the barbarian and the woman, both on one beast, led the way.

Peaks and valleys passed before them, and still larger peaks of mountains and lesser volcanoes loomed. Wind blew threateningly.

Soon, Vesenthal thought he could touch the four moons of Xulthal. Below him and above him was only darkness, and then he saw the tallest apogee of the mountains.

"Look," Aesika said to the barbarian. "Who is that who sits and slumbers?" She then laughed. She pointed at this zenith to show how, directly below it, was carved the gargantuan form of the Lord of the Planet, on its throne of black gneiss, with its many snakish arms and body stretching thousands of miles downwards.

Vesenthal shut his eyes in fear as the thing's huge top loomed before him and vanished, as the worm-bird flew over and past the tallest peak.

"Such a large image was not sculpted by mortal hands," Udian Andkar said.

The woman from behind him answered, "No, darling, only his gigantic ancient priests, who perform his secret rites under the ground, could have done such a wonder."

Passing the highest summits, they saw how peaks of smaller mountains awaited them, curiously placed as if in a circular pattern, like living earth walls.

Atop three of those mountain peaks, the worms circled and dropped their riders, each vast distances apart, and flew away. The three humanoids were placed in a triangular pattern on the circle of mountains.

* * *

Not the wastes, thought Vesenthal, of this fearsome and always savage world of Xulthal, with life flitting and death near, of mostly rocky terrain, molten and hot and—in places—demon cold, of few comforts, small oceans, raging weathers and frightful fears, and illumed by the cold light of a dim star, could strike his heart with such tremors as now he felt, atop these dark-wooded, desolate, rock-ribbed steeps.

Below him, he knew not how far the abysses plummeted. Above him, the stars and moons seemed bigger and bloated.

He knew that somewhere, in the far black mountains, like dots connecting a triangle, the barbarian and the woman stood atop their own blasted pinnacles.

Near him was a step of stone, butting against the pine-bending winds that blew from the gaping chasm.

With growing trepidation, he soon listened to the sorcerous woman say, "Do not be alarmed that you can hear me across these tremendous distances. The technology of the Elder Ones was such that even the Atudiani Collective would marvel at it. Those stone markers that you see, inscribed with strange hieroglyphs of an antique world, are the high places from which the long-gone Elder Ones first grabbed and imprisoned the Lord of Xulthal, and pulled him ferociously from the stars. Step at my word on top of them, quickly, to see and marvel at what happens. But do not step off them at any time, for then the spell will be broken and all shall be lost." Then she commanded forcefully, "Step on the jut of stone now!"

Vesenthal did so, with blood beating fast, and instantly felt dizzy. The world moved, the wind blew harder, strange buzzing noises assailed his ears. From the fathomless pit between the circle of mountains, a light of varied colours shot out, and engulfed them all. The distances did—and yet, at the same time, did not—come together. He saw Udian Andkar and the female serpent where they were on their own obsidian stones. The great spiralling mountains encircled him, yet with this new distortion of vision, he saw them clearly, vast and yet near. Then, from the profundity of the abyss, he saw a great storied throne emerge, whose towering crest touched the sky, on it sitting the eidolon of horror, its zenith touching the stars.

Such a monstrous thing, the necromancer thought, as he looked up. It was higher than a mountain and was undefeatable by insects such as they were. He regretted now his foolhardy decision, and wept at his certain death. Indeed, the throne and the creature on it dwarfed the tallest peak. It was a miles-long hologram.

"See that I was right!" he heard Aesika scream gloatingly. "He sleeps and pays no heed to us at all!"

The necromancer was shaken out of his fear by these words. Slowly, hope crept back into his heart as, with each passing moment, the figure on the throne remained idle and aloft of any mundane occurrence. It was a king of eternity, and its thoughts dwelt only in those spheres.

"Now, necromancer!" the abbess yelled urgently. "Place the teleportation mechanism by the Sleeper!"

Vesenthal was wide awake to the plan they had agreed on. He did not know if it would work, but, with vital and renewed hope, he placed all doubt aside. The woman had said she had fixed the mechanism. Even though they had not tested it, out of the faintest fear its power might attract the Old One's notice before they had a chance to use it, now with confidence in the woman, the necromancer moved to place the object in front of the Sleeper. The woman had said that what the entity's devilish image felt likewise affected the Sleeper under the planet. They hoped that the teleportation mechanism, enhanced by the cosmic powers of the old builders of the prison, would teleport the beast far from them.

Magically, as he moved his hands closer to the abyss, they grew distortedly bigger. Even though he remained the same size, his hands and the object grew huge, and became a part of the hologram, scaled so that the object looked as it would if it were actual-size by the throne.

Amazed, he took his hands away. They shrank to normal size. He began to modulate his voice and say the words they had all agreed would activate the mechanism.

But nothing happened.

Except for the first movement of the Dark One on his throne.

* * *

Now, frenzied, the barbarian took his heavy sword out of its sheath, panther-quick, and heaved his arms in an arc, so that its cutting edge might cleave the monster by its top. The sword grew massively large, because of a distortion of vision and matter, while it swung ever forward over the great chasm in the midst of the sentinel of mountains, becoming mysteriously part of the hologram, until the barbarian saw he carried a mammoth, miles-long blade in his hand. As it moved in less than a second towards the entity, the barbarian anticipated joy to think it might cleave a mountain. But, quick as he was in his wild lustful rage, the tentacle appendages at the sides of the Sleeping One were quicker. Before he finished his shout, a tentacle blocked the sky above him, and others thrashed before him, with lance-sharp teeth within the maws at their tips, one limb knocking the impossibly large sword out of his hands, sending it careening down the Iglios mountainside.

He looked not at the blade, though, but in awe instead at the flailing, planet-thick limbs, like constellations, which seemed to come shy of brushing against the stars above.

"By the lesser gods of Xulthal!" he yelled, "what have we awakened?"

* * *

On the Old One's holographic trunk, eyes—or what seemed eyes or something else; Vesenthal was not sure—opened like voids in the dark, while he saw the gigantic blade of the barbarian fall. The creature turned its uppermost top, which culminated in craggy peaks like a crown, towards him, and motionless remained with potential energy.

His people, aeons before, had mastered words that commanded matter for short periods of time. With this skill, the necromancer began to construct an insectoid, a feat which had earned him his title, since the ignorant races of Xulthal believed he, in fact, resurrected the dead. Sand, atom, bark, stone, and pebble morphed into molecule and organ as, little by little, chitin, limb and carapace joined, until a wailing, gumless wraith emerged from the blood-red dirt, and stood by Vesenthal on his stone step. Then the serpent woman told him what to do. Controlling its mind, he hurled it forward, without it leaving the step. This motion caused a gargantuan representation of it to form, which began to grapple with the other thing on the peerless throne.

Seeing this, the barbarian, after tensing his muscles while remaining on the stone, with thought-intent also threw himself against the waving tentacles. His hologram hit the thing as a tree hits a solid wall. Hologram hands grabbed tentacle and feet kicked alien flesh as he manoeuvred on the stone. With each movement, the scene shifted before him in impossible views, while his representation fought. He saw, inexplicably, both through his own eyes and through his hologram's eyes. Mountaintops moved from north to south, coalescing, then separating from each other. First, he was in front of the thing, then in back, then on top, bigger than a moon. So the fight went on, as the serpent woman also joined in, wielding a dagger with which she tried to stab the monstrosity.

The two males and the female fought bravely, until flashes of extreme energy hit them where they stood, and their battling images crumbled. A power held them to the stones, paralysed, while the shadowed entity on the throne, now undisturbed, stretched its many tentacle arms into the sky and began to spin them. Helplessly, witnessing forces they did not understand, the three felt and saw as wind coalesced above the tentacles. Air as wind swept past them, drawn like a magnet, and trees and detritus were pulled towards the epicentre, while clouds also closed in and spun, and great lights tore the black sky above. The mountains rumbled and shook, while a massive whirlpool or maelstrom formed above them all, and the thing on the throne sat in massive splendour, connecting earth with the heavens now opened, within whose spinning was reflected an alien sky.

Then they felt in non-sounds, yet knew it was happening somehow, a great laughter from the god. With it did the three come to ultimately respect the true dimensions and cosmic power of the thing.

Their mouths were allowed to scream as realisation of their doom hit them.

The teleportation device suddenly became operative, and flashed a beam, which the Old One drew to himself. With greater power, he directed it out towards the open hole in the sky, as other beams hit the three, and they were drawn into the light. Then they saw themselves above the Old One, coursing away, as the hole in the sky closed below them.

* * *

Vesenthal, between gasps of fear, wondered desperately while he was being teleported through hyperspace, whether the grinning thing—for he recalled dimly a slit that seemed to grin where its nose should have been—had, in its cosmic power, actually granted them their escape. But also he remembered from legends how even its pleasing rewards were monstrous and alien. So he screamed more.

And screamed he still as his mind melted, and was lost, in the mind of a dumb sea-beast on a far planet of water.

The serpent woman, whether in reward or punishment she never knew, found herself alone in hyperspace, in which for aeons she floated, not knowing either light or rest.

As for Udian Andkar, he, many years later, proud and battle-scarred and the first High Emperor of the Atlanteans on a planet named 'Earth,' sat on a throne in glory by a wide ocean, with white-and-black hair falling over his face, and wondered thoughtfully at his life and at the strange enigmatic turns it had taken. He thought of his former companions on Xulthal, and if they had been as fortunately rewarded as he.

It was a reward he was granted, he was sure, not because of laws regarding punishments fitting their crimes or of rewards justly dealt, but because of incomprehensible judgements, based on pure cosmic whimsy.

A Monster in the Midst

Le Vicomte Triste to le Grand Duc

Now that the world is going to hell, I think how I should have shot you with my gun and not my wit, oh, so long ago over our game of *écarté*. But, oh, well, what's a vicomte to do, monsieur?

You do remember my faithful clockwork man? Of course you must. He lies how the world will soon lie, dead and undone by his master, oozing mucous and fungal matter. They will say: It was the glorious 158th year of our glorious mushroom age, when it all came to nothing. Or, hopefully, someone will say it. Hopefully, it will not be you. I will not, henceforth, address you as you so like, by the title of Monsieur le Grand Duc, but simply as monsieur, as I deem more appropriate, and as is still good etiquette, despite the diminishment of title.

Eight months ago, I remember watching my man grab great handfuls of fungal matter, and fill my steamcarriage and himself with the lumpy fuel. I winced, as you no doubt remember my disgust at the filthy growths and their smell, so sweet to most, so putrid to *moi*. It was with even greater trepidation that I witnessed how ravenously he stuffed himself with the new toxic outgrowths of the fungus. The stupid automaton had practically filled his head with some of the slimier and more liquescent green transmutations of the substance, so that it oozed over him and hung off his chin in flabby waves of solid jelly.

Then I noted how one of my valet's eyes glowed with a lust and yearning unsettling to behold. He walked toward the clockwork man and dipped a greedy, jerking finger, like a great plowing oar, into the massy substance of my man's egg-like head, and then proceeded to hungrily lick the loathsome substance off his own finger, like a slobbering animal. His eyes took on a glossy, idiotic cast and he fell over.

I knew, of course, that he was now under the hypnotic fatal sleep of the green fungus and its slime. It had but recently manifested itself and I was closely studying it, to make a scientific treatise for L'École Mycologique, which I was readying to present at our next meeting.

I observed how, almost instantaneously, my valet's lower jaw began to putrefy and turn into mush. In seconds, his jaw was a fetid liquid. Soon, monsieur, the man was liquid himself. I was alarmed to find this new anomalous metamorphic by-product of the green fungus. Up until then, it had only worked as a sort of opiate that led to death in about ninety-five percent of its consumers. The other five percent, who awoke, described its effects as hallucinatory, a shamanistic type of experience, which involved travelling to strange, exotic locales...or perhaps other worlds...seeing queer dark beings and culminating in an encounter with a strange, green star-shaped or jellyfish-like entity that imparted (as far as I am aware) no wisdom, but merely was, and pulsated at the centre of a gigantic mushroom world. This was the first observation that I made and that was later observed and confirmed by all of Europe, including yourself. Later (as you know), I also documented how a strong compulsion affected some innocents to eat of the substance: how only some takers were liquefied; how, of those who awoke from its effects, a small percentage were transformed into a new aesthetic of the grotesque; and how the survivors of the opiate soon started their own cult, centred around the green godling (May God in Heaven have mercy on their souls). The frighteningly deformed members are held in high esteem, now. The most monstrous are high priests, of which there are some whispers...dare I say it...that there are even some who are unnamable in their horror, and who are considered demi-gods, the highest masters of earth's great chain of being.

But that is all too far in the past.

You are aware, monsieur, how, 19 days ago, I presented myself before L'École Mycologique, with a petition to seek out the source, if there was one, for the green fungal menace. I only asked for a vast, steam-powered airship from the King's royal navy, and permission to leave early to attend a *mécanique* performance of both Moliere's *Les Precieuses Ridicules* and Beaumarchais' *Le Mariage de Figaro*, at the Theatre-Francais. I was nearly denied all three requests, by you. But thankfully (or not, as it would seem), your dissenting vote, and that of your colleagues in your absences, was annulled by our esteemed secretary of L'Academie des Sciences, the Marquis de Condorcet.

In two days' time, I was ready to leave on my mission, monsieur.

I dressed for the occasion in a wine-dark, silk-velvet suit of the highest courtly fashion, the richly embroidered coat high-collared, and the waistcoat opulently decorated with diamonds for buttons. I also wore shoes and breech buckles, and a jewelled scabbard at my side, a white flounced frill at the neck and sleeves and, atop my head, an auburn, small-yet-stylish, lightly powdered wig with, of course (since I was, in a sense, going to war), a military cocked hat of fine fabric atop the wig. My clockwork man and valets were also dressed impeccably.

At our farewell, damsels wept to see me go and Mademoiselle Tussaud fainted horribly. Do tell the poor creature not to wait for me.

I stood at the stern of the ship, a chambered cannongun slung over my left shoulder. After saluting the officers, the pageantry and science members, and our King Louis and Queen Marie Antoinette, who had both come especially from Versailles to see me go, I asked the helmsman to circle Paris once and then to head off into the bright, cerulean sky.

Cheering crowds followed us, trumpeters trumpeted gaily below, and French flags waved proudly. We flew over large buildings, streets, cabs, coaches, parks, vendors, the Louvre, the districts, the filthy populace—in short, over everything. I saw street urchins and city-workers picking and cleaning the membranous film of fungi which grew on the walls and on the ground, on trees everywhere, and threatened to engulf the city, if it were left to spread unchecked. Here and there, I noted drooling supine bodies, no doubt victims of their own uncontrollable urges for the deadly green slime mold.

In no time, our steamship and attached aerostat, with its three accompanying smaller dirigibles, flew over the naval harbour. We cruised calmly onto the Seine and followed the course of the river. I read alarm and fear in some of the men, but that was of no great concern to me, since I reasoned my adventurous spirit was enough joy for everyone.

* * *

"*Vive la France! Vive la liberté!*" I yelled, as I stood courageously at the bow of the ship, a good strong breeze blowing through my wig. A young boy, a sullen naval student named 'Napoleon,' was so touched by my enthusiasm for this liberty and patriotism that I felt, that he also joined me in hollering passionately at the sky.

It was a clear day, with only a few clouds not far above us and a hot sun flaring down. We travelled at a good nautical pace, the sailors keeping the coals and fungus burning. The combined steam allowed the overhead large aerostat to easily bear the burden of our heavily ironclad warship.

In no time, we flew onto the Atlantic Ocean and I marvelled nauseated to behold, outstretched before me in all directions, a vast, viscous, bobbing desert of slime and mushroom. Indeed, here it was impressed on me nakedly and powerfully, how much of our earth the organism was truly lord of!

By day, as we travelled, all I saw was the mold and, far away through my spyglass, almost as if purposely keeping a distance, barely discernible seagulls that to my scientific mind did not look or fly quite like seagulls should. By night, the green, intrusive slime glowed eerily, and cast a greenish light on the silent world.

When everyone else was asleep, I would look through my spyglass, alone and hidden, at the gruesome film that covered the ocean, which, in places, was elevated and more compacted into solid islands of sponge or smaller iceberg-like mounds. As I looked at the fungus in the dark, I discerned in places, either beneath it in the water or, more horribly, of the stuff itself, amorphous shapes that, to my mind, seemed to be following our fast-moving ship. I liked it not.

Because of this, one day, I said to the captain, "Capitaine, I command you to change course immediately. I believe we are being followed. By changing course, it might confuse our pursuers and cause them, or it, either to lose interest in us or lose track of us. We shall reach our destination from another direction."

To which he answered, flushed, "Monsieur le Vicomte! To do so we would have to recalibrate our computational astrolabe and also more than likely extend our journey! This will not sit well with our helmsman in the former, nor with our men in the latter. How sure are you that we are being followed?"

"I am not sure at all. But I command it."

After this brief exchange, he quickly changed to an indirect route, and I am sure that it was because of this caution on my part that the first leg of my journey was saved.

***

My second leg began one morning, when we arrived near our destination. An officer of the watch spotted a column of black smoke, ascending from the horizon of our port side. Cautiously we neared the source of the smoke, the helmsman causing the steam from the aerostat balloon to lower us so we could have a better view, once we realised the site was of no danger.

Below us were three navy warships, ironclads like our own, still smouldering from a recent tragedy, and all black and burnt and devoid of crew. Their bulks were enmeshed and floating on a great plateau of gruesome jelly. Their aerostats were burnt to ashes. These three ships were the titanic hulls of empires, namely, England's, Spain's, and Russia's. No doubt, ours would have made a fourth.

Later in the day, the captain said to me, "It is certain they did not destroy each other. Their cannons never fired a shot, from what our investigations can tell. Apparently, two ships are old and the Russian ship more recent. It must have fallen or crashed into the other two."

Not wishing to put the crew into any more danger, nor finding myself with time to fully delve into this mystery, I decided to disembark.

The captain asked me if I had any suspicions as to what had happened to the Russian ship.

I said, with certainty, "Sabotage."

* * *

And so, the third and last leg of my journey began.

Call it madness, or an egocentric wish to be thought a hero, or perhaps a too-great love for my fellow man, but that very day, I left, accompanied only by my clockwork man. We left inside a metal machine that I had transported onto the ship, one of my own new experimental inventions, which I called a 'submarine.'

The fungus near the ship was compact and solid, so that my submarine, walking and resembling a half-monkey, half-octopus creature, took us on a vast journey atop that pustulous landscape.

My mécanique man told me where to go. You ask why, perhaps? Because, monsieur, in my skill with automata, I had installed in my man a means by which he could, like a hound, track the source of our predicament. He merely had to fill his head with the vile substance and instantly he felt the source, like a beacon. Do not be surprised at this, since you yourself are aware of my prodigious scientific skill with the construction of servile robots.

Sometime during mid-day, I looked behind me and, through the glass dome atop the submersible, which housed us and the control panels, I saw shadows following us at a far distance. I could not make out their shapes exactly, but something in how they moved made me shiver. I sped up my construct.

It was not long before my man told me to stop and dive into the mushroom island. I looked up at the hot sun and bade it farewell, before I plunged my ironcast into the flesh of the slime.

It dug into the substance, shredding the organism's tissues with its many arms as we travelled, until the submarine broke into clear water below the mass. It swam at top speed, like an octopus, beneath the Atlantic; schools of shiny and lightning-fast fish passing by it. I marvelled.

Following thick filaments of fungi down, eventually, we reached a hole. Falling into it, after a few hours, we emerged in a cave, hundreds of feet under the ocean.

I was surprised to find readings that told me there was oxygen here. After a curious exploration of my surroundings, my automaton pointed out our new direction. It was a tunnel, but the tunnel's entrance was too small to fit our vehicle; so, climbing out of the walking cephalopod, we continued the journey on foot.

* * *

While in the tunnel, we were illumed by the glowing green slime. I despised being so close to the disgusting stuff. We passed, to my shock, a hideously smelling, decomposing corpse, which I quickly surmised was a Yankee—no doubt, I morbidly joked, unaware of his recent triumph over England in his revolutionary war. As I wondered what new surprises were in store for me, we neared the end of the tunnel and, monsieur, surprised I was, indeed, to behold what next I saw.

Exiting the tunnel, we beheld a monstrously massive cavern, undulating and alive with the slime—at its centre, vibrating horribly, a cyclopean green-wheeled or starfish-shaped mushroom. It was attached to the rest of the fungus and slime, like a many-tentacled thing, and I was sure it was the fruiting source of the green ooze. There it hung, like a pulsing, grotesque spider in its own web. It was

JULIO TORO SAN MARTIN

the brain of the world-conquering membranous scum. The deity of the hallucinators' mushroom world, which was our own world! God-like, indeed, it was!

Suddenly, I felt a powerful blow to my head. I collapsed—weak, bleeding and dizzy—onto the goo. Before I fainted, I saw a thick grey and yeasty slop of a leg step into my line of vision.

* * *

I awoke to a strange chanting directed towards that contamination at the centre of our world. Beside me I saw, lying also, my clockwork man.

I was, no doubt, in the clutches of the green godling's insane cult. I was forgotten for the moment as they praised it.

Never have you seen, monsieur, such a depraved motley of diseased humanity. They stood like stunted sponge things, for "human" I dare not term them, comprised of growths and deformities too hideous to enumerate, and covered with green goo of an unclean corruption. They stepped towards the fungoid entity. With each step, their bodies quaked, so much so that I feared their cellular integrity might collapse. Then a marvellous thing happened.

They began to disintegrate!

The huge cavern was filled with their moans as they putrefied and turned to slop. The stoutest, I saw turn and try to escape. I knew then this was not part of their plan. The god was incomprehensibly destroying its own worshippers!

What was happening? Bravely, I stepped toward the malevolent thing. Nothing happened.

I surmised that the mushroom-mind had evolved consciousness from the parent mindless fungus over years in isolation and had then, instinctively for survival, spread its green slime and tissue like a cancer, over the parent species and even through it, taking it over, compromising the parent species' own integrity, transforming the parent's flesh in places into itself. All this while, it possessed nothing more than a simple, primitive brain, being defensively instinctual and unthinking like an animal, and unaware of anything except its own kind.

Realising this, I picked up my cannongun, which one of the mushroom beings had carried, and walked towards the pulsating tumour. Though suspended, it seemed to squat before me like a malicious imp, spokes of fungal rays radiating from it in all directions. I touched its gobsmooth and slippery flesh. It glowed green. In places, a muck of impurity dripped unsettlingly from it. Everything about it aroused deep disgust in my being. Surely, this was life antithetical to man. And yet, oh, yet, it was an awe-inspiring sight. Here was a baby, a new-born life-form, lush with fecundity, first of its kind, the earth-circling lord of this world. I petted it, imagining its thought processes to be like those of a dog. Then, taking aim for humanity, I blasted it out of the animal kingdom.

I will not lie, I will not say it wept, or screamed, or thrashed and hurled about in agony, as it burnt mightily on fire. It merely burnt, soundlessly, pulsing erratically, though once I think I did detect, for a second, the faintest outline of a distorted, anguished, semi-human face appear and then disappear on its surface. Perhaps it did this for my benefit. Once it was a charred husk, it burst, releasing smoke, and then it flattened out like an airless bag.

I rejoiced at how easy it was to destroy! Then the cellular deterioration of the fungus around me started.

* * *

My clockwork man and I ran in fear. The fertile, luxuriantly tropical mushroom vibrancy around us was disintegrating, as if the vital life of the fungal body, with the centre no longer there to pump life through its veins, was dying. And so I learned the dead entity was not only the fungus' mind, but also its heart.

I felt as if rich oxygen and warmth, the very humidity of the air, were being sucked out of the cavern.

When we reached my submersible, I saw it was damaged—no doubt by those cultists who had followed us and who were now dead.

We managed to make it back to the mushroom island before the machine completely broke down. I saw then how the island was also slowly deteriorating. I noted how thin filaments of fungus, resembling seaweed, and also thin slime, interconnected to other excremental fungal islands. These islands, too, were falling apart. What an immense arterial network the god had a hold of on this earth! And it was all dying!

Was I hero or villain?

As I sat contemplating all this new information, I heard my clockwork man's gears beside me, whirring and clattering. Then, for the first time in ages, I heard through the gramophone embedded in his chest, a small artificial laugh, which grew louder and louder.

"What are you laughing at?" I yelled at him, disgusted.

He struggled to use speech tubes long in disuse. Slowly, a sentence began to emerge. "Master is blind," he said.

I was incensed at his statement and yet, afraid. "How so?" I asked, secretly dreading his answer.

He spasmed. I could hear his computational box clunking in his chest.

Then he answered me. "Monsieur has not taken into consideration all the tools available to him from the current sciences. When the fungus first appeared, it rapidly spread and destroyed most of the greenery and trees of the earth, while also becoming an important source of fuel and food, among other things, for your species, which greatly changed your world. Those green plants I previously mentioned, it is thought they originally supplied earth with oxygen, which your species breathes to survive. The conquering fungus mutated and took over this process, for reasons I cannot fathom. By destroying it, you have destroyed yourself, for when the fungus is dead, the earth will be depleted greatly of its oxygen. Master is a good roboticist, but a poor mycologist and botanist. He is also a poor strategist." After saying this, he began to laugh again.

The reasonableness of my servant's logic frightened me. I screamed at him, "And how long have you theorised of this possible outcome? Speak!"

"Since the day we left France."

I then picked up my cannongun and struck him hard, until he was nothing but a mess of rolling gears and dented metal.

* * *

Since that day, I have seen this island decrease, I estimate, by nearly six percent of its mass, and the process still continues.

I will send this letter with one of the seagull-beasts I have captured, in hopes that it might reach you, monsieur, since you are accounted France's greatest mycologist.

I wonder what the new face of the earth will bring with it in the coming years. What catastrophes will come? Shall we all die or not?

My hours I spend, sometimes blaming myself for our predicament, sometimes blaming others.

One morning, I saw, far in the distance, a great mound of decaying jelly arise out of the ocean. It looked like a volcano. It erupted and threw millions of spore-like things far into the sky. What this could mean I know not.

Though, that night, I did dream I walked the fungal island at night, alone. As I looked at the sky, I saw a horrendously large and pulsating moon, all green and dripping green slime. I pictured it as an eye looking down at me. With this thought, I covered my eyes.

July 23, 17_

Imagination

Phantasia, that in one place never stays,
But must forever be traversing through
Realms of dreamlands the forceful mind makes true;
Arise in me strong, and bulwarks erase,
To build in me your Heliconian throne;
And fly, from where the fleet-footed nymphs
In coverts hide, and heroes, their triumphs
Celebrate in emprises far from home.
Go where witches and fantastic gods dwell,
Enamoured of sorcerous rites, and hippogriffs
Swoop by cities grown of strange accruements.
Fly the airy zone of earth's azure cell,
To outer worlds of alien hieroglyphs,
And take me, Goddess, a willing celebrant!

The Lost Letter of Lucian of Samosata, Concerning Apollinaris and the Star Ones: A Fragment

INTRODUCTORY NOTE: This fragment was unearthed at the beginning of the Twentieth Century in Ancona, Magna Graecia, at an archaeological site that also brought to light various texts on hermetic magic, gnostic treatises, an incomplete papyri of Greek poems (which was probably an early fragment of an anthology later to be incorporated into the Byzantine Anthologia Graeca); also fragments of a text by Porphyry and two specimens of Latin Literature: one various leaves of elegies by Tibullus and the other an almost complete codex of Vergil's Aeneid.

Immediately this single text found itself as the major focus of the excavation. Also the deaths soon after of its discoverers, Professors Dusza and Foerstner, under mysterious and unwholesome circumstances, one being completely and thoroughly drained of blood, only helped to add to its notoriety among researchers.

As it stands, the letter purports to be the work of the Roman era satirist Lucian of Samosata, who lived during the second century of the Common Era. However, that author's intrenchant skepticism in regards to the existence of the gods and to religion and the supernatural in general, is at extreme odds with the later portions of the text. This has led to an almost unanimous consensus that the letter is a highly duplicitous forgery. To add more weight to this judgment is the belief that it contains a world-view of the universe perhaps too foreign to the thinking of men of an earlier time and uses a mythology which many students of cults and hidden theologies consider outré and blasphemous.

Yet, if radiocarbon dating is to be relied on, and it has indeed been tested and dated to within the time-frame of Lucian, then we must be prepared to entertain with humility notions that are not at all salutary to the well-being of humankind in general; namely, that perhaps the myths of Cthulhu (in the letter referred to by the sobriquet Tulu) are indeed true, and mankind was visited in earlier times by advanced outside forces hostile to him. It is this very notion which has led many to doubt its authenticity.

The text, as far as study has been able to show, using stylometric testing, is consistent with the word usage and phraseology of the known authentic writings of Lucian; the Greek writing, under paleographic analysis, is proper for the time; and under close scrutiny the letter in terms of personal idiosyncrasies fits in well with his other letters.

In terms of genre it appears to be a mishmash of his common letter style with influences of perhaps the *Satyricon* of Petronius and the Greek novel-romances, of which his own *True Story* is an example. Some scholars go even so far as to suggest Lucian speaks more in his own voice in this letter, without stringent genre convention, because it is indeed a personal letter and was never meant for publication.

This, among other findings, gives credence to its authenticity, in opposition to the proofs and nay-says of its detractors.

The translation herein given was made in the mid-70's of the last century by a Dr. Kavanagh of the Oxford Institute of Archaeology. Being a firm believer in its fraudulent nature, he took many liberties with its translation as an inside joke, not least of all having adopted a low style then and now common in mass-market literature, of which he took a guilty pleasure.

I apologize, and will strive to soon enough give an accurate translation, free from all whimsical flourish.

It should also be noted that though Lucian, or Pseudo-Lucian, as the author of the letter is more commonly referred to, references the Star Ones as aquatic, this should be interpreted to be a surmise of his, due to how he perceived things with his limited knowledge as the events presented themselves to him.

This in no wise diminishes the authenticity of the letter.

Prof. T.T. Macaulay

* * *

Newly translated, from the Greek, by J.S. Kavanagh, and further revised for Appendix XXXVI of Book III of the *Collected Works of Lucian*, in the Ellis Jonson Classical Library collection.

Lucian to Cronius. Greetings.

You ask me to give you a detailed portrait of the man, whose death, or what passed for it, is the subject of my story. This I will attempt to do, though it is not an easy task. In all my travels (of which there have been many) I have never met his like or equal in all the races of men I have been fortunate in my life to make an acquaintance with. Men may live many lives and yet never see another Apollinaris. In the fullness of his youth, he was more god than man, and I do not lie when I say that he possessed that essence of nobility of physique the greatest sculptors have attempted to emulate in their works. Phidias, Praxiteles, Lysippos worked their art as if they had Apollinaris in their view, though he was not to be born until hundreds of years after their time. Plato says this world is but the shadow of the perfect forms; as such, Apollinaris was the light to show us what such things might be. All men are not the same, and not all men are born to rule; he was of that race the exalted times brought forth that Homer sings about in his eternal tomes. Athletic since his early youth, he took great pleasure in the exercise and condition of his body, saying the outward form should be as caveat to the eyes; meaning to inspire awe by your presence inspires others to be followers. In all his movements he had those subtle touches actors, statesmen, orators have; his affectations were of a grace and singular. When he spoke in public he carried himself with the dignity of the Emperor, and addressed the masses as if he was their father. He was all poise and fire, and even when he walked in private, he would salute men by raising an arm in a stately style. He was not short, but of a medium height, and yet seemed taller than his equals. His beardless face, delicate, girlish, and yet manly in its beauty, defies complete description. His cheeks were of a reddish tint and his skin of a tone orangey and tanned. His lips were full, and yet not large, and his nose was perfectly proportioned. Oval-like were his eyes, which could cast forth serenity, poise, mirth, and gravitas, depending on his mood. Over this dangled light-colored brownish locks of hair, which when cut, depending on its growth, showed either curls or a haphazard look. At times he wore a thin bandanna, more for the look than for any real need of it. To speak of his mind is to speak of things closer to the gods than mortal men are, for like the gods, he showed himself inscrutable in his thoughts.

There you have the portrait of the man, Cronius, and if I have lavished too much in his praises, it is only to show the traits and dignity that could draw so many to him, because if I did not do this, no one would believe that such a charlatan-so-called, as I will here present, could ever have commanded a following, much less be thought of as a friend of any gods, even his own Star Ones.

Now then, in my youth, and not long after I had left Commagene, I journeyed to Messenia and stayed in the fishing town of Abia. It was then infested with talk of Apollinaris' Star Ones. I was on my way to visit with Demetrius the philosopher, in Rome, and took this stop-over as a chance to witness this phenomenon. Abia, as I now remember it, Cronius, was deeply wooded and brooded with a quiet timelessness over the sea, so much so that nothing but wild nature disturbed at times its indolent sleep.

While I was there, rumor said that one of Apollinaris' Star Ones had recently washed ashore, and I was taken to the spot in the Mediterranean where this miracle was supposed to have occurred. I was told by a local, how one night, disciples of Apollinaris had gathered by the shore and, after having chanted incomprehensibilities, a sort of dome or smooth mountain-top emerged from far out in the sea. Later, the Star God washed up on the shore. I asked to speak to anyone who had observed this first hand, but was told by the man how the youth who had observed this soon after became a disciple himself of Apollinaris, and now refused to speak to outside inquirers.

Witness, Cronius, what I thought then! I thought how barefaced charlatanry is displayed for all who know how to discern it! Was it not obvious that the youth and the charlatan were together somehow involved in some gullery?

I asked the fellow to take me to where the witness lived, but just then some noise startled and terrified him from the brush nearby, and he said that he would not speak anymore. I tried to hold him and coerce him into talking, but in panic he managed to escape my grasp and run quickly from me. Curious, I went towards the brush where the noise had come from and saw nothing.

Later, an aged fisherman, who reminded me, though less elegantly, of the aedile P. Hosidius Urbicus, after I had paid him a few denarii, assured me that the supposed god was kept like a 'sacred and secret thing' in the house of Apollinaris.

Also, at this time, unbeknownst to me, a god-fearing rich woman by the name of Violentilla, from Carteia, had also landed at Abia. We found ourselves headed in the same direction, and during our journey I could not help but notice that though she was dressed luxuriantly, her face was veiled, allowing one to glimpse but lovingly only on eyes of the brightest emerald.

As we conversed, she turned to me and said, "Why do you not ask why my face is veiled? I know you want to."

I had not, I said demurely, out of respect for her person.

"Very well, then I shall tell you. My face is horribly scarred from a terrible accident I suffered in the amphitheatre of my city at a young age. Zeus, Asclepius, and the other gods have so far remained silent. No god has answered my prayers for healing. Then, last summer, my guardian spirit commanded me to come here and meet with Apollinaris. The old gods are dead, it said to me. It told me that I should expect nothing from them."

Near Apollinaris' house I left her to go on alone, followed by her train of slaves and sycophants.

I was greatly angered that such gullible souls should be deceived by the ruse of rascals like Apollinaris.

Sometime later, a slave came to bring me into the villa. It appears, Cronius, that the rascal had recognized me from our previous encounter.

I soon found myself in Apollinaris' house, waiting for him, with the slave. This slave was a strangely pestilent fellow that I immediately took a dislike to. His curious face, resembling too horribly and closely, more than I thought possible, that of a dusky grouper fish, upset me greatly. The slave was reticent to any question I put to him, and perhaps after noticing my discomfort in his presence, he soon enough shuffled off, rather disconsolately, leaving me alone.

Disturbed, I waited in this rather spacious and opulent villa (for how many citizens had not Apollinaris by then fleeced of their wealth?) and noticed on some walls recently painted frescoes, which were a veritable gallery of his foreign philosophical and mythological perversions.

As I looked at them, to my right, a strange pantomime was played before my eyes. The fish-faced slave appeared with Apollinaris, who made as if to hit his servant with a wand of Hermes. But before he could, the man ran away, weeping. All this while, Apollinaris stood immovable as a rock, and once the slave had left, he walked up towards me, throwing away his wand, as if nothing had happened!

We greeted each other. I had originally intended to confront him about his false teachings, but because of his charm and intelligence and my own inexperience, he quickly took over the conversation. We spoke of many things, but the most pertinent to my story, I will here transcribe.

"In Ovid's *Metamorphosis*," he explained to me calmly, "and in the stories of our native Greece, whether one speak of Niobe or Philomena, Narcissus, Syrinx or Aesacus, it is transformation which informs the main, or should I say, the very root of the narrative. It is of this paramount metamorphosis, or transformative experience, not symbolically, not treated to amuse, but as a truth, that I teach. "

As he talked, Cronius, he subtly began to lead me deeper into the exterior of his house. I feigned a sort of submission and interest in his person, in order to gain admittance into his antechambers, which, out of curiosity, I wished to see.

"Was it not, Lucian, in Smyrna and then in Pergamum, in their respective agoras, that you first spoke out loudly and forcefully against me? Will you now see and learn that you were wrong?"

I answered yes as he took me deeper into his house.

While we walked, I observed and was quite amused to see how even though his wealth was obvious, he wore a simple dirty tunic, as if to seem a poor beggar.

Entering a small damp room, with a rather large rock in the midst of it, he stretched out his arms theatrically, and then this Heracles proceeded to move, with great effort, the boulder.

After his large frame moved the obstruction, we continued down steps carved into the earth, our way being lit through the airy shaft by a torch he carried.

We reached a man-made tunnel, lit in the distance with wall torches. Through this earthen cave tunnel we proceeded to walk. I dimly heard the playing of instruments.

"Like Isis and Demeter," he said, "and the wine of Dionysius, the Mysteries of the Star Ones promise us liberation from this world. But the after-life of the Star Ones is not for human flesh, nor is our form desirable to have in their sphere, for our form is not pleasing to them. We must be transformed."

He then showed me, in a corner, a plant of ill-favored grandeur, which grew crooked under the earth. Its most fantastic feature was its height, for it was man-sized.

He looked at it, and said, "The forms of the gods are multifoliate and varied, and the initiate must not quake in fear to become as they are, in order to gain of their immortality. And yet, the most of mankind will not like the forms, the true forms of the gods; therefore is my message only for the few, and its true implications passed on in secret, lest outsiders destroy us in their ignorance and fear."

We continued walking and entered a large rocky cavern, from which the music came, and where I saw disciples of Apollinaris practicing his perverse rites under a full glow of torches. It is well that these mysteries were done under the earth, away from goodly eyes and the full light of shame. Men and women swarmed upon each other in revelry, all either naked or in extravagant regalia, unseemly painted and drunk, as if in a festival. They held up cuttlefish and other sea creatures, and wallowed with them, sidling them across their bodies and kissing them reverently. It was a mass of writhing humanity, from between whose moving arms and legs tentacles protruded like in a scene from Hades.

Leaving this barbarity, we entered another passageway and continued our journey. The music and noise was fading behind me when I noticed, in front, a strange shape lurking in the shadows. As we neared it, I realized it was the fish-faced slave I had previously seen, resting against a wall and staring, without blinking, at nothing. Slime covered him. His face, under the dancing torch-shadows, gave me the impression of being now even more like a dusky grouper's and only remotely human.

"Let us pass him," Apollinaris said, "and leave him to his gestation period."

We came to a locked door that he quickly opened and, passing through it, I realized we were in a cavern, with a pool of sea-water in it. I heard the wind blowing and light shining at us from two opposing openings to the Mediterranean, from some distance ahead of us. Reflected light glimmered eerily on the cave roof.

"Behold," he said, and pointed at the water. "Behold, the god!"

And indeed, there lay before us, a massive mass of boneless mottled flesh, creased like a mound of garments, comprised of polypi and tentacles, which was some sort of sea-creature, or rather, because of its size, to my thinking, a pleroma of squid or octopi or tubeworm, piled together and stinking atrociously like age and the depths of the sea. It was in the water and I did not know how much more this abomination stretched out underneath the pool.

This then was his Star God—the agglomerated catch of a fisherman's net! The foul-smelling heaped refuse of a wharf!

He ran into the water, and towards the visible bulky pile and, thrusting both hands into it, began to yell, "Hear you, terrible and shaggy, large-toothed Azotus, my Khaos, who lulls blindly in front of queer dancing devils and are centered in the middle of our cosmos; and also you, strange dark winged-ones, who delight in impaling nymphae, as well as heroes, in sacrifice; and you, bestial gods, who travel from over-large stars, hear me; and especially you, monstrous, octopus-headed Tulu, in your own towering Olympus, from which you once pronounced dooms from a throne while under Oceanus, upon your Star-Spawn, as you rested your chin on a seaweed-infested hand, through whose fingers coiled and twisted, like writhing tongues, massively pink tentacles, hear me! Accept this sacrifice which I bring, Tulu, my Zeus and Poseidon! Raise your trident, raise the clouds and thunder, awaken this Star-Spawn! Awaken it!"

Well, Cronius, as you can imagine, I could not bear anymore of this tomfoolery. Laugh when you read at what I next did, as I also laughed then!

While this quack, who fancied himself some sort of magician, was busy talking to the decomposing mound and invoking his made-up gods to bring it to life, in great spirits I ran towards the open door and slammed it hard on him, quickly locking it also! I wanted the faker to suffer for his crimes and to swim to some shore and, gasping and wet, remember me and the justice I had dealt him!

The revelers had left and so had his slave, so I was happy to know we were alone and for certain no one would help him. I heard him clearly as he yelled from the other side of the door, "Open, Lucian, open! The Star Ones, who came from the sky and now rest under the sea and under mountains and lonely places, are real, and I will show you one, alive, if you will but just let me! Come, Lucian, and see!"

"Save your empty words, story-teller," I said to him. "Go and tell your lies to the fishes you so adore, for I will never open this door to a phony. Go and pray to your unbelievable gods, that you do not drown as you swim to freedom!"

I then heard a groan of some kind, and the charlatan, now putting his full skills as an actor to the fore, shone in his next performance. "Lucian, open! Open! It rises! By Zeus, how beautiful it looks! How gigantic this Titan is! But why do you look at me so?" Then his voice changed to one of desperation and fear! How artfully he acted the part! I felt like I was listening to one of the great actors of the age, worthy to be performing a work of Aeschylus! "Lucian, open! Open!" he continued. "I admit it! Yes, I do! I admit it was all gullery! All of it –just open the door! Yes, I am a faker! Open the door! I am not the sacrifice! Beast!"

***

When Apollinaris' screams became too intolerable for me to bear—for mark, Cronius, the man raved and screamed too much even for an actor, for he was like one in the throes of a grand doom; and when I heard a bestial and indescribable growling, loud as a horn, and which I hope never to hear again, then out of curiosity I opened the door a tiny fraction, to take a peep through to the other side.

I saw how the water in the pool foamed monstrously, like a raging fire, and how Apollinaris was himself caught up in the tentacles of some gigantic sea-beast! His broken body thrashed about mercilessly in the creature's demonic grip! Blood splattered everywhere. What the creature was I could not really see, since its body was underwater, and what I saw, I am sure, was but just the tips of the thing!

Horrible was the sight of his flailing skin, which as much as the monster shook him, seemed to be dislocating from his body as a strange liquid, with an unsupportable odor, seeped from tiny holes on him. His skin soon took on the appearance of a soft sack placed over a bone-frame.

He yelled until the tentacles took him into the water, and I heard him no more.

***

It was then I knew he was no charlatan. It was then that I became acutely aware of the hidden beasts and beings that watch and lurk behind the common places of man, in dark woods, or secret mountaintops, or even behind the stars themselves. It was all as Epicurus had imagined, except much, much more horrible.

Later, as I watched the sea from the ship carrying me to Italy, a few of the sailors began to holler that not far off in the distance, it appeared that a great fish was following us. I went to where they were, and indeed it was so. The fish, itself of a gigantic size and like a grouper, came right up to the stern and followed us with a purpose. Many averred this fish was kin to the dolphin who had saved the poet Arion in the old stories. I was not so sure. I was convinced the great thing looked at me with eyes of recognition. This fish was no kin to dolphins. As we watched it, till it tired of following us, I felt a great fear, as if nothing in the world was to be trusted, and that rational nature had lost its battle against some order outside itself, during my stop. I was like an anchorless and rudderless ship.

"Is it true what the men are saying?" I heard an abrupt voice say from beside me. "Were we being followed by a giant grouper fish?"

I turned, to see a most beautiful face looking out across the sea. If Helen of Troy and Aphrodite had stood there before me, I could not have been more mesmerized. The voice was familiar, but it was those unforgettable emerald eyes which were the most familiar.

"Violentilla," I said, "I see you no longer wear the veil."

"The gods, the new gods, have answered my prayers. I saw you in the caverns of Apollinaris. Did the new gods also answer your prayers, Lucian?"

For some reason, Cronius, I hesitated with my answer. I could not help but think this experience we had shared was against nature and was evil. This power was of an ancient provenance in which men had no part. It was then that my dual natures were born. Though only slightly understanding, I knew it was my duty to shield humankind from the knowledge of this evil, and moreso has this feeling been strengthened in me as I have learned more throughout the years. Better that they should live in ignorance than despair in the truth. In public, I disbelieve; in secret, I tremble.

"Unfortunately," I said to her, "I found nothing but a charlatan in Abia."

She laughed and said, "You cannot mean you found yourself?" After a few seconds she grew solemn again and said, "The cult is real. I am going to the Lake of Nemi, near Rome, to participate in the rites of the Dying King and of the King in Yellow. It may chance that we will meet again, Lucian. Perhaps one day, when the stars are right."

"Yes," I said, "Perhaps when the stars are right we will meet again."

I smiled, and as I looked at her I saw in her eyes, flash rapidly, malignant faces where no faces should be. She smiled, a cruel bestial smile, and then left and made her way to the prow.

Wizened, Cronius, a few weeks later I entered the harbor of Mitylene, on a hot, sunny day in June. The merchant vessel I travelled in, only stopped for a few days, and I continued my journey towards Rome.

My travels in Italy were most worrisome, as have my days and nights been since.

One day, while touring the northwest of Italy with Demetrius and his students, I happened to overhear some sailors discussing a frightening occurrence which had happened to them while crossing the sea from Massilia. Apparently, their ship had been attacked by some type of gigantic sea creature, with arms as many as the Hydra's heads, and which they never got a good look at, since the bulk of the thing had been mercifully under the water. They did not know why it had stopped attacking them, but were greatly relieved that it had. Could this have been the same star-spawn that Apollinaris in his madness had revived from its sleep? The sailor's description of its arms struck terror in all the standers-by, and glad I was that I did not see the whole thing in its entirety, and did not know the full extent of what brooded in those black seas that surround our homes.

When they left one among the people exclaimed that it had undoubtedly been Briareus, one of the hundred-armed ones, come to extract some horrible vengeance upon the land. When I saw how frightened everyone was, how the children cowered helplessly under their parents' shades, I immediately stood up and calmed them, saying many things in a declamation, until the sailors were accounted no more than drunkards and tellers of tall-tales and worthless fellows.

Also one night, in Faesulae, Cronius, while I alone explored an olive grove, in which lay exposed to the warm breezes a splendid mausoleum, which was surrounded by marble statues of exquisite workmanship, I was surprised by the vampiress. (*Note: The original reads* lamia. *This is but one of the instances among many which I have chosen to highlight where the translator, Dr. Kavanagh, translates freely from the original to give to the account a more modern and sensational tinge.*) Alas, Cronius, even though dead, the work of Apollinaris was not yet over! Listen to what I learned. There was an inscription on the building, yet before I could reach it, from the shadows of the all-pervasive and twisted olive trees, a form quickly moved, and hid behind one of the columns of the façade. Seeing my entrance to the tomb now blocked, like a frightened hare, I calculated a retreat into the shading fronds of the trees. Yet I did not move as the vampiress, with blood dripping from those ghastly lips, like a feline licked them, and from under the façade, stepped out. Oh goddess, to condescend to grace us mortals with your presence! What semi-deity from the fathomless Outside now stepped to the earth! Ah Violentilla! How grotesque and yet so lovely! Her eyes, two emerald jewels, shone like priceless gems, and her black high-topped hair of curls and braids, weaved how [...].

[This is where the fragmented text ends.]

***

POSTSCRIPT: The publisher wishes to draw attention to the fact that Thomas Talman Macaulay, the preparer of this text, disappeared during the time that this small text was being readied for publication. He also wishes to castigate severely the pranksters who no doubt worked evilly to unhinge the poor, frail man. He wants whoever they may be to know that the police have been contacted, and are working meticulously to apprehend them, and to find the professor. If any foul play was involved, the publisher wants them to be sure that their nefarious deed will be found out.

His last known whereabouts was a subway station somewhere in London and his last known communication was an email to this publisher, which read:

Do not publish the letter! I repeat: do not publish the letter! It's better if it remains hidden, secret and accursed! I will not make my own translation of the thing! I want nothing more to do with it! When next I can see the original I will destroy it! It's better that mankind have no inkling of these things and that they never know of those creatures from dark abysses which haunt the spaces between worlds! I have seen the woman three times now—twice alone and now with a male companion! I have no doubt that they delight in my torment and do this as a sort of amusement! The second time I saw her she was in my room on the roof looking down at me when I had just woken up from sleep! You must believe me! Oh, the terrible things she whispered to me as I lay motionless. Last night they entered my room while I was having tea. It is him! I have no doubt! By what strange means can they walk through doors and traverse the streets unguessed at? And by what witchcraft does he now live? It is Apollinaris! They spoke of the secret sign, of Leng, and of the soon to be convergence of the stars and of my impending sacrifice on smoking altars, when the demoniacal city of R'lyeh rises from the sea! How my sacrifice shall be I do not want to think on! I must get away! I must flee and disappear totally! I do not want to see the Star Ones rule again! They delight in blood as she delights in blood. Blood rich in life and vaster than the sea! Her appetites are insatiable! I grow weak! Remember: do not publish the text! We are helpless to stop anything! Let it be forgotten, as it once was before! Star Ones, Star Spawns, Star Wretches, begone! Their gods are unholy! Iä! Iä! The Goat of a Thousand Young! Ghatanothoa! Great Tulu! Byakhee! I feel their presence even in this subway. **That is not dead which can eternal lie, and with strange aeons even death may die**! Those eyes of emerald! Such a terrible beauty!

* * *

The publisher wishes to ask anyone with information to contact the London police immediately, so that Prof. T.T. Macaulay may soon come home safe and sound.

The Travel of Epaenetus the Wise, or the Missing Lord

Introduction

Discovered during an archaeological dig at the site of the ancient city of Naukratis, Egypt, in the 1930s, the fragment named *The Travel of Epaenetus the Wise*, initially published in a flawed translation under its variant title of *The Tract of the Missing Lord*[1], is one of the most tantalizing gnostic texts thus far found from Antiquity. Written in Greek sometime between the first and third centuries of the Common Era, it is unusual in being a gnostic text devoid of any seeming syncretic affinities with Christianity, and for its peculiar treatment of the worlds as taught in the cosmology of Democritus, and for its use of apocalyptic themes. Others have also detected a hint of ditheism in the work. Praised for its oblique and imaginative content, the fragment affords us a small window at aspects of an ancient world as yet hidden from us.

---

[1] Butler, Andrew (trans.), *The Tract of the Missing Lord: A Conjectural Translation and Assessment*, privately-printed monograph, 1939.

THE TEXT
Translated by Dr. Peter Kavanagh

Note: Lacunae are indicated by square brackets, with unreadable or missing text indicated with an ellipsis and with reconstructed text inserted. Pointed brackets indicate a conjectural translation or insertion of text for cleaner reading.

* * *

[...]. [...] and we waited for seven cycles and on the seventh cycle we sat together fasting awaiting any word from the Lord of Tesh, Heb, Narnath and Pith, in the vale of Carnath, which lies west of the river Zuma. And as we fasted, the heavens were opened and we beheld a great living appendage, like a twisting rope, dangle down as if from a great creature, and this appendage began to swell and open like the petals of an inverted flower or cuttlefish, and from its midst fell Epaenetus, as the baby calf falls when birthed from its mother.

And Nonus, the Roman, asked him, "What have you seen, Epaenetus?

But Epaenetus would not speak of what he had seen.

Again, the Roman asked him, "What have you [seen, Epaenetus?]"

But, this time, Epaenetus said, "I will not speak of it until seven more cycles have passed."

And so we waited and when seven more cycles had passed, he said to us, "Ask?"

I was the first to ask, and said, "Lo, master, in the last aeon of aeons does the grass grow on the earth as plentifully as we have heard [it] grows by the shores of the meadows of Tesh?"

"Nay," Epaenetus answered. "In the last aeon of aeons there is no grass on the earth like in the meadows of Tesh."

And the Egyptian asked him, "Lo, master, in the last aeon of aeons are there beasts in the sea or air or [on the] ground?"

"Nay," Epaenetus answered, "In the last aeon of aeons there are no beasts in the sea or air or [on the] ground."

And the Samnite asked him, "Lo, master, in the last aeon of aeons is Man to be found on the earth?"

And Epaenetus answered, "Nay, in the last aeon of aeons there is no Man to be found on the earth. What grows is not grass and the beasts are not the same beasts." Then, he turned and said, "Ask me no more."

* * *

Later, he said to us, "In Pith, world of the lower heavens, there are two suns seen in the sky and four moons which dance in the night, and these four spin a full revolution in the sky, first one, then the others being atop, before the night ends. In Pith, the day sky is always red and the evenings purple and on one half of the world are found great forests of green and azure and <orange>, and as for the rest, it is desert and ocean. And the priests of the ochre headdress yearly hold sacrifice to their god, Y'chyniccus, and this god is great and terrible, for its arms sprawl through all the worlds, and one travels through its person, but first one must satiate its appetite with a sacrifice, lest one be devoured in its innards. In the temple of the god, which is a mighty structure supported by massive white columns and decorated with marble statues and friezes depicting the history of Tesh, Heb, and Narnath and in which are located the Scrolls of Pith, that tell of the history of that world and of other worlds far removed, dwells a high priest alone. The high priest serves his function in the temple for only one year, after which, when his term is ended, he willingly sacrifices himself, so that one fortunate supplicant may travel to other worlds.

I went to him, for the high priest is renowned by the people and the nobles and the kings as one with great wisdom, and asked whether he had seen or could tell me of the lost Lord, for I had not seen him for a long time, and he asked who my Lord was.

I said he is the fount of all being, who is above all and dwells in perfection in eternity, nameless and in ineffable light. From him all purity comes and to him nothing impure can go. From him the councils and rulers and materials emerged at the first and also the cosmocrator, who, in ignorance, created the worlds and all we see. Tesh, Heb, Narnath, Pith and Earth were special to him because a fraction of the light was still preserved in them, I further explained.

Then, he took me into the spacious naos of the temple, where, instead of a marble representation, lay the form of Y'chyniccus itself, stretching into infinity. In the dim interior, lit by torchlight and surrounded by splendid colonnades, the high priest threw himself into the wide open [maw] of the hungry god. Now grown calm, I also entered its maw and, after losing myself in darkness, emerged eventually out of one of the god's appendages into new space.

I emerged into chaos [...]. [...] a flute [...]. [...] danced wildly those gods of cosmic size [...]. [...] the shadow outside the light [...].

I asked the lesser demon where the Father of All had gone. [...].

"What god of light?" he asked.

I further [...]. [...]. [...].

[...]. [...] and the lesser demon laughed and laughed and said to me, "The god of light is fled and will not come again. Worship instead him whose feet rest upon suns extinguished and from whom darkness rises. Behold, your new god!" I trembled [...].

Then, I said to Epaenetus, "But, master, was this in the past, the present, or the future? How is it the [...][?]"

[Here the fragment ends.]

The Second Lost Letter of Lucian of Samosata, or the Night of Pan

From *The Homeric Hymns: A New Prose Translation; and Essays, Literary and Mythological* by Andrew Lang, published in 1899.

EDITOR'S NOTE: This is a translation of complete, recently discovered letters, purporting to be by the 2nd Century Greco-Roman satirist, Lucian of Samosata, undertaken by Dr. Kavanagh, of the Oxford Institute of Archaeology. Guessing as to their order of composition, we have decided to label this the second letter. The discovery was made near the ancient port city of Ostia Antica, near Rome. More will be published in the future as time allows. L.D.

From Lucian to Cronius, greetings.

To answer your last letter, I will state this plainly: the existence of the gods I deny, while I fear them, and call all men crazy who traffic in their lies, while I wholeheartedly believe in them. To better give you an understanding of my predicament, I will tell you a tale that will illustrate my philosophy, and at the same time make you better acquainted with the true nature of things.

As you know, by the peaks of Mount Hermon in the Panion, and to the Acropolis, and further still to sacred Parnassus, since ancient times has been worshipped the god Pan, that

dear son of Hermes, the goat-footed, the two-horned, the lover of the din of revel, who haunts the wooded dells with dancing nymphs that tread the crests of the steep cliffs,...the pastoral God of the long wild hair.

* * *

So far has his worship spread, in fact, that his shrines are found throughout Italy, and there is even a temple to him on the Tibur in Rome. Unknown, however, are the sacred shrines dedicated to him on the alpine peaks far to the north, in those places where few cultured men have dared to venture. But is it so strange that this should be so? Isn't it true that this god, who is imagined as roaming undetected by large shaded trees and by still lakes far from civilization, should find such a place congenial to himself, for cannot you picture him in such solitary surroundings, playing his pipes joyously undisturbed, late into the night, on those dark-green mountains? In other words, Cronius, don't those wooded leagues scarcely populated seem like a place befitting Pan?

Well, to move on, I'll describe the setting where I first heard this marvelous history. It was on one of my long-ago journeys to Rome, where I was to attend to some business with Fronto and also spend some time at his leisure gardens. While still several stades away from my destination, night creeping on, I decided to stop at an inn. It was a pleasant enough place, not as boorish as those in the capital, or as pleasant an establishment as those in Attica. The host was a genial person and much taken with philosophy, so that I did not fear him for a cutthroat. I ate porridge alone and after, while sitting at my table, a fellow traveller entered, who sat on a stool at a table opposite from mine. He was as old as Nestor, yet still carried himself with the strength and vitality of a young man, and was accompanied by a large black dog. Where I had thought the man the veritable image of the wise counselor, this beast I thought the very image of the guardian of Hades, Cerberus. These were denizens of the night not to be trifled with. After their meals, they rested as if they didn't have a care in the world. Indeed, few men I wager would have dared to traffic with such a dangerous-looking pair. I took him for an ex-gladiator, who had gained his freedom when young, but as luck would have it, I was soon presented with an occasion to find out the truth about him. It turns out my Nestor comparison was not far from the mark.

When I was ready to head to my room, the man said to me, "Always have I served Mars and Bellona, and seldom Bacchus. With a man of peace such as I see before me I would like to have a drink. Come here, young sir, I will satisfy your curiosity."

It is said that because of curiosity Pandora opened the chest which let out every evil into the world; by this we learn what a wrecking passion curiosity can be. I'm sure you won't be surprised to learn, Cronius, that your friend was led by curiosity. Whatever evil might come, I sat at his table and drank wine with him.

As we talked, I learned much about him. His name was Arruns and he had been forty years in the Imperial army, beginning his military career on the Danube, and serving under Trajan in Dacia and in Parthia. When Hadrian became Emperor, he'd seen battle against Bar Kokhba. When not in battle, he'd spent his time stationed in garrisons, in time rising in rank to become the eagle-standard bearer of a legion.

His dog, whom I learned was also old, while we talked mostly slept, but I was warned by the man not to think his friend was helpless.

"An old Molossian," he said. "I named him Agamemnon, because I think it a very martial and sonorous name and worthy of his deeds. He is a gentle soul, now declining in years; but watch, he has been a soldier. Also a guard, farm-hound, and terror of the mountainous Alpes Poeninae. An old fire still burns in him. I'd feel sorry for the man who tempts him too much, or who intended harm to my person."

We continued to talk, as the shadows lengthened outside, and eventually came to the subject of the gods. I told him that, much like Anaxagoras, I didn't believe the gods existed, at least not in the way they were presented by the lying poets. He grew silent at this revelation, and I was worried that I had upset him. I tried to change the subject, but as I talked, I noticed that his demeanor now denoted a man trying to conceal some extreme agitation.

Our conversation dying down, I decided to excuse myself when he abruptly said, "It is dark outside. Yet we must part tomorrow. Perhaps it is time I tell this tale I have scarcely mentioned these past few years. It is night, and the fire is burning low, and Agamemnon rests comfortably by our side, tired yet alert. We are safe, for there are some spirits in this world, and in the world after, who fear dogs. Who knows why? Perhaps it is their natural devotion or love, which perturbs these spirits, or the dog's natural goodness, which confuses these spirits and acts as a bulwark to them. I don't know. I only know many a bugbear has fled when Agamemnon has but flexed an ear."

Since I did not need to wake up early the next morning, I told him that I would be delighted to hear his story. As the old man got comfortable on his stool, I noticed the dog, Agamemnon, rouse slightly and move his head, so that his eyes looked perfectly at the inn's entrance door.

Then, with the room in silence, the man began.

* * *

Not long after I had retired from the army, about seven years ago, I had the fortune to meet up with a military tribune I'd served under when a young man. He was by now a patrician, who of course long ago had completed his *cursus honorum*. Well, this man was a well-respected senator in Rome, by the name of Marcus Trebius Torquatus, a name which I am sure a bright fellow like yourself is familiar with. We got to talking, and the subject turned to our respective farms: I owned a small one in the southern countryside, acquired through my military career, and he owned a country estate, far away near Germania. Also, like most people I meet, he was impressed with Agamemnon. The dog was then in his prime, you understand, and much more sturdy, robust and energetic than now. I laughed to see him run rings around us, and scare the men, women and children in the Forum. Not a bystander stood nearby that didn't look at us askance. Eventually, he stood by the senator alert and obedient, and my old friend told me that he owned guard dogs on his farm, but none as intelligent as Agamemnon. I explained to him that I had trained him myself, since he was a little pup, and before you knew it, because of this, I had been invited to Marcus' estate, to enjoy myself and also to train his own dogs, to be as great farm dogs as he imagined Agamemnon to be, and as he indeed was, and still is, despite his age. I thought this a blessing from Mercury.

I left my nephew in charge of my small plot of land and that very spring I headed north. The senator stayed in Rome. I planned to stay no longer than the first few days of autumn, and then return to my farm in southern Italy.

The journey took us north by wagon, through roads rarely travelled. There were five of us, not counting Agamemnon, the other four being country slaves belonging to Marcus. We were jovial enough, until we reached the Poeninus Mons pass on the Alps, and entered desolate and wild country valleys.

There is, my friend, a strange feeling of loneliness, when one has voyaged far, and left behind all one knows of family and friends and local buildings and landmarks, and despite having been in the army stationed in far garrisons, I felt this loneliness as I left Italy behind me, and voyaged deep into those lands of grim barbarism. I am sure you felt it when you left Greece, though not to such an extent as I did, since Italy is still civilized country.

As we journeyed deeper, we passed the solitary temple erected by Claudius to Jupiter. I was distraught to see it recede in the distance, as I looked before me at hills and valleys that our ancestors had barely penetrated.

I was discomforted to notice that my travelling companions, despite being from this place, also seemed to share my uneasiness. I would have thought them elated to be travelling to their home, as I was sad for leaving mine.

At times, when they spoke amongst themselves, I'm sure I heard the words 'sixty' or 'sixtieth year' cross their lips in hushed tones.

To not make you think, Lucian, that I am being a bit over-dramatic, I'm going to tell you in all honesty what I saw on one of those days in which we voyaged. Sure it can be explained away, but it is, let us say, strange, and then felt most unsettling, like when one is in a temple, and is certain the god is actually present in the marble, and it is alive and looking at you, and will soon talk.

As we moved, we noticed a peculiar cloud formation form high above us in the sky, and it took on the appearance of a man's face. At first, I thought I was seeing one of the gods, like Jupiter or Neptune perhaps. But when the aspect changed to one of the infernal gods, and great horns sprouted from his head, I couldn't credit this thought anymore. This cloud-face, as it drifted away, also gave the peculiar impression of looking at us, for as we moved and as it moved, the front always faced us, no matter in what direction we turned. It eventually disappeared over some hills.

I was both impressed and perturbed at this, but was more alarmed to see my companions in the harshest throes of panic. They did not look at the cloud, and muttered prayers, until the cloud, or should I say the man, was blocked from viewing us by the hills.

Agamemnon himself did not like this latter half of our voyage, and stayed close to me.

Eventually, we came to a green valley in the Alpes Poeninae province. All around us were hills and trees and high mountains. By the road, and near the estate walls, we saw dirty men and women in rags, poor creatures that my companions showed an aversion to, and which they said were citizens from the mountains. These people, I noticed, knelt and prayed to a portable god, which from my distance resembled a faun or satyr, but wildly made and chaotic, being obviously fashioned with less skill than our craftsmen make their idols. It won't be any falsehood on my part to say that while I looked at the thing, I thought it slightly moved. At the time, I explained it away as a fanciful trick played upon my eyes, but with what was to happen afterwards, I'm not so sure about that. Once again, I heard the men grumble something about the sixtieth year, and Agamemnon growled and barked.

We passed the front gate of the villa rustica, leaving the native citizens outside, and were welcomed by the head slave, a man in his fifties named Publius, and by his wife, Livilla. Once I'd settled myself in, I learned that I was the only freeman on the premises—everyone else was a slave. None of Marcus' relatives or immediate family was present. My arrival was unexpected, and the head slaves were astonished to see me. I introduced myself with a letter carrying the master's seal, and my travelling companions also made my introduction, so that in no time, Publius and his wife were on friendly terms with me.

The estate itself was large, but not on the scale of a latifundia, though it was self-sufficient and made profit. Publius showed me around, and I saw all the livestock and produce, and was amazed at the orderly way in which everything was handled.

I saw the dogs that protected the premises, great hulking beasts, and I looked forward to my time working with them.

I met many of the workers: slaves from all over the empire, but mostly from the stock of the native Helvetti and Salassi tribes. In the evening, I had a simple yet delicious meal with the slaves that I treated like my hosts. Though I will tell you, young man, during this whole time I couldn't completely shake the feeling that something was not right. Things seemed a bit too forced; there was something not healthy, though I couldn't articulate what it was. I would later learn that I had arrived at a time when momentous things had been happening, and which would all come to a boil the next day. I had arrived, in a sense, in the middle of things, in just the way our great epics start.

When night arrived, Publius showed me to my bedroom on the second floor. It was a spacious room, with decorated walls, and a large window facing the west wall in the distance, over which was a wooded area with tall trees. The bed was high, with a step, and there was a table nearby for my lamp. Since even in the military

Agamemnon had accompanied me as a guard, he slept on the floor, and not in the kennel.

It was past midnight, when I was awakened by the sound of panpipes playing outside my window. I went to the window and told whoever it was to hush, but was startled and confused when I realized the noise was seemingly coming from the sky. It was a clear night, and the full moon was out, but I could make out no one outside. Just as abruptly as the playing had started, it ended, and I returned to my bed, extremely tired and determined to get to the bottom of this in the morning. I must have slept maybe an hour when once again I was awakened, this time by an odd bellowing sound. It came from all directions, in minute intervals, and this time I lit my lamp and went angrily to the window. Once again, I was confronted with a quiet night, and was puzzled that no one else was startled by this noise. As far as I was able to tell, everyone slept soundly. Even the dogs were quiet, except for Agamemnon, who was dutifully by my side. I put out the wick, and once more returned to my bed, but my sleep was now troubled by unusual nightmares. Most were confused and jumbled, and I no longer have a complete memory of them, except for one. I dreamt, or perhaps did not, that a strange creature crawled up the outside of my room, and rested its head just outside my window. I awoke, and saw its outline, with great horns protruding from its head. Dazed, I yelled at it, and it hissed back, and I remember Agamemnon barking hectically at it. I then felt extremely tired, and went back to sleep, or perhaps was asleep all along, I am not sure. My night was undisturbed from then on. It was a blessing from Somnus.

In the morning I ate breakfast at a table, and after, in a foul mood, demanded of Publius and his wife an explanation for the night's occurrences. At first, they denied knowing anything, or hearing anything, but after I had made it clear to them that I would not be trifled with, lied to, or thought crazy, they unburdened their hearts to me. And what a black wellspring of filth broke forth!

"We are at our wit's end, sir," Publius said. "I too once saw the shape with horns, and red eyes, staring through our windows. And worse. It was walking on hind goat-legs, out by the far forest, and near the pars rustica in the evening."

"We would leave this place if we could," Livilla added. "But we are slaves, and our master is harsh, and would be displeased with us. This whole place is accursed."

"Why do you say that?" I asked.

Publius looked at me sorely, saying, "We will tell what we know, if you promise to tell master Marcus all that is occurring here, so that he will not be angry with us if we decide to abandon this place. Being his good friend, he will surely listen to you and believe you."

"I might help you, if I find it necessary," I said. "What is it I must tell him?"

I gave them permission to sit at my table, and Livilla spoke with great gravity in her demeanor. "About a month ago, the mountain people started flaming fires, and singing, high up in the forests. We asked the slaves who'd been born here what this meant, but they wouldn't answer us. We told them Marcus would punish them severely if they held back, but even this threat wouldn't loosen their tongues. They were more afraid to talk than of the threat of punishments.

"After a week, the fires and singing stopped, and some of the mountain people in ecstasies came down, singing and dancing wildly, and worshipping openly idols of a god we can only surmise was Pan.

"May Jupiter and the gods help us, for it was then that the troubles in the house started!

"Every night, for four nights, we heard footsteps walking through the place in darkness, only these footsteps were like hard objects pattering on the ground. Now they're not here, but we used to have two bronze statues of fauns, placed in the peristyle. Every morning we'd find the statues moved from where we'd placed them the night before. I do not lie when I say that they always seemed to have subtle changes to them, such as a head slightly tilted in a position different than it was before, or an arm in a slightly more elevated position. Then, one day, a young girl who used to help the cooks swore she would never enter the house again. When we asked her why, she said that she had seen the statues move, smirk at her as if in mockery, and bound out the doors, and into the thickets outside.

"When we searched for them, all over the estate, we found nothing.

"Speaking of the girl, there is also another girl who said she saw one afternoon, not far from here, and by the small hills, a troop of grotesque wolves or goats, dancing upright to the sound of a puzzling flute sound.

"Publius himself saw a peculiar creature, as well have many others.

"Then, last week, the piping sounds coming from the sky started, together with the loud bellowing noises. They were loud, increasing in frequency, until just the night before your arrival. Last night they'd diminished in loudness. You wouldn't have wanted to hear the whole cacophonous sound.

"I could go on, but the most distressing occurrence can barely be articulated."

She went silent, and wept, and her husband put an arm around her to comfort her. After this touching demonstration, he continued, "What she finds hard to say is that a human baby was born during this time, which died a few days after, who never ate or stopped crying. She was pitiful, and to put it mildly—an abomination. Her legs below the calves were those of a goat, and her face was that of the selfsame animal. The rest of her was human. We buried her, and wept."

Incredulous, I asked to speak with the mother, to find out how this had happened. But Publius said, "You cannot. She will never answer you. The mother is one of the goats on the farm."

We exhumed the body, so that I might verify what the slaves told me. When I saw that it was true, I was shocked, and we quickly reburied the small corpse.

I was angry, disgusted, and beside myself with amazement. I've often heard the stories of the gods and of their wondrous doings, and how they have sometimes sired their offspring on mortal creatures, but never had I expected to see such a thing for myself. For I was convinced this was something to do with the higher powers, and that the whole countryside was under the bewitchment, careful watch, and control of some unfathomable god. How do you fight against such a power? What reasonable strategy can be mustered against what you do not understand? Indeed, cannot understand, since it is not of this world. I have never felt so helpless and afraid.

After much thought, I decided to appease the gods, to have them fight our battles for us, since we were weak. I ordered sacrifices to be made to our more powerful gods: Jupiter, Neptune and Pluto. I ordered everyone to help, and soon the preparations were under way.

I was busy working when news reached my ears that several of the slaves had secretly fled with eight girls as captives, into the forested mountains. Reports also reached my ears that wild hairy men were also seen with them.

I knew Marcus would be angry to lose property, so I ordered the slaves to make the sacrifices, while with another group, comprised of Greeks and Romans, I would chase after the kidnappers.

We took a few swords, spears, and farm implements to use as weapons, setting off with eleven of our strongest men.

* * *

As we marched, I asked one of the slaves what the hairy men looked like.

He said, "They were tall, rambunctious, with pointy ears and small horns, some with and some without beards, and with tails and hairy matted ram hind-legs. They walked briskly in a jumping manner. Their long faces alone inspired fear in us."

We tracked them as best we could, but soon enough this wasn't necessary. At dusk drums started beating from high in the mountains. These villains didn't care who followed them. This certainly showed a brazenness in our foes. I prayed the sacrifices in the farm had begun and that our gods, pleased, were rousing to our cause.

I was troubled, but I didn't let the men know, though I knew they must have suspected something was wrong. They were not stupid. What enemy lets his position be known unless he is laying a trap? I also knew you do not steal slaves you intend to return, and so it was my duty to retrieve them. Even if the women had gone willingly, they had gone without permission, and this was tantamount to escaping.

My best tactic was to come upon our enemies unexpectedly, silently, hidden. I knew they expected us, but they didn't know exactly when.

Up we maneuvered, as the night slowly set in and the full moon came out. Dark it was, with only those hadean drums beating constantly. I inspired my men to keep moving, to keep them from bolting.

Eventually, we felt a huge warmness reach our tired bodies, and saw through the black trees a brilliant light cast from a red-flaming fire. I ordered them to hide in the undergrowth and to advance slowly. We heard drums, flutes, lutes, cymbals and loud chanting, which was at times cut by desperate screams.

When I was close enough to peer at the scene I saw a frenzied sight. What horror is this, I thought? Is this some new cult wishing to spread its worship into the civilized world, as once the terror-filled cult of ecstatic Dionysus had done from the east? For I could only compare what I saw to a group of maenads or Corybants in their fervorous excitement, such as we hear cause them to tear animals apart, or castrate themselves. The mountain people jumped and hollered and wallowed on the ground around a huge stone platform, whose back part showed a flame of incredible height.

The fearful slave girls were tied on the platform, before an altar, at which officiated some high priest of sorts. He was bare-breasted and clothed in pelts that stretched from his shoulders and circled his midpoint like a swaddling-cloth, sporting a tail at his back. A hairy hood covered his head, and from this hood huge ram-horns protruded. He held a cup up to the sky, from time to time drinking from it, as if from a sacred chalice. His mouth was stained red, and I thought it not unmixed wine, but blood.

He was terrible, but more terrible were the forms which writhed and twisted with the slaves and mountainfolk. These things did not wear a costume. They were man-beasts, fauns, or as you'd say in your Greek language, Lucian, satyrs. I will tell you, our artists have never truly captured their horror. These creatures too were in raptures and didn't notice us.

It was plain to me that we were not expected. I think all the previous experiences on the farm had been induced to cause enough fear so that no one ventured into these hills. Something important was going to happen tonight.

They hadn't counted, however, on a military man visiting at this time.

We continued watching in a trance, until the hooded high priest chanted something to the sky, and tremendous clouds with tremendous speed commenced to cover it. In no time black mist roiled over us, as from this mist a shape began to take form.

The thing was of a huge size, with smoky legs that dangled over us in a swaying motion. Mouths appeared and reappeared everywhere across its barely tenuous body, and from its head, shaped like that of a gigantic goat, a loud bellowing noise sounded.

Through the frenzy of the thing's voice, and the noise of the celebrants, I heard the high priest, yelling, "Shub-Niggurath! Shub-Niggurath! Black Goat of a Thousand Young! Do as it has been done since before the Golden Race, since before men walked the earth, since before the Olympian gods took sceptre over the world! Do as it was done when Chaos ruled! Do as it has been done so that it may also be done to these slaves we offer to the Great One! Help us build our army! Help us defeat Rome!"

I noticed the more he said what I imagined was the infernal god's name, the more solid it became, so coming out of my shock, with no time to lose, I thought of action, and taking a long spear, broke my cover and quickly with all my might hurled the thing at the chanting priest!

The spear arced through the air and hit him straight in his bare chest, embedding itself in his soft flesh.

The thing in the sky immediately turned its head to look at me, giving a loud bellow. And as its head angrily hovered and bellowed ferociously near me like a wild animal, it dispersed, writhing into nothingness.

The priest meanwhile fell, clutching the spear, trying to remove it, as the fauns and unprepared mountainfolk looked at him dumbfounded.

Then, I grabbed a sword and rushed at the crowd; my only thought was to kill the high priest and rescue the captive slave girls.

I wish I could say that the men I'd brought followed me into the fray, but they remained frightened and in shock. It took my loud command, and my chopping off of a celebrant's hand, to rouse them.

With this action, they rushed into the general confusion, fighting the unprepared mountainfolk.

There was outright turmoil, with men and women yelling and running everywhere, as my men thrust and hacked at whatever they saw. Some of the celebrants put up a fight, but more of them fled into the wilderness. The fauns were our greatest challenge. These things, larger than us, with the speed, strength, and ferocity of feral animals and the intelligence of men, attacked us, their giant claws a match for our weapons.

I thrust at whatever came near me, while making my way to the front altar. The fauns scratched and bit at me, but I also gave in turn with my sword. In time I was full of blood and panting for breath. My heart heaved in my chest.

Around me, I saw wounded fauns and also some of my dismembered men, whose heads and limbs had been hacked and hurled around and whose entrails even from the boughs of gory trees hung. So great was the strength and ferocity of the fauns!

When I reached the altar, I hacked unmercifully at the goat-skinned priest. With a gaping hole in his chest, he didn't put up much resistance. To finish him off for good, I decapitated him, and threw his head into the wilderness.

The rites were over. The fauns fled into the darkness.

I ran to the slave girls, yelling, "We have saved you!" I cut their ropes. They were relieved and wept with joy.

Then, lowly at first, but gradually increasing, piping sounds were heard in the sky. Soon, it was as if a thousand panpipes were sounding by the stars.

Slowly, the music began to move. It subtly shifted its centre. It moved away over the hills, like an invisible vessel. And it was headed in the direction of our farm.

Our night was not yet over.

* * *

I ordered my only three remaining men, and the women, to follow me, and together we all headed after the chorus playing in the night sky.

As we hurried down, drums began to beat incessantly in the darkness, with loud chants filling the air. Chants of, "Io! Io! Pan! Pan! Io! Io! Pan!"

In our mad rush we had to detour constantly, for bizarre women, either hiding behind trees or a part of them, appeared constantly, and tried to touch or hinder us. They were, as far as I noticed in the darkness, green and the color of bark, their flesh filled with leaves and branches, and of the texture of trees. I surmise now they must have been wood nymphs. These dryads also sang to Pan, as always incessantly the drums beat.

When we escaped from the forest, we heard loud screams coming from the farm in the far distance. Though almost dead with fright, tiredness, and injury, we coaxed our bodies to move onwards.

The nearer we got, the louder the commotion became, as did the piping sound, now inside the compound. Over the wall I saw a black mist roiling like smoke, and my first instinctive thought was that a great fire had broken out.

The gate was open, with slaves outside, and rushing through it we saw the cause of all this mayhem.

A black cloud had settled on the slaves' quarters, and it stirred as if alive. I have never seen anything so dark in all my life, young man. It was not only like mist, but as if a break or hole in the world had opened, showing a doorway to somewhere else.

I quickly asked Livilla what was occurring. She replied, "We were asleep, with only a few slaves on watch, when the piping noise commenced again. Then this cloud fell on the slaves as they slept. Most managed to escape, but many were trapped within."

"We must go and get them," I said.

"It is impossible. We have tried. The cloud burns like a hot fire at its outer edges, and inhaling it stings like the cut of a knife."

I stood planning my next move, when abruptly the air was pierced with the loud whine of an animal, a dog to be precise.

"What is that?" I demanded, dreading the answer.

"I did not want to tell you, sir. But when the mist first arrived, your dog bolted into the quarters, and was trapped when the cloud finally settled."

Loud growlings now came from the darkness, barks, and the screams of men and women.

"Your dog is trapped. It is impossible to go in," Publius continued, sadly.

I was beside myself with confusion. Agamemnon was my friend; I had brought him up since he had been a few months old. He was my child. My grief getting the best of me, I braved the cloud. I was unthinking. I tried to pierce through the darkness, but the mist burned me like a thousand fires. Still I tried to fight it. I hacked at air. Wisps of smoke merely coiled around my sword's edges. Tears ran down my face as I hacked desperately.

Who can fight a god and win? The god was exacting a terrible revenge against us for having dared to stand against it. This was the punishment for our irreverence. The gods, the good gods of our fathers, had disowned us in our hour of need. Or perhaps they had never existed at all.

As I tried to breach the smoke, others joined me. Sweat and tears and loud lamentations filled the sky all around us. Men and women wailed for loved ones trapped within.

Then a loud yell rent the sky and echoed throughout the barren countryside. We were stilled in our tracks. This was the voice of no earthly thing. It came from the cloud, and yet, simultaneously from all directions.

The cloud receded. It shrank. Like smoke it seeped through crevices, and inwards through windows, and the gaps between the building's doors and their frames.

Through a window I heard a bark as a shape barreled through it, crashing frantically on the ground. Then, it bounded enthusiastically towards me. I wept with joy and relief.

The dog, though tired, bloody, and injured, with great gashes throughout its muscular body, licked my face and fell on top of me.

As this happened, from the building the cloud emerged in black stringy wisps, forming above, then lowering, to coalesce into a great shape before us. It must have stood fifteen feet high.

It was dawn, and we beheld as it took on many forms, from man to woman to animal, until finally, ending in the shape we were all familiar with. Enormous horns grew from an aquiline face, situated on a man's body, possessing protruding claws and goat legs. Red eyes leered, and though its smoky body was black, we discerned on it features common to beast and man, such as skin and fur.

Agamemnon growled at the thing as it paid no attention to us, but merely studied its small antagonist.

It was then that I noticed that all the animals on the farm were positioned in a stance of obeisance and facing the great beast: body low to the ground, head tilted downwards. All, except for Agamemnon, who stood firm, meeting the thing's stare squarely, as he continued growling.

We cannot know what passed between them as they stared at each other. It was some communion foreign to our understanding, for I am sure they communicated.

Seconds, which seemed like hours, passed, until the big beast looked away, and I believe, I cannot be certain, smirked and smiled, and then dissolved, its monstrous frame blending with the air, becoming as nothing. It was gone.

I cannot help but think that the dog saved us, that Agamemnon had won some mysterious battle we had no part in on that day. The more surprising, since I could have torn him apart with my bare hands if I wanted to, and yet he defeated a god!

He came towards me, and stood by me humbly, as he has always done when our work is over, and sat, like nothing had happened.

Now answer me, Lucian, what do you think occurred on that farm so far away?

* * *

When he finished telling me his tale, Cronius, I couldn't help but stare mystified at Agamemnon, as he slept soundly on the floor.

I slowly ran the soldier's story in my mind, then answered with, "There were two deities in the countryside you visited. One I will call Shubb, and the other Pan. These two gods since ancient times have copulated, and I will venture to call their offspring by the generic term of the Thousand Young. This meeting was most likely enacted every sixtieth year. The spells of the celebrants in more recent ages likely determined the location of this encounter. The mountainfolk worshipped Pan, and taking advantage of this event, gave slave girls to the god's lust so that offspring would be born that they could use to their own advantage. These are creatures separate from the Thousand Young. They plan to unleash an army of these satyrs against Rome. When Pan's ritual was disturbed, the god went against the farm, as a divine punishment. His lust, I wager, needed to be quenched. The sign of Pan's presence was the sound of panpipes playing. The sign of Shubb was the loud bellow. Have I guessed correctly?"

Arruns leaned close to me and said, "You are astute, young man. Listen to the end of my tale. You'd think that I left that place immediately, but I ended up staying until the autumn. I trained the dogs as I was instructed. The troublemakers fled, and I never heard from them again.

"I learned once Agamemnon had entered the slave's quarters that he had protected those inside. But unfortunately, the god had managed to interact with two maidens despite this. Still, he fought the god as best he knew.

"A week after the horrendous event, the two slave girls showed signs of pregnancy. In two months they were at full term. What was born we locked in the kennel, and moved the dogs into the main house.

"On the locked wooden doors, whenever I got near the kennel, great kicks were given. They were like the hooved kicks of a large animal, like a horse.

"Days before I left the farm, the doors were kicked open, and it was reported to me that two creatures on goat-legs were seen running on the hills before disappearing into the forest.

"I don't need to explain to you that the creatures' mothers never wanted to see them or talk about them.

"So what do you think, Lucian? Do you believe now in the gods?"

I come at last, Cronius, to the very exposition of my predicament. What was I to answer? This man was honest and good and I doubted not his story, yet was I to call him a liar? For as I have said many times, though I believe in the gods in private, I deny them in public, so that those who hear me may live quiet and peaceful lives, unaware of the great menaces that threaten to overwhelm them every day. Better for them to live in ignorance and be happy than have knowledge and live in fear, especially when the knowledge will in no way help them, since the coming of the Old Ones is inevitable. We can just try to postpone it as much as we can—can we not?

Trying not to rouse the man's anger through my skills in rhetoric, I explained to him that though I believed he thought his story true, I thought other more reasonable explanations were preferable. I told him gods didn't rule behind the scenes, but that what appeared to our eyes was all there was. What we see every day in the world is what is true. Our senses do not deceive us, our minds do. As do our fears, our hopes, and our dreams.

The night was late and we parted amicably. Yet the man shrewdly said to me, "I do not think you believe in what you have told me. So I will caution you: Be vigilant against things that shouldn't be in human form, and yet are. And just in case you are wondering, the Emperor knows of this threat. Good night, young man. Tomorrow night I go to visit Proculus Viburnius Marco. I say his name so that you may avoid the bearer for as long as you live."

The old soldier picked up his sleeping dog and went to his room. I never saw him again. Today the name he mentioned gives me the shudders, but at that time I didn't know who it was, or what evil it portended. You will be glad to know, Cronius, that no evil befell the soldier the next night, as far as I know, and I will tell you why in a second. Just writing Proculus' name makes my body ache, just like when I remember Violentilla and the old wound pains me.

Well, the next day I continued on to Rome, and met with Fronto and did all I had set out to do.

* * *

Years later, when I was grown in wisdom, recalling the old soldier, I decided to pay a visit to his farm. I knew of course that he was long dead, but I went anyways out of curiosity.

In Bruttium, near the Gulf of Scylacium, I arrived at a little farm in an out of the way place. I asked for the man, and the owner of the farm told me that I must be looking for the person buried with the unkempt marker by a large tree nearby. The new owner was not a relative. I went to it, and indeed, I saw two markers, long abandoned and forgotten. One epitaph was simply written, and said only the name Arruns Sertorius Calidus, and marked the years of his lonesome passage through this world, and his profession. He had died a few years after our meeting.

The other was elegantly written, in a voice which I was familiar with. It read:

Here rests good Agamemnon,
Not present at his birth, I was present at his death,
A friend to the friendly, loyal to the loyal,
He gave much and loved long.
Soldier, farmhand, guard, jack-of-all-trades,
Lover of the fields, captain of his hearth,
And terror of the mountains.

R'lyeh: Two Irregular Sonnets

1. The City

Through dim uncounted years the silence rolled,
Through Palaeogene ages fraught with fear;
No light shone, on that colossal bier
Of star-stone quarried steps and turrets old.
The Pacific mightily the wreck concealed
Of Elder gods and their city, stilled;
None guessed, none from ancient prophecies distilled,
What was to come, what was to be revealed.
Till from the ocean burst the sleeping city,
And nightmare centuries with it to the world.
"R'lyeh!" its acolytes boomed forth, unfurled,
In manic utterance, without tear or pity.
For now the reign of men had come to pass
To unimaginable hordes of flabby mass.

2. The High Priest

All along the star-spawned gods had lain
Within their ghostly city beneath the waves,
Dreaming in their crypts, sepulchers and graves,
In peaceful repose from their former reign.
All was quiet in the murky depths
This frightful silence of the deep, and sea-beasts,
Who without voice enjoin in noiseless feasts,
Were there, with brainless pastimes to be kept.
One god - Cthulhu - dreamt greater dreams than all.
In delightful darkness was his mind rapt

On promises the stars had made, and so slept
More peaceful in those eon-haunted halls.
"Who is your Chief?" he asked. "You," the gods did say.
His kraken-head was pleased and chuckled where it lay.

Periphery

People always thought that when the world ended, it would be with fire and brimstone and weeping and gnashing of teeth. A certain group certainly thought so, but they were solely disappointed. The world didn't end for them, nor for anyone else. Some people witnessed the city with all wrong angles rise out of the ocean, together with the tentacle-faced creature writhing within it, and there were some earthquakes in Antarctica, and other anomalies across the world, but overall, it was kept secret, and nothing made it into the mainstream six o'clock news. I belong to a group on Reddit that has a thread that discusses the phenomenon. The thread is over five thousand comments long. When it happened, I was one of those who'd witnessed a strange thing, but didn't know what was going on until the internet and the Reddit post came along. Since then we've pieced it all together.

The Cthulhu Apocalypse occurred during one evening and night in August, in the year nineteen-eighty-three.

At the time I was eleven years old. But before I go on, I should tell you first that I'm not going to write about everything that went on; I'm mostly going to concentrate on what happened to me. I was far from ground zero, so I think it's best that I write what I know firsthand. You can find other testimonies, and a fuller history of the main events, elsewhere. This is mostly about my experience that occurred at the peripheries. Imagine it like you're reading a story about World War 2 (except it's a secret war), and instead of it being set in Europe or the Pacific, it's set a world away, and involves how the war affects a young kid in a suburban neighborhood nowhere near the war.

Well, to start, when the apocalypse occurred, I lived in Canada (like I still do), in the west end of Toronto. My family lived in a typical four-bedroom, two-story house, complete with basement, garage, backyard and attic. We were an ordinary family, comprised of my parents, myself, my mother's parents and my two younger sisters.

My days were normally spent after school doing homework and then playing outside for a little while. When July came and summer vacation started, I alternated my activities between bicycle riding, ball hockey, soccer, and going to the pool or playing Atari at my house, or Intellivision or Coleco at other kids' houses. Sometimes, when I was playing outside, my two sisters joined me. In the evenings, usually, my parents and grandparents watched television or movies that my father had eagerly rented to play on his expensive Betamax machine. He was a fan of the video player, and we weren't so much as allowed to say the word VHS in his presence without him going into some esoteric mumbo-jumbo about how Beta was a better VCR. We weren't even allowed to touch it. My bedroom was directly above the living room, and sometimes I was sent up there when my parents were going to watch a movie they didn't want me to see, though this rarely happened. I was usually not allowed to watch a movie, depending on how my parents were feeling at the time. I'd been allowed to watch *Friday the 13* and *Porky's*, but conversely, I hadn't been allowed to watch *Alien* or *The Blue Lagoon*. My sisters were only allowed to watch Disney movies, usually the same ones, repeated over and over again.

One time, when my mom had objected to me watching the movie *Ilsa, She Wolf of the SS*, saying I could watch the movie when I was 14 (which I did), I had been upstairs and heard a loud bump in the attic. Part of the attic was directly above my bedroom. I was immediately startled from reading a Fantastic Four comic (one of the issues where they voyage into the Negative Zone) and looked up. I waited to see if it happened again. After a few seconds it did, but this time louder.

Extremely frightened, I quickly ran downstairs like a speeding jackrabbit.

* * *

I'll stop here to describe something of what was going on in other parts of the world at this time, to give you a perspective on things. Remember, since none of this was on the news, I wouldn't know about any of this until the internet came along, and the Reddit post thirty-two years later. The world was a different place then, a larger world made up of separate bubbles located within it, and a smaller place for those inside those bubbles. The internet wasn't around to connect those separate bubbles into a coherent whole instantaneously. Nor did social media sites exist to connect individuals worldwide in an instant.

I would later learn that close to the time I was running downstairs, around the town of Innsmouth, a fault began to appear. Strange crab creatures were seen to fly away from Vermont, and a weird statue in the house of a Brazilian millionaire began to bleed green blood. A town in Papua New Guinea was attacked by giant worms, and poltergeist effects were reported in random places around the globe.

This is just some of the things that were occurring. More of them can be found on Reddit, or on the internet if you are curious to know more.

* * *

"You know your father gets mad when he's interrupted from watching one of his movies," my grandfather said to me as we climbed up the stairs to the attic. "You shouldn't have come down screaming like a maniac."

"But there's something in the attic. I heard it loud," I contested.

"Well, if you don't want to get yelled at again, next time come down more quietly. It's probably just a cat or a rat or a raccoon rummaging up there. There's probably a hole it came in through that we're going to have to find."

After he said this, I couldn't bring myself to believe that the sound I'd heard had been caused by a cat or a rat or a raccoon. It didn't sound right. It sounded more like a heavy ball and sliding long arms. Maybe a spider?

A huge, gigantic, glutinous spider, dragging its bulk across the floor. Or an octopus perhaps?

Though now that I think about it all these years later, I'd actually never heard what a cat or a rat or a raccoon sounded like in my attic. I couldn't, therefore, have known that it wasn't any of those things, though I remember now thinking it most definitely wasn't.

While we were walking upstairs, the thought of something hairy crossed my mind. Something hairy, with three fingers, that didn't want to be found. Something that, if found, would become very, very angry.

When I told my grandfather my worries, he laughed, and said, "This is your overactive imagination again. It's what happens when you watch too many movies and read too many comic books. The mind starts living in fantasy. It becomes lazy and doesn't know what to do with itself. You should play outside more than you usually do. That'll clear you up. This is the same like when you were younger, and you thought there was someone under your bed and in your closet. When you described what it was, you described something right out of the *Planet of the Apes* movie." He then chuckled out loud. "Now you think we have a three-fingered little hairy man living in our attic."

We kept climbing up, past my bedroom floor, until we reached the attic door. My grandfather pushed the attic door, but it only opened slightly.

"Hello," he said. "It seems there's something blocking the door."

Puzzled, he bent down, and put his hand around the floor of the door to grab what was obstructing it. The attic was dark, and we couldn't see anything through the slight crack between the door, and the side casing.

"Hello," he said again, then paused, worried. "It seems there's something here. Maybe a hand or foot. Except, it's furry, and large."

***

In another part of the world, a few hours before, the strange city with wrong angles began its tumultuous re-emergence into the world from its watery grave. Later, seismologists detected a mad shaking of the icy ground near the interior of Antarctica. Planes from three different countries were sent out to investigate these occurrences.

Over Laos, a hole opened in the sky, and a forest in Germany mysteriously caught fire. Backpackers later said they'd seen strangely-dressed people dancing in the forest and then disappear into thin air.

***

When my grandfather said 'furry' I thought of the hairy imp I had imagined, and my heart almost came out of my mouth. Suddenly he yelled, and flung a white furry thing down the stairs. I screamed, and jumped quickly to the side. My grandfather started laughing. I took a closer look at the thing, and saw it was a flip-flop.

"You kids are so impressionable these days. It probably fell behind the door when your parents were lugging boxes of old clothes down yesterday. Or maybe a cat dropped it. We'll find out."

He opened the door, and turned on the light switch. The attic was spacious, with a slanting roof meeting in the middle, light-blue painted walls, and a single window facing the main street. Shelves lined the sides and old boxes and plastic crates were stacked everywhere. Toys, decorations, and antique junk lay sprawled across the floor.

"Well, there doesn't seem to be anything here. Let's take a look around."

We searched the attic but didn't find anything out of the ordinary.

"It is rather chilly. I think air must be getting in here somehow, so there must be a hole somewhere. Whatever was in here is gone. Though I think you were asleep and dreaming."

"I was wide awake and reading a comic book!" I protested.

"That's it," he said, more to himself than to me, as he looked around the silent room. "Dreaming—while reading comic books."

I went back to my room, as my grandfather kept walking downstairs to continue watching the movie. A few seconds later, I heard laughter coming from the living room, and I knew they weren't laughing at the movie *Ilsa, She Wolf of the SS.*

* * *

Shutter 3657 (he hasn't given his real name) writes on Reddit that he was a young Marine in nineteen-eighty-three. He describes the size of the risen city, which he saw from a military expeditionary vessel he was on as being roughly the size of Manhattan Island. Any trawler or fishing ship that had been anywhere near the thing when it started surfacing was surely gone after, destroyed or lost on its monolithic towers and aberrations of architecture. These structures grew outwards in all directions, and were possessed of inconceivable angles, like a mad designer's feverish dream, as if the designer had been Dali, or some other crazed surrealist. At its zenith, rising out of this miasma of stone outcroppings, like an inhuman pyramid, rested a building, a temple of sorts, from which wild, guttural sounds emanated, echoing and travelling as if from outside our universe.

***

It was now past nine o'clock outside, and nearly dark, when I decided to listen to the radio. I was still shaken from my previous experience, and kept running through my mind what could have made the loud, bumping noises upstairs. What comes in and out of a house without being noticed? A ghost? A goblin? A gremlin? No. Nothing. My grandfather was right. I was being irrational. It must have been some poor animal that had wandered accidentally in and then run off.

Now more relaxed, I started to draw superheroes.

While I was doing this, and listening to Culture Club singing on the radio, a sudden image of a small, hairy thing, with three fingers on each hand and a blood-shot yellow eye, larger than the other eye; this large eye almost poking out of its face, and staring at me intently through my bedroom roof from the attic, hit me hard, and almost paralyzed me with fright.

I slowly got off my bed, not daring to look up at the roof, and with a loud, beating heart, and nerves fit to break, slowly walked out of my room, and panicked and hysterical, ran down the stairs again.

***

At around nine it's estimated that the American town of Innsmouth, in Massachusetts, fell into the Atlantic Ocean. It just broke off from the rest of the continent and slid into the ocean, to disappear forever.

I say it disappeared because others say it disappeared. No one nowadays, except for a tiny few, even remembers that Innsmouth ever existed. It's been wiped out from memory, in some sort of cosmic amnesia.

***

"I want to wait in my room," I said to my grandfather, as he looked at me with worry, anger and exasperation written all over his face.

"Oh," he said in turn, surprised. "There's nothing there, you know. It's all in your head. You should face your fears. But I'll check. You'll see. Everything is okay."

He walked away, and I immediately regretted my decision. I was such a coward. I should have gone with him, to protect him as best I could from that lurking thing in the attic. Together, we had a fighting chance of survival. But...I was the one it wanted. Without me my grandfather was safe. I hoped this was true...and hope made it certain.

"I'm almost upstairs!" my grandfather yelled down, having decided to keep me updated on his excursion.

It's almost comical now when I think about it.

A few seconds later, he yelled, "I'm opening the attic door!"

It's then that I heard a whoosh sound, like wind blowing, or more correctly, like a sucking sound, like something being sucked quickly into a big, hungry giant's mouth, and then I heard a door slamming shut.

I softly whispered, "Grandpa, grandpa." But received no reply.

I walked back into my room, and looked up at the ceiling. Instantaneously, I once more had an unbeckoned image hit me hard inside my head. It nearly knocked me off my feet.

In my imagination, I saw the hairy imp drag my defenseless grandfather with its long, skinny arms into the darkness of the attic. Then it gave a high jump, as if in triumph. As I thought this, I heard a loud thump in the attic. After, something horrible began to happen. The creature faded into darkness, as did my unconscious grandfather.

A bulging thing appeared. It steadily materialized. First I saw small wings on it. Then two claws appeared. Green scales began to glitter all over its body. Soon, it was larger than a sixty-story building and its head resembled a coiling octopus, with tentacles flailing everywhere. It was in a passage of some sort, made of ancient stone which dripped water, and I sensed that it was about to unleash itself on the world. It gave one of the most horrendous screams I have ever heard, and this startled me so much that without thinking, I ran out of my room and up the stairs towards the attic.

I had to save my grandfather. I was an unthinking animal, all adrenaline and fright.

When I got to the attic door, I opened it, and saw a humongous eye blocking my way into the room. Through the doorway all I saw was a pupil, and somehow I knew this was the pupil of the octopus-headed creature I had seen in my mind. I stepped back in fright.

I knew it saw me. But how could this be? How was the thing in my attic? Then it moved, the eye disappeared, and I saw a blue sky, and water everywhere in the distance.

The automatic submachine gun and assault rifle fire started, and once again I ran downstairs.

***

Shutter 3657 writes that when the Marines landed on the just risen city, close to its top, having been let down by a helicopter, the slimy stone underneath their feet felt both hard and soft. A texture that sank a bit when you stepped on it, but that also gave the impression of having an otherworldly resilience.

His team, one of many that were dropped off around the city, climbed up the abnormal cliffs and juttings of the city, which they followed up in a path that zigzagged like a contorted snake. Planes and helicopters circled the city, and far down below, he saw the warships –warships which had been near the area, and had been sent from a few different countries. He could smell the ocean and the wetness in the air.

When his team had almost reached the top, where a mighty door was situated near the tip of the pyramid, a great sky-reaching scream was heard, and a maniacal thing opened the vast doors, and squeezed through its aperture. He remembers a massive shadow blotting out the night sky, coils of tentacles flexing in all directions, and an immense claw swatting at the sun.

Then his whole team in unison began to fire on the thing with their submachine guns and assault rifles.

***

I waited breathlessly, as my father was about to open the attic door. He looked at me, and I could tell he was holding back his fury.

"This is the last time you interrupt us, Mikey. If I don't find anything in here, you're grounded for two weeks. And where is your grandfather again?"

"I told you already," I answered, sobbing. "The hairy man took him."

My father looked like he was about to yell, but instead decided to try the door. He opened it quickly, and we saw nothing. No vast eye, or landscape of endless water.

I heaved a sigh of relief.

He turned on the light switch and it illumed the normal attic, with shelves and boxes and junk scattered everywhere.

He looked at me and said, "See, there's nothing here."

On the instant, a hand appeared out of nowhere, and grabbed my father and pulled him into the room. I remember the hairiness of it and the long slim arm it was attached to.

The attic door slammed shut as I ran desperately into my room.

I hid under my bed covers, and after a few minutes, just as I had decided to go downstairs to tell my mom and grandmother what was happening, I heard a pebble hit my bedroom window. Then another...and another.

I cautiously made my way to the window and peeked outside. It was already dark, and all the streetlights were on. No cars were passing by and the street was empty of people. Everybody was indoors.

Another pebble hit the window.

I looked in the direction it came from, and saw a terrifying sight. By the front bushes, in the darkness, I saw a hairy manlike thing; its head was its whole hairy body, and two arms and legs jutted out of this head. It resembled an egg with arms and legs, like a furry Humpty-Dumpty. One eye was popping and yellow, and the other was heavy-lidded and almost closed. Its mouth drooped downwards, and its nose was long and aquiline.

My father was propped up against the creature, like a baby held in its arms. His face sagged, all life gone out of it. And the creature played intently with his head and lower jaw, opening and closing my father's mouth. He looked like nothing but a lifeless sack of blood and meat, like a grotesque ventriloquist's dummy.

This was finally too much. I ran downstairs and told my mother and grandmother everything.

Terrified out of my mind, I went upstairs to the attic with them, to check it, but we found nothing. We also checked around the house, and also found nothing. If it wasn't that my father and grandfather were missing, I would have thought I was crazy. We stayed awake all night but they never returned. Everything was calm outside.

Meanwhile, a world away, daylight time, which was night for us, showed the opposite of calm for them.

* * *

The Marines' weaponry was useless against the creature. So was the jet and helicopter fire. Nothing the warships threw at the creature harmed it either. The creature didn't even notice them. After its initial chaotic behavior, it just looked at everything with what appeared to be detachment.

Sometime during this skirmish, the Marines found themselves under attack, from a small group of men and women who had been hiding on the island. They were quickly overpowered.

The pests later stated they were worshippers of the giant creature, which they thought of as a god. A god named Cthulhu. They, and their antecedents in the cult, had always been awaiting the god's great awakening, when it would destroy the earth and make them rulers with him on a new earth. They'd travelled to the spot the city would rise from to help the god out of his million year entombment.

It appears their beliefs were quite mistaken. For one thing, it didn't help them win their battle against the Marines—not even lifting one finger to help them. Later, in custody, a few of these cultists committed suicide.

Eventually, a hole opened up above the creature. Through it were seen the outlines of a strange universe. Cthulhu flew into it, and disappeared from our worldly view. We seemed to be of no concern, or interest, to this incredibly old, and incredibly powerful being.

Then, a tremendous commotion was heard, and from doors unnoticed before, a mass of these same gigantic creatures followed him into the rip in our universe. Shutter 3657 says it was quite a sight to see. He will never forget it for as long as he lives. A few Japanese warplanes are reported to have followed the monsters into the portal. Nothing has ever been heard from them.

Immediately, the city began to disintegrate and blend into the ocean. Everyone evacuated, and soon nothing of it was left to see. With Cthulhu gone, it wasn't held together anymore.

Yet Cthulhu and his sleeping minions weren't the only ones to disappear off the face of the earth. Reports say that all over the world portals opened, and creatures that had lurked hidden in mankind's darkest dreams and nightmares were seen to all of a sudden take visible form, and disappear into their own portals—creatures such as gorgons, griffins, satyrs, nymphs, and others of the air and water and forests. Giant worms, shoggoths, alien lifeforms all disappeared. Even all the old gods from antiquity are said to have departed with Cthulhu.

The world was cleansed of magic.

With nothing more to do, the few representatives of the nations which had managed to make it to the spot left, and returned to whatever they had been previously doing.

They were all sworn to secrecy.

* * *

As for my family, we waited until morning, and then my mother called the police. A missing persons report was filed two days later.

Miraculously, my father and grandfather reappeared three weeks later, calling from the airport to say they'd be arriving by taxi.

We waited for them outside the house. When they arrived, they both looked pale and frightened, my father especially so.

Before he entered the house, grandfather looked at me long and hard, and said, "Don't ever ask me to go into the attic again."

* * *

Apparently, they had found themselves on the risen city just before Cthulhu left our universe. I imagine then that our attic had also been a portal.

As for what the creature in the attic was, I have no idea, though many have given me suggestions.

Whatever it was, I'm sure it resides now with Cthulhu, far from our world and its mundane concerns.

Recently I've managed to acquire a new copy of the Necronomicon—the book the cultists said spoke of Cthulhu and the other gods, and the creatures which had departed our earth. I compared it to an old copy I'd also acquired. Apparently, new words have been added to the newer version.

These words are:

Gone they have from the mountains of the world, in Leng their voices are no more, the waters do not contain them, nor do the forests hear them when they pass. Gone they have to the stars, returned once more to their home; gone once more to the darkness above, where men cannot go.

Settled

What was the name? For the life of her, she couldn't remember. She'd thought highly of the exhibit and the work of art, but now, funnily, couldn't remember its name.

She knew it had been somewhere on exhibit in London before the war. Then, when the Nazi bombs started falling, it had been moved to a private collection outside the city. At the end of the war, her husband had found it amid the ruins. Apparently, relocation hadn't saved it from the bombs. After numerous thorough inquiries, no owner was found, so he had it shipped to the States.

Well, she wasn't about to drop the conversation just because she couldn't remember the name. Already Alice had moved on to another topic, yet Mona wanted so much to show her the thing.

Looking outside, Mona listened to the wind blowing the unsettled yellow and orange leaves that had fallen from the trees, and in dim autumn's wake, felt the slowly encroaching cold and greater oncoming darkness, far removed from summer's sultriness.

If she wanted to show Alice, she would have to do it quickly, in case Alice decided to leave earlier than usual because of the weather.

"The pumpkins this year," Alice said, "are smaller than last year's crop. I've searched all around, but one really must go to the countryside to shop for the best ones, don't you think?"

"I really don't know about that sort of thing," Mona answered. "When I was younger, my father and older brothers and sisters took care of the shopping, and now that I'm married, Mr. Macready does the buying for pumpkins." She paused for a second, then continued in a lighter tone, "My, but you did say we get a lot of traffic here during Halloween, didn't you?"

"Oh, yes!" Alice said, barely containing her enthusiasm. "It's a regular fair around here. The children come from all parts looking for candy. You do give out candy and enjoy it—Halloween, I mean?"

"I suppose," Mona said. "Now that the boarder's gone and Mr. Macready won't be getting back from Europe for some time, I'll have to do something to keep away the boredom. Yes, I think I will give out candy."

Mentioning how alone she was brought back a slight twinge of the depression she had been feeling. With Mr. Macready working in London as a building contractor, and the boarder, his business at the university now finished, back home in the Southwest, it was only Alice, dear Alice, and her frequent visits—except recently, when she'd gone on vacation—which provided Mona with at least some company.

When she'd moved here with her newlywed husband from Alabama, she hadn't expected this to come about: no husband, no children, no job and no expectation of finding one, and no friends, except for Alice and a handful of acquaintances who rarely visited, if ever. It was enough to drive any sane person to depression, and to cling onto any scrap of companionship that could be found.

So when Alice said she was leaving, Mona wouldn't have it. Besides, she hadn't yet shown Alice the exhibit piece her husband had sent her.

"Oh, Alice, must you go?" Mona asked. "Can't you stay for supper?"

"If it will make you feel better, I can stay a while longer."

"Oh, it most definitely will! You can help me cook!" Mona said, her face brightening. "But first, do let me show you the exhibit piece. It's a simply marvelous thing. They say it was made by an artist in the '30s. He was said at the time to be absolutely, deliciously deranged. But isn't that what they say of all true geniuses, dear Alice?"

She led Alice to the basement door.

"We keep it down here. It's much larger than you would imagine. I feel rather ashamed, but I can't remember the piece's name for the life of me. As I've said, it was rather popular during the '30s. I really can't go on showing you without sharing any real information with you. Do wait for me while I go search for one of the newspapers that Mr. Macready sent me along with the piece. Its name and more of its history are in them."

Alice opened the door and turned on the stairway lights.

"My, but you're in a hurry!" Mona said. "Though you have been a dear, offering to stay until after supper. Do you want to go on ahead and wait for me downstairs? Very well, do mind your step on the way down, while I go search for that paper. I shouldn't be more than a few seconds."

Alice walked briskly down the steps and stopped at the bottom, since the rest of the basement was still in darkness. Not wanting to waste too much time, she decided to go on ahead, feeling in the darkness for the overhead pull-chain light switch.

From upstairs, she heard Mona yelling clearly. "I do appreciate you staying, Alice. You can't imagine how depressing this time of year can be for someone without company. I suppose it can be a time of quiet contemplation for others, but not for me. I think it's simply beastly. The days getting shorter, the outside world emptying of people, the colors growing dullish and gray, everything dying and slowly turning cold, like the inside of a bland, frozen refrigerator. It's beastly!"

After groping and almost giving up, Alice found the chain and pulled it. The overhead light bulb lit up spectacularly, forcing the blackness to retreat a short distance away.

She was surprised at how large the basement was! There were still vast sections in darkness. In a corner, she saw two pairs of ripped-up men's shoes, neatly placed side-by-side. For some reason she couldn't quite grasp, she found the display deeply strange and unsettling.

Mona's voice was coming closer. "The newspaper says the piece was originally on display in Southwark Street, London. It's a representation of an obscure totem creature from Nome, Alaska, based on some barely-known legend from the place. You can read about it all in more detail soon."

Alice noticed some kind of symbol in blood-red paint on a crossbeam above. This was all deathly strange. As she moved closer to the outer darkness, she thought she might be able to make out the outline of something hiding in the shadows.

Was it an elephant's trunk she had glimpsed? And three shiny glazed things, perhaps eyes or massive marbles, coming closer? There was definitely something in the darkness...moving.

She was turning to leave, when something hit her hard across the head. Dizzying pain sent her sprawling to the ground. Looking up, she had just enough time to see Mona rushing across the basement and up the stairs, carrying a hammer in her hand, stopping only to turn off the lights.

In seconds, Alice was in total darkness, tasting blood on her lips. Something was slowly crawling, or slouching toward her. Not sure what else to do, Alice started yelling for help. "Help me! Someone, please! Mona! Help me! Anyone!"

She heard Mona upstairs, moving around in the kitchen and running water. Was she getting supper ready? Even after what had just happened? The kitchen radio blared on.

Suddenly, a terrible, fishy stench reached her nose, and horrible slopping sounds started to inch toward her. Whatever it was, she could tell that it was big.

All her bodily defenses told her to flee, so she got up, and flung herself in the direction of the stairs with all her might. She crashed straight into them, banging herself up. Pain flashed across her shins and nose, yet she immediately got up and ran blindly up the stairs. Hammering into the door, she reached for the handle and tried desperately to twist it, but it wouldn't budge. The door was locked.

The sound of the Andrews Sisters singing on the other side blended with her own words as she screamed, "For God's sake, Mona, let me out! You can't do this! Frederick knows that I came to see you today! People will come here, you can count on that! What about my daughter? Think of her! I was supposed to go to Washington tomorrow to visit my brother, who's a senator! Do you understand, Mona? He won't let this go! Oh please, Mona! Please!"

Mona calmly put down the knife she was using to chop vegetables for the chicken stew, and made her way to the basement door, rather bored. She quickly began to chastise Alice.

"Do be a dear and hush now, Alice. All this fuss is just serving to make you all flustered. The thing in the basement, it...I know that I'm not myself lately, but...it gets inside your head, strange-like. You think they're your ideas. I can't explain it, right; it's strange. Now, do be a good dear and hush. I promise it won't hurt for long."

Alice heard as Mona went back to the kitchen and resumed cooking. She slowly slunk down by the door and started to weep uncontrollably.

From the bottom steps, something began to make its way up to her.

* * *

Mona sat alone eating supper and lamented the fact she always ate alone. First, the boarder didn't come for supper anymore, then Mr. Macready, and now Alice. Outside, she saw the new-fallen night, heard the howling wind crashing against the window glass, and grew despondent about her lonesome predicament.

She hated this time of year, hated what it represented to the soul. She felt as fragile as a weathered leaf, like she would crumble if pressed too hard. She couldn't—wouldn't—forgive Alice for leaving her alone like this, just her and her supper.

At least the children and their laughter during Halloween would bring some jubilation to her world. Their ringing, merry voices carrying within them the promise of spring and regeneration, when all things are made new again after the death of autumn and winter, would bring her some joy. This was some happiness to look forward to, some companionship.

She'd most definitely have to invite some children into the house—perhaps for supper! It was definitely what it would want. She'd do this before hibernating for the winter, before turning herself off, before awaiting nothing but the spring, before dying temporarily, drowning herself in sorrow, and drink.

The thing in the basement was quiet, now. It usually did this after a feast. Mona sensed it in her head and was strangely calmed.

She got up and went to look for Alice.

"Are you done being dead yet?" she asked.

When she found Alice, she would pick her up and hang her on a coat rack, and talk to her. It was simple to do, since the creature usually broke all its food's bones as it sucked sustenance from the inside. Then she'd have Alice all to herself.

She carefully unlocked the basement door and peered into the darkness. Alice lay in a heap in a corner. As she inched nearer, a hand reached out to grasp her ankle, and grabbing onto it, yanked hard. This couldn't be! Alice should have been dead!

Mona lost her balance and tumbled down, falling and hitting herself horribly against the steps. Her neck was twisted in a very awkward way.

Now, at the bottom of the steps, she waited calmly for her end. There was no fear, only expectation. The thing, subtly controlling her mind, didn't want her to struggle.

Mona gasped as hundreds of sucking filaments appeared from the dark, and embraced and attached themselves to her. Then, the gentle feeding began.

In flashes, Mona saw what the creature had seen in its long life. Dizzying planets swam before her. Uncountable acolytes praised and worshipped it on worlds now dead. She saw this and much more, and was astounded. But it wasn't to last.

Soon, the squeezing and breaking began, and the mashing of her insides commenced. As she slowly felt her life leaving her, she finally remembered the thing's name. She thought this quite comical, quite deranged even. But of course, how could she have forgotten?

Its name was Ran-Tegoth.

***

The well-dressed woman who boarded the airplane a week later was rather strange and yet distinguished, with an air of steely purpose about her. She sat in first class, and wore dark glasses and extraneous makeup, as if to cover some unsightly blemishes. Most took her for a socialite.

She spoke of traveling to many places, and of a brother she had, a senator. No one guessed she was leaving her daughter and husband behind—her whole life, in fact—to start a new life. The only items she carried with her from her old life were a carry-on bag and a huge container, in another plane's cargo hold.

The metal container was roughly the size of a small car. It was marked hazardous and dangerous and was not to be opened. The creature rested inside.

Alice was much more suited for its purposes. Mona could never have offered it much. She was already dead, even while alive. It needed something more vivacious, more adventurous, something with more opportunities to offer.

By 9:45 p.m., the plane was airborne, bound for Washington, D.C.

***

No one ever found the grotesquely punctured, loose skin-bag thing that had been dumped inside the garbage can in front of the Macready residence—the thing which once had been Mona Macready.

Two Collaborative Sonnets

1. Darkness Comes to Erebus
(Written in collaboration with Hank Simmons)

Wake my soul, darkness comes to Erebus—
Dormant renaissance of a new earthen crust—
Where vibrant burn your fires dangerous;
Where we think we all will die, but someone must
Wake my soul from Erebus, dormant since
The coming of an age befitting this.
Charge my sword, to cleave the deathless prince,
And free our land with my steel's bitter kiss
Of that dark renaissance imperatorial;
Our hearts confused but redolent and true
Will swiftly strike that throne marmoreal,
Illuminating darkness we've passed through.
So wake my soul, while dark Ashtor sleeps,
And free me from his black infernal keep.

2. The Cursed
(Written in collaboration with Hank Simmons)

Old woods, where darkness lay, a livid dream,
Partaking of a black and bitter draught;
Where cursed men howled in lycanthropic scream,
At tug of Luna's foul gleam throughout.
Your blasted trunks, uprooted from their stems,
By those within and those without the earth,
Housed living corpses, unsightly ghoulish gems;
That, blasphemously, ascending from their berths,

Crept, as I, into the newer homes of men;
Malefic and intent on evil gain;
Their crimson hearths warmer than your haunted glens.
Migration hence we cannot now refrain.
Our paws rest lightly on town and city beds,
While we flense the skin from their owners' heads.

Beastmen of Beringia

What had the men of the south to do with me? They were not my people. I would have hunted them down and cut them from the land if it had been up to me.

***

"Yig," the old wizard often said, while he sat beside the summoning fire, fingering his necklace of colored stones—that haughty, wrinkled and wretched old man. "Why must you always look for excuses to fight? We are in a new land. We must look for ways of peace. It may be that our new neighbors are more powerful than we think. The ways of friendship must be our course, lest we find ourselves exterminated."

How I hated that haughty, wrinkled and wretched old wizard. Because of his magic he thought he was my match, thought he was my equal, but my people respected him, so I let him prate. *Yig is Yig.* In time, I would have my turn upon him.

***

The world I'd been born into was one of almost perennial winters, relieved only by short mild summers. Legend said that once my people had walked the ground without heavy furs, that the air had been as hot as burning fires, and the earth as green as the towering conifers, but I laughed at this; I believed they were empty dreams spoken by fools, the earth had always been this way and always would be, a great pain of white snow and frozen earth.

This was the epoch of the great ice, when continental glaciers covered the world.

In my youth, with just two short wooden pikes, alone, I had hunted and killed a large saber-toothed cat. It was because of this that

I'd become a legend among my people. I was like a father to them. They were like my children.

At that time, I stood taller than any man of my tribe. My father was one of our important men, and if I wished to be like him, one day I would have to prove myself, so that our elders could die in peace when it was their turn to rest with our kin.

That morning I would prove myself. I put on my dire wolf furs, arranged my weapons on my body, and set out. My frosty breath came forth slowly from my tense mouth, like a smoky ghost, the grey sun of morning shone hazily through the clouds, the brittle underbrush cracked softly under my soft tread. The wild roar then, when the monstrous, large-toothed beast lunged at me from behind some snowy pine trees, and I drank in the moment as I lunged also exultantly to greet it, muscles rippling from forth our two heavy bodies, as we both fought a contest to the death, each one of us fighting against the rabid, will-to-live of the other, until I impaled the smilodon against a tree with a quick thrust of my cold hand, using one of the sharp wooden sticks I carried. I smelled, almost tasted, the delicious scent of its warm blood, as it cascaded down forcefully from the creature's thick neck, melting the snow below.

That monster never stood a chance.

***

The Gwarns were the people of ice and snow. Strong as rocks and lustful for life. They were the supermen I had not seen in many years. When they came, the year of the Sundering and in the year that I killed the saber-toothed cat, I marveled at them. Tribe legend said that my immediate family was part Gwarn itself and that sometimes it showed itself, as it now did in my prodigious strength.

They appeared loping that cold summer out of the fog and flurries, a horde of them, as we celebrated our Festival of Births, and while children were readying to enact the storming of the ice hills of the moon by the sun god's retinue. Well-built beasts the Gwarns were, possessed of varied-colored hairs, which grew thick upon them. Their jaws protruded. Their foreheads sloped forwards into heavy, bushy brows, shadowing leering, intense eyes and large, bulbous noses. Their hairy wide mouths grinned, and I knew they grinned because of our smallness and weakness. Huroc was the second in power in our band after me, and yet his hands were like a child's hands when compared to those of the Gwarns.

Through the fog, as they advanced, I saw they were dressed in bushy furs, and a few held tied to ropes, gigantic and snarling, bulldog bears. Beasts commanding beasts, I thought. Atop their heads, the Gwarns wore great pelt-caps, embedded with heavy tusks and horns, and they carried weapons of long, sharp ivory, and wide wooden clubs nailed with strange, sharp teeth.

These Gwarns were not entirely like the former Gwarns I'd known. It had always been unsettling for me to be in close proximity to them. They moved and reacted differently than us; they were more ape-like, though close to us, a type of us. These Gwarns, however, I saw were of a different order than the others. Their teeth were sharper. They were taller. Stockier. In my gloomy temper I wished nothing more than to keep them away from me. They inspired something akin to fear in me. When the youngsters in our band saw them, they ran and hid, or else cowered frightened where they stood.

The old wizard walked up to them and, through his power of languages, managed to communicate. When they left, the old man said to us, "They call themselves the Children of Morkoo. They only want to dwell in peace with us and to share the foraging grounds for a time. Come next summer or earlier, they promise to leave."

The wizard managed to convince the elders that accommodation was preferable to hostility. All the trouble that was to come afterwards I blame on the old man.

* * *

When I was born, I was imprinted on my inner thigh with the Sigil of the Shamans, by the old wizard. Only three of us received this honor at our births: myself, Nazree, and Arakhan.

This mark set us apart as successors to the wizard. As babies he inspected us to see if we had the seed, the initial power, the spark that in time could be nourished to grow and expand and make us powerful wizards.

I did well in my first studies, though later I was denied my birth-right.

One day, Kulkut—such was the hated old man's name—called me to him and said, "Are you sure this is the path you wish to take?"

I didn't know what to say. Often I'd preferred hunting to my studies, but still I'd found my studies pleasurable.

"Soon," he continued, "it will be time for you three to stand against each other in the game that will decide your ultimate fates as my students. Only one, Yig, can continue further studies. Do you in truth wish to compete? You were chosen and until now have been forced to come to my classes, it has not been your choice, but now I give you a choice. Leave if you wish. Go and run free with the wild beasts, and play in the ice with the boys at war, let your sullen temper take you where it will. I discharge you, with all honor, from your duties to me. I will speak well of you to the elders, and will have you placed with our top hunters."

I thought well about what he said. I thought of my pleasures in hunting. In the end, I decided to compete.

* * *

The game was simple. We were taught childish spells and diagrams, for Kulkut said that words and diagrams, when wielded by one with the gift for magic, made wizardry work. For others without the gift, nothing happened. These spells were designed to enable us to find a precious gemstone hidden somewhere in the nearby cold and desolate woods.

Suffice it to say that when we went out tracking the gem, I was the one to find it buried in the frozen earth. Yet when I returned to the spot after telling the wizard what I had done, after he had hurried on ahead of me to the spot, I saw the traitorous wretch hide the gem in his warm clothing and then say to me that I, in fact, had not found anything. He made of me a liar. When I left angry and disheartened he hid the object somewhere else, and Arakhan later found it and he became his apprentice.

I hated the old man afterwards, and my anger will never fade. I am Yig and I am always the same. Time cannot change me.

* * *

In the year of the Sundering winter came in summer, and much harsher, brutal and colder than we had ever known. Our grey world turned darker, violent winds blew feverishly, and the snow marked the earth like a thick white blanket. The dark clouds hid the sun from our eyes constantly, so that I forgot what its brilliance looked like. Always the blinding snow blew. Our elders had never seen an age like it. Food grew scarce and hunting became difficult. More and more children began to starve and weep through nights and days of sullen bleakness. We feared the end of all life had come.

One evening, the gust-blown snow sheets found four lonely interlopers crossing with sleds through its icy wake. Dressed in warm furs, their hot exhalations cut through the chilly air like hard knives. These four were myself, the wizard, Nazree, and Huroc. Nazree brought along her pack of sagacious hunting dogs. Our eyes saw only curtains of white flakes, which stormed against us, stung our eyes, and made visibility nearly impossible. Onwards we trekked, trudging through the treacherous and high-hefted snow, with desperation on our minds and hunger in our stomachs. No beast was intuited, either level with us or in the sky above.

"If we are denied," Kulkut said to us, "we will have to break camp immediately and go elsewhere. I am certain that northwest from here there are more of our kin. Whether we stay or walk in the snow, we will die if we have no food. We must find our kin."

Because of the weather and our arduous march, I heard him as if from faraway, and looked at him grimly.

Near nightfall, the wizard led us to the campground of the Gwarns, which was somewhat cleared of snow and surrounded a dark, ominous cave. Their temporary home was vast and wide, with many makeshift animal skin tents spread throughout it. Low fires were barely burning, and because of the minimal number of Gwarns we saw, we guessed most of them had already retired for the night. We were, however, startled to see an inordinate number of bulldog bears sleeping and tied to posts throughout the camp.

As we watched, giant stooping shapes carrying fire-lit torches came to us out of the haze of blowing snow.

Once near us they looked down upon us with haughty, sneering eyes. When they baulked in their uncouth language, I saw jagged, sharpened teeth and smelt the fetid air that came from their cavernous mouths. Their faces were covered with thick, heavy-set, hoary beards.

We asked them for food, but they denied us, saying they themselves were in need of food and could not spare any. I pointed at all the bears they possessed, but they would not move from their position. In-between words they grunted and muttered the name, "Morkoo."

I would have attacked them right there, but the old man prevented me. He thanked them, and he led us away. He was the leader of the expedition, he told me, and that I should never say anything when he talked.

Later, because Nazree and Huroc were also mad, we snuck back in darkness to the Gwarn camp while the old man slept. We left him dreaming, since he was good at dreaming.

Everyone was asleep, and over a great bear I stabbed mightily with my obsidian blade into its exposed throat. My skill was such that it died without making a sound.

As we cut it into pieces, and put those bloody slabs onto sleds, we caught the sound of something in the nearby cave moving, and heard a deeply disturbing voice. It was loud, and sounded as if a bear suddenly had grown the vocal instruments of a man. The thing yelled in a growly and raspy voice in our own language, "You will die for your wrong, intruders!"

Then that which rested in the cave came out, and even though we were in darkness, by the outline of its monstrosity, we could tell it was the work of some sorcery.

Ape-like it ran ferociously forwards, with shards of broken horns rammed violently into its skull. With hands bigger than those of a giant sloth, it batted at us with large swipes. In the dark and cold, startled, I jumped on its back, and as I struggled, I tried to wrest its black cloak off, and was uneased to find the fur I pulled was stuck to the thing and would not come off. Then I realized the thing was gowned in heavy shaggy fur! The hoar-frost gleamed white, and icicles were matted into it. This was no atypical Gwarn. In our struggle I found myself staring at its gigantic serrated teeth, and saw clearly for a while its incongruous face, marked by bushy eyebrows and small yellow eyes. Its face was as if a Gwarn and a bear were fusing into each other, and each part did not know what it wanted to become yet! I could not tell where Gwarn ended and bear began!

By now Gwarns had begun to appear from their shelters, and chanted, "Morkoo! Morkoo! Father!"

The creature bit into me savagely, and I bit into it. I pummeled its head and shoulders as it roared brazenly into the wintry dark. Nazree's dogs jumped on the thing, their long sharp canines ripping into it, their survival instincts on high alert. Nazree and Huroc slashed at the thing with singing axes and blades. Somehow, as we all fought like desperate wild beasts, the thing and I both tumbled hard onto the red snow. With the fall I managed to loosen myself from its clutches, and then we all ran frenziedly into the woods.

It stayed behind, but Gwarns followed us into the forest, like hungry wolves. We fought bravely and desperately, trudging against the snow bed. Neither dagger, spear, quiver, or formidable axe was spared in its usage against the chasing behemoths.

In the end we managed to escape. When we finally rested, falling like dead into the high snow, Nazree was greatly saddened to find out two of her dogs had died, albeit heroically, in the melee.

* * *

"There will be deaths, many deaths." Kulkut said to me as we walked back to our camp. "This may be the grim death of us all."

As I looked before me all I saw was the endless death of winter.

"We needed food," I said to him. "Weak, our people cannot walk through this frozen hell. A little food would have given them hope and strength."

"At what cost, Yig? You three slaughtered many Gwarns. They are many and will follow us. Not all of our band is fit for this further test of our strength. You have brought more doom upon us."

"Go weep somewhere else, old man. What good has your wizardry been? It hasn't helped us. At least with a little bear meat we would have died with something in our stomachs."

"Do you love your people, Yig?" the old weak wizard said to me.

"Perhaps more than you do, old man," I said to him.

* * *

We fought across the snow drifts of Beringia and into the unknown lands of North America, always pursued by the tireless Gwarns. The wizard took up the mantle of a warrior, and proved himself adequately well as a magician on the field. He tired easily, however, and his apprentice, Arakhan, had not yet attained any proficiency in the art to prove an asset. At times, we heard the lamentation and funeral drums of the Gwarns, who had never forgotten their fallen. Mostly we heard their beats of war.

We headed east, and not northwest, where the wizard had said more of our clan were, since the Gwarns had blocked this route of escape for us, and with their numbers forced us always east, ever east.

Eventually, they stopped their chase. We imagined it was because they feared to go any further into what was unfamiliar and uncertain territory for them.

By this time, more than half of our band had succumbed to injuries and diseases, due to weakness and famine. Most of our elders had died and we'd left them behind, eternally frozen in the ice, and as markers of our passage. Because of this I, along with others, was voted into the council to replace them.

In time, in these new lands, food appeared more abundantly, and some of the snow melted. We followed the animals deeper east, and then south. Our strength returned and one day we met the men of the south.

* * *

"Yig," Kulkut said to me for the hundredth time at the council circle, "why must you always look for excuses to fight? We are in a new land. We must look for ways of peace. It may be that our new neighbors are more powerful than we think. The ways of friendship must be our course, lest we find ourselves exterminated." He became quiet, and picked up a prong to tend the fire, which summoned the spirits of our deceased elders to our meetings.

For the hundredth time I answered him the same way, though this time I meant for this to be the last council meeting on this matter.

"The first day," I said, "I saw them running past us, I saw how they were dressed similar to the Gwarns of Morkoo. I will never forget what those beasts did to us. These men are somehow of the same band; that is why they are dressed the same. I have seen my father, my mother, my brother and sisters die because of those brutes. I will not allow our band to suffer in the same way again."

"You only council bloodshed."

"Kill them first before they kill us. If we must be friends, it must be the friendship of the hunter for the prey. Only this mind will allow us to survive."

All in the council I sensed were in some agreement with me, and divided between my words and the wizard's.

Ever since we had entered this new land, we had been alone except for the wild animals. One day a group of men from the south hurriedly crossed our campground, and without authorization from the council of elders, I had proceeded to hunt them down and cut them from the land. They wore garments too similar to Morkoo's beasts, I thought.

The old wizard and some in the council called my actions madness. I laughed at their words, since my actions were not yet as mad as I wished.

Soon, more of the men came and camped near us. The wizard wanted us to send an embassy to them. That night I put his plans to rest by sneaking into the southern men's campsite, as a dark wraith of destruction. I killed most of them, quenching my anger with their deaths. I impaled some of them horrendously on long spears. Some I let escape to tell others of the demon in the woods. In this way I hoped to spread fear of our woods among those brutes.

The next day, when my actions were found out, I said to the wizard, "Is this madness enough?"

I had kept one man as a prisoner for myself to extract information from. The old wizard wouldn't help me with his gift for languages during my interrogations, but there are ways to tell when a man is saying something of importance, without such trifles.

After days of torture, I knew the man was saying something of value.

The whites of his eyes shone brightly with fear as I dragged him in by the hair, since he could no longer walk. He'd once been a man, is all I will say on the matter. One sight of my raised hand is all it took for the man to begin to whine and curl into himself. His bruised, broken and bloody body was piteous to some of the members of the council.

He spoke gibberish, in between labored breaths. I'd by now gotten used to the rhythm of his words, so that I knew he repeated the same sentences over and over again. I asked the old wizard to interpret for the council what the man said.

The wizard looked at me somberly and said, "He says: I don't understand you. What do you want, monster? I will do anything. Stop. I will never rise against the city of Kataan again, if that is what you want. Stop. I promise. I swear. Please stop."

I asked Kulkut what a city was. He explained that it was a great group of immovable tribes, numberless tribes, living together in set boundaries.

I said there must be great stores of food there, and great materials. Surely if we asked, we would be given some. Or we could take it. After all, this city was not of our kin.

I commanded the old man to tell the prisoner that we were not allies of the Kataan, and for him to take us where the city was. The prisoner said that he refused, that he would never go back. When I moved to harm him, the old wizard stood up to my face.

"I will not abide this abuse any longer," Kulkut said angrily. "You are evil, Yig! What you do to this man is cruel! Listen, all of you! We must never go to Kataan. The path of the city men is not our path!"

The wizard asked for a vote. He wanted to cast me out of the council and for us to leave immediately back to our kin. The council, however, voted in my favor. Their curiosity, too, was aroused. They too wanted to see this city. They too wanted to see what materials and food they could get. They would tolerate me, they said, for now.

I was amused.

Kulkut said he was leaving. That he would not abide by their decision. I was stubborn with what I wanted. I yelled at him to leave. I said all were free to leave who did not want to abide by the council's decision.

Many left with the old man that very night. Among them were Arakhan, Nazree, and Huroc. I smiled to see the old man go sorrow-stricken with his rag-tag train. I laughed to see him weak and finally defeated.

He and his band were no longer of my kin.

* * *

Together with two companions, I was sent by the council to scout the city and file an intelligence report of its look, its strength, demeanor and materials. Later, we would decide what further to do.

The prisoner gave us directions to the border of the city's foraging grounds before I killed him.

When we were near the border, we hid in a patch of woodland and looked out at the vast expanse of snow-fields before us.

In the distance, we saw a cleared path, and two massive standing black, jutting rocks to either side of it. Atop the rocks were men and Gwarns, and by the rocks were giant mastodons and woolly mammoths; these animals being ridden by both men and Gwarns. It was an unholy alliance, I said.

The men and Gwarns wore black leather armor, heavy furry boots, and were equipped with spears, atlatls, daggers, axes, shields, slings and other sharp instruments of ivory, stone, and wood. Their heads were protected by black pelt-helmets massively studded with mammoth ivory. They were cloaked in thin furry capes. Later I was to learn this was the last outpost of the southern men's civilization.

Further in the distance, I saw a stone two-story building. It was the first I had ever seen in my life.

The men asked me what to do. We were curious to see what was inside the building. If we just walked up to the post it could be dangerous, since the guards might kill us or take us prisoner. Besides, we did not know how many more were inside the building. I decided to wait until nighttime, to see if something then could be done. If not, we would find a way around the post and continue our journey.

* * *

When night came, the great weight of cold fell upon us. In the sky, I admired the emergence of the stars and constellations, and those ever-fixed friends, Kochab and Pherkad.

Below, the men stayed at their posts, while others surrounded the building. In the immensity of silence, I felt like a lone snow-drift in the wasteland.

Heavy clouds gathered quickly above us, to shade us in a greater shadow, and gusting winds began to shake the uppermost treetops. In no time we were in the midst of a howling blizzard.

We shook with fear in the swirling eddies, and covered ourselves tightly, and huddled sitting to keep ourselves warm and safe from frostbite.

The dark and blowing snow became a wall between us and the world. We saw nothing.

Sometime, in this raging tempest, as I shivered and was covered in ice and snow, I began to hallucinate. Or so I thought. Out of the blizzard I saw a man looking at me, and coming towards me, floating above the ground.

He was dressed in crude garments, and his long white hair did not flow wildly with the wind. He glowed, and somehow I saw through him.

I heard a voice in my head say, "Welcome, barbarian. What brings you to these lonesome ways so far from your people? You are confused? Under the everlasting arch of heaven there are many mysteries, and I am but one of them. Come, follow me, and I will show you the stone building nigh here, and the great flint-cities of the south. Why fear? You are stronger than me, are you not? Come, and I will lead you past the guards."

By all that's strong and fearless in the world, I swear, I followed the ghastly specter. I left my two companions shivering on the spot.

I followed him past the rocky outpost, past the freezing, sleeping guards. I followed past the treacherous open tundra, and to the stone-built building. I entered it, and climbed up stairs. I was delighted to be out of the storming snow.

On the second floor he walked through a gated cell. Looking through the stout wooden bars, I saw a man tied by tightly wound ropes. He was the same as the specter.

He had suffered much at the hands of his captors.

"Come," he said weakly, "if you can. All my strength I have used to cause a deep sleep on my captors. The rest of my strength was used in summoning my minions, which you have killed or frightened away, foolish barbarian. These bonds you see are enchanted bonds put on by one greater than myself, and which I cannot break. But need I explain more? Help me escape, and I will be indebted to you. My name is Xaqqua, and my sorcerous powers you will find of great use to you."

Like one in a dream, I broke the bars with my bare hands, using my prodigious strength, and entered his cell.

I walked up to Xaqqua as he showed me wonders: great cities built in the midst of unfathomable ice, hidden cities dwelling serenely under the earth, vast monolithic cities of men and women to the far south, where there was scarcely any glaciation, and the world was luxuriantly green; he showed me mighty countries of teeming peoples; sky-reaching palaces and temples, full of riches too great to number. And it could all be mine, if I just let him escape and helped a beast-spirit enter into him.

"I had a general named Morkoo, the Father of Bears. You will be my new general. Together we will attack Kataan again. And then, further south, Aztlan, and all the other decadent kingdoms that follow. We will build an empire.

"I have saved the most powerful spirit for the last."

I untied the sorcerer's bonds. I cut my wrists and saw my blood pool at his feet as he chanted his summoning spell. The blood rose and wheeled into a vortex. Through it, I saw enormous gaseous clouds, alien worlds and stupendous stars. The vortex moved far through time and space, past numberless galaxies, and rested atop a loathsome world the sorcerer called Xulthal. Here I saw ancient cities of columned marble, and dark gods worshipped by non-human votaries.

I saw a colossal piebald shape which brooded alone in a purple jungle among tottering temples.

I laughed, and grabbed the weak sorcerer like a toy, and proceeded to choke him forcefully with my swarthy hands. With my inherent and latent magical powers, I was immune to most of his controlling spell. Something—the piebald shape—slithered from that other dimension and entered into me as the dead sorcerer fell at my feet.

Weak and stupid sorcerer, did he really think that Yig would serve another?

* * *

Once outside, I mused that I had much to learn of that new world to the south, at whose threshold I now found myself.

When I returned to my people, I found all of them had changed and were now non-humanoid. To each of us the gift is different.

I headed back into the forest, with them following me. They were my children.

Before leading them south, I tracked and snuck, in darkness, into my great enemy's tent.

He will now teach me the magical arts he had denied me all those years ago.

Later, with those new skills, I entered Kataan, Aztlan and all the other continental cities, well prepared to do my mischief.

Senators, nobles, kings and queens, with their luxuriant robes and jewels, knelt at my feet.

Yet now, in darkness, as he slept, I cut out his tongue, so that he couldn't use words to make spells against me. In the silence of his tent, I tied his arms and legs with the magical bands that were used against Xaqqua.

Kulkut was now helpless.

With my strong arms I parted the tent to see if his people were still asleep amidst the vast desolate snows. They were. Then I proceeded to do my business.

It was now my time to have my turn upon him.

I sniffed his feet with my nose. Then, little by little, I opened my mouth, and swallowed them. My head deformed, expanded and elongated, like a balloon. I worked my way up his knees and torso.

Soon, he was in my belly, screaming hellishly with delicious torture in my gastric juices.

Eventually, through telepathy, a gift of the serpent-mind, he taught me everything.

I wriggled out of his tent; my lower serpent half wreathed its slippery and freckled gleaming mail around a tree, and climbed up. I heard the old man's bones break.

Hanging down, I opened my arms and summoned my tribe, who were, unlike my gigantic proportions, normal-sized serpents. Their tiny shapes came through the ice, and also wriggled up the tree. They began to worship me.

I looked at all before me, past the ice-sheets, and far into the world of the south that I would someday conquer.

I was a god. I was Yig, the Father of Serpents.

The Lost City of the Neanderthals

I reclined leisurely on a soft adorned couch in the city of Uruk, the greatest of all the cities of the Sumerians. Beside me, on his purple couch, sat Gilgamesh, the king who had brought the city to its pre-eminent glory.

Outside, and below in the courtyard, I heard the gently titillating laughter of the court's noblewomen—or concubines; what they were at any given time depended solely on the king's whims, for he did as he pleased and no man dared to stop him, since to stand against the savage king was foolishness. It was because of this also that no guardsmen kept watch over us, or were posted outside the room's doors.

I myself had seen him fight and defeat eleven powerful men in sport, with his hands purposely tied behind his back and with his eyes blindfolded.

This day, his black beard, cut square and braided, hung elegantly on a face frozen in perpetual gloom. With one gigantic hand he held a goblet of ale, and with the other he played restlessly with the blazing jewels filling his treasure chest.

"What foolishness for a man's work to be done," he all of a sudden said. "The cities fear me, my enemies stay far from me, and there are no more monsters to slay. What I wouldn't give for the taste of danger again, Enkidu."

That he called me by my proper name, and not his customary 'brother,' warned me that his restlessness was growing ever stronger. This boded trouble for the kingdom, for the restless and wild lion is a danger to both friend and foe alike.

I got up and looked out the window, over the city, at the great temples of the gods. I clutched tightly the medallion hanging by my chest—the medallion I had sworn never to part with.

As I did so, I said, "Great king, your people build mighty temples for the gods. They do this to honor them, both as masters and as creators, and it is good that they do this, but as for me, I know that they had no hand in creating my people. I need not honor them as creators."

I saw a fire flash in his eyes, and just as quickly subside. Luckily I was his friend, or even now I would be feeling his fury. Gilgamesh was two-thirds god and did not like to hear his parentage insulted.

The one-third of him that was human gave him flesh and the man's voice, which answered sarcastically, "Are they not? Is that so? If you know such a thing, tell me then, just who are your creators?"

"There is a city, great king, to the east, known as the City of the Neanderthals. It lies deep under the Zagros Mountains and was already old when your people were young.

"In time to them was born a great warrior, who made himself king by force, and who, yearning for ever greater glory, led his people on an expedition deep into the nether regions of the earth.

"There, it is whispered, he found terrible tablets fashioned by gods ancient and unknown. It is said just reading the tablets drove him mad. He grew darker in countenance, learned blasphemous secrets and magic, while becoming long-lived.

"Through epochs of ice and of fire he ruled on his throne--ageless and eternal.

"During this time a malevolent though came to him. He decided he would create slaves as powerful as Neanderthals, yet weak of mind, to lord over and do with as he pleased.

"And so, as men breed dogs, and with sorceries learned from the eldritch tablets, his heinous experiments began. He bred, or tried to, Neanderthal with Voormis and Gnophkehs, with Denisovan and Antecessor and others. He did this since in those days, Neanderthals weren't the only near-men on the earth.

"Eventually, after many failed attempts and abominations were made, my people were born. We were men, though hairy like the rest of the beasts. He had failed, though, in one respect. Our intelligence was just as great or greater than the intelligence of the Neanderthals.

"In time, we rebelled against the hard yoke of slavery and fought a war against our rulers, but were defeated. Our yoke after became doubly hard, my dread king. Under Atlu's harsh rule our backs and will were broken.

"To this brood of slaves in time I was born, but fortunately, I managed to escape. The only one who had ever done so. Tearfully, I left my family behind.

"Like a wild beast I roamed with all the other wild beasts in the wilderness, far from civilization, content in my new-found freedom, until I was caught and shaved and brought to you, brought to civilization, my lord, to be your subject and your comrade.

"This, then, is where my people came from, my dread king--from Atlu's dark forges."

Immediately, upon finishing my story, Gilgamesh got up and asked, "Is Atlu still alive?"

"He is," I answered. "And still rules."

He called his servants, and gave them orders. When they returned they brought his battle armour. Since my king was a giant, it took two men to just carry his bronze shield.

When he was finished dressing, and held his sickle-sword in one hand and his battle-axe in the other, he said to me, "By Ninsun, you will take me to Atlu, brother. I will kill this savage man and stake his head upon my battlements. We will have glory again, and bards shall sing of our deeds."

"And we shall liberate my people," I added, as I knelt before his towering form in front of me, and as I also clutched tightly and anxiously the medallion I always wore around my neck.

***

When we went past the soaring city gates, bastioned with towers, that very afternoon, the whole populace of Uruk came out to cheer us, from high on the parapets. We ran, since Gilgamesh considered the use of donkeys a useless thing, when his own legs could carry him just as ably.

At first we followed the marshlands and swamps, running parallel with the Euphrates River, and after veered off the river's course and headed into the hot deserted wilderness, where patches of dry bushes and scarcely-fronded trees were scattered everywhere we looked.

Eventually, the tall sprawling Zagros Mountains appeared before us, with tops lonely in their majesty and touching the azure sky.

"This is the secret entrance," I whispered to Gilgamesh, after we had swerved through rugged inclines up the side of a mountain and at a craggy ledge had come to a hidden hole. Like wriggling worms we crawled through it to a rocky cavern, inside of which was situated one of the gateways to the city. Fluorescent dull-green stones illumed the place.

Climbing down from the hole, we cautiously made our way to the slightly open door. Before we had a chance to hide, however, we noticed a man appear silently from out of the shadows.

We stood still, watching him alertly.

Beside me I sensed Gilgamesh's muscles tense; he was like a coiled snake with a fatally-venomed bite, ready to strike.

The stranger moved sluggishly towards us. He was dressed in a wrapped grey garment, a dirty skirt, and was jewelled in gold and lapis lazuli. Around his wrists he wore silver bracelets and from his ears hung elegant silver earrings.

When I finally got a clear view of his face I noticed it was thin, long, with bloodless cracked lips and deeply sunken eyes. He resembled more a wraith or a lich than a living man. My right hand tensed strongly on the hilt of my sickle-sword.

"Help me," he said in a low, hoarse, drawn-out voice, as he kept moving towards us from the shadows. "Friends, I am a merchant of Shuruppak. I set out to explore for riches when my caravan was ambushed. I alone survived."

His eyes were glazed over, and as he spoke his outstretched hand touched his head, then his other hand followed suit. In the egg white of his right eye I thought I caught a quick glimpse of a tiny, segmented appendage, which only flashed for a moment.

The mummy-like man relaxed like one dead, his head sagged to one side, and he said monotonously and sadly, "My head is full of spiders."

Then he fell, and as he did so, from his mouth, a vibrantly yellow ball appeared and began to bulge outwards, his dry mouth widening, until its sides ripped violently, and a score of spider legs flailed out like grasping fingers and jumped towards Gilgamesh.

In an instant, with his axe, Gilgamesh swiped, giving a great smack to the ball with legs, and as the creature fell with a thud to the ground, he cleaved it. With a second motion, as the man lay on the floor moaning, he cracked the man's skull open also. Out of his broken crimson head a plethora of little yellow spiders streamed out.

Abruptly then the gate's doors creaked, and a wall of yellow spiders broke through them. They were gigantic, with long prehensile legs that kicked a cloud of heavy choking dust into the air.

Seeing them, Gilgamesh and I jumped to the high roof. We held on with all our might to its veined crevices. Beneath us the creatures swarmed and scuttled, and in no time had enlarged the hole on the side of the mountain, until they burst out on the other side like a gushing cataract.

When we saw they were gone, we jumped down.

If we'd been normal men, our quest, undoubtedly, would have been already over.

* * *

We continued walking cautiously down the passageway, our nerves on daggers' edges.

We crossed through shafts that led to yawning caverns of dangling stalactites and soaring stalagmites.

Eventually our worries lessened. We began to run again, our way lit only by the faint phosphorescence of the green stones.

When we came to a crossway, we stopped and hid. We were sure that we had heard the sound of something creaking slowly in the distance. Our hearts beat loudly to our ears. A terrible moment gripped us. We hid ever deeper in the shadows.

As we waited, with the stones overhead now giving a reddish glare, we saw a monstrosity emerge.

The ebon thing was bloated, and possessed the mottled slimy flesh of a toad. Six insectoid legs sprouted from its sides, culminating in feet that ended in damaged and bruised human heads. On its front, two stalks emerged from where its eyes should have been, and these extremities also ended in human heads. All the gruesome heads looked dumbly before them, their open mouths making a blathering and a moaning sound. From a wide mouth on the creature's front, a dangling saliva-dripping tongue caressed the ground.

We were in no doubt that this was one of Atlu's evil experiments.

This creature towed a wagon, on which was seated regally a gigantic baboon.

This proud, aloof character was dressed in bronze armour, carrying a ponderous sword in one arm. With the other arm, it carried a buckler-shield. Tied around its neck and falling over its massive shoulders hung a spotted leopard cloak, studded with metal disks. It looked ahead with a cruel smirking grimace, obviously taking pleasure in the other creature's distress.

As the wagon passed, the baboon screeched suddenly and jumped off the wagon. It moved its massive body with facile agility, and when it stood straight, we noticed its height was equal with ours.

It bounded erratically close to us, and suddenly stretched out a muscled arm with lightning-speed and grabbed Gilgamesh by the neck, pulling him out forcefully from the rocky formation that he had been hiding behind.

Not wasting any time, Gilgamesh punched the hulking beast hard in the middle of its plated chest, catching it off guard, causing it to drop him as it strived to catch great mouthfuls of air into its pained lungs.

Gilgamesh was quickly on his feet again when I reached him. I stood firmly planted beside him as he unsheathed his sword.

The baboon bared its sharp teeth at us from its dog-like muzzle. Its close-set red eyes furrowed and burned with rage. Its brown mane and cape bristled with potent energy.

The primate growled menacingly as it steadily made its way towards us, with sword unsheathed.

"It's mine," Gilgamesh said.

The two champions then rushed headlong against each other, like wild horses, their nostrils chortling rutilant air. Their two swords swung down madly against their protective shields, bursting into a thousand pieces as the shields, receiving the full impact of the brunt force, also likewise burst.

Now without their swords, the baboon and Gilgamesh jumped back, and threw away what was left of their shields. Gilgamesh did the same with his battle-axe and spear.

Viciously they engaged in hand-to-hand combat, testing to the utmost their naked strength. As they fought, punching, wrestling, and grating clenched teeth, black-scarlet blood began to cover their formidable bodies.

Eventually Gilgamesh, from behind the giant creature's back, locked its ponderous arms. It raged, but Gilgamesh would not let it go.

"My lord is wrong about you!' it yelled with hatred and gore spitting from its mouth. "Never have I met a champion like you! Kill me if you want to survive, for I'll never stop until you're dead!"

Gilgamesh complied with the request, by savagely breaking the sapient baboon's neck.

We both stood over the creature, wondering who he was. No doubt, he had been a great champion in his world.

The other creature, seeing its tormentor dead, without a word continued its sorrowful trek alone, in the direction we had come.

* * *

Gilgamesh didn't say a word as I continued to lead him downwards into the shades. Abruptly, at a turn, he accosted me suddenly with his sweaty and bloody hands.

I was surprised.

He made me face him as he proceeded to look with a cunning, burning gaze into my eyes.

"Atlu obviously sent that baboon and knows we are here," he growled at me. "If this is a trap you're leading me into, be aware that I'll kill you, even if you are my friend."

Before I could protest my innocence, he had taken his heavy hands from off my broad arms and was disappearing down the dark tunnel.

As he went, I could hear him snarling.

I'd formerly been a shaggy beast, being still considered a beast by some, but now, at this moment, I wondered truly who the man was, and who the beast.

* * *

Eventually, the caverns became smoother.

At what appeared to be a hole some way above us, I decided to climb up, to look through it. The hole turned out to be a window that showed a stone-paved sandy road on the other side. When I looked straight up, I saw high above us, where the sky should have been, the vast rocky expanse of the earthen firmament.

"We're inside the city," I said. "We inadvertently took a tunnel that led directly into it. I must have made a mistake somewhere. It has been so long since I left this city. Ah, Gilgamesh, how I wish I could have shown you the city's splendor from the open terraces of the roof of this world."

We continued, and I was surprised to see nobody.

Gilgamesh only glared at me suspiciously.

After a while, we entered a huge room made of colorful sandstone, its walls decorated with sculpted hieroglyphs and painted fading frescoes.

One of the ancient panels told the story of Atlu. It showed him conquering the city, and lording over temple priests and elders, and taking what he wanted of maid and wealth. Other scenes showed him indulging in great contests of strength, and going on dangerous adventures. He was also shown initiating stupendous building projects.

Gilgamesh studied these closely.

On another wall, we saw murals with impressions of an earlier time, showing a hirsute Neanderthal, battling monsters and hefting great titanic rocks over his head, which he hurled from a hill onto a lush tropical world below. No doubt he had been a forgotten hero from earth's murky past.

On another wall, we saw the histories of the Neanderthals' gods and maps of their temples.

***

When we exited the complex, we found ourselves high up, looking down on a scene of astonishing magnitude.

The vast metropolis sported tiered terraces, plazas, domed buildings and gigantic up-thrusting towers. All were crumbling. Irrigation arches, which were still functioning, watered the sparse trees and vegetation. Far away we saw fields still yielding their plenty.

We followed a well-worn road, now familiar to me, seeing nothing but destroyed cupolas and empty sandblasted streets. Lichen and encroaching moss covered obscenely the ancient houses and buildings.

As we walked, whispering winds originating from we knew not where, brushed by us suggestively, as if with the malign intention of protective ghosts. From dark windows, these ghosts seemed to watch us from behind the ebon veil of long-gone misty time.

Sometimes, here and there, we caught the grimy sight of osseous cadavers that looked human, and others that were less than human. By these dead bodies lay armor, and weapons layered with green-black rust.

After a while, Gilgamesh and I came to a massively ornate palace, canopied with great spires and gated by thick, red sandstone columns. The entrance was reached by climbing stupendously high paved stairs to a portico, at which were flung open cyclopean doors.

In front of them rested a chiseled throne.

This was no doubt the high-built citadel of Atlu himself, built in dark time from carven bedrock and mud-baked brick by sore-laden workers, and terrifying demons summoned out of musty books.

On the imposing white marble throne, which was encrusted with glittering gems and diamonds, and situated between two columns, sat ensorcelled Atlu, leering down cunningly at the world.

Long flowing white hair hung over his massive shoulders, and trailed over the seat of his regal throne. His hands tensed tightly on the tips of his armrests.

On his lap, I saw a turquoise cloth.

His heavy wrinkled brows shadowed his clean-shaven protruding jowls and wide-flaring nostrils.

He was a man with much of the ape in him, possessed of the truncated lower half of such a beast, and a large, stocky upper body, and though the heavily stooping posture and senescent body was in its decline, there was the power of immortality, like the power of an ancient monument defying time, written in every inch of his frame.

His venerable, nearly hairless body was not covered with any cloth or saffron robe, but with just a bulkily wrapped loincloth.

Disgustingly behind him rose a tall wooden pole with a rotting head staked on it.

It was neither man nor Neanderthal, but more reptilian in appearance, of a verdigris color, with scaly skin dangling off the serrated neck. There was a man-like quality to the face that made it seem more hideous.

To each side of Atlu stood amassed an army of ferocious Neanderthals, arrayed in leather shoulder-guards, and armor of bronze. Like mad things these apish warriors hollered and jumped threateningly, flinging gibbering words at the red-lit sky.

I could not help but be transfixed by the sight.

My imagination carried me back through dim uncounted ages, to when this city was still populous and in the prime of its glory. People of all classes I pictured surrounding the colossal palace, as far as I could see, with cohorts of soldiers in pageantry, flying banners in celebration of their young monarch.

Atlu I saw at the top of the stairs, on his throne, proud and strong, loud blaring trumpets reaching his satisfied ears. The festive atmosphere and colorful gleaming city were quickly subsumed, however, by the lonely and grey present, as the shining past was dispersed by Atlu's loud bestial voice.

"Come out from your hiding places, intruders," he said. "Why have you come to destroy the peace that we finally enjoy? Go back to that outer world of restless change."

Haughtily Gilgamesh stepped out from behind a crumbled wall, and yelled defiantly, "I have come for no other reason than to kill you, and to gain glory thereby!"

Angered at being threatened, Atlu's eyes lit up like fulgurous flames while his face darkened, like when the moon quenches the light of the sun in an eclipse, and said, "Avaunt, slaves! My people have been sore aggrieved these many years in endless battle with the loathsome serpent-men of red-lit Yoth deep below, but now with our victory, be sure that your cities above will someday too fall beneath the victorious march of our thirsty blades.

"I bid you leave, Sumerian, to better prepare for that day, when we soak knee-deep in your blood."

Gilgamesh laughed a booming laugh that cast frightening echoes throughout the hollow air, and answered grimly and hotly, "Those are the words of a coward. I stand firm in my resolve. Stand and fight, coward, or meekly lay your head upon the ground that I may chop it."

Gilgamesh then stood squarely and straight, feet firmly planted on the ground, as he held his battle-axe at the ready.

Atlu gave a loud yelp, thumped his arms, and grunted repeatedly, as his face went from contorted expressions of preposterousness to anger in an apish manner. When his thumping arms finally rested, he lifted one arm from an armrest, and merely pointed at us nonchalantly.

At the signal, the savoring Neanderthals at his sides jumped and gibbered ferociously, and began to rush down in two disorderly rows of oncoming doom.

"You take the ones on the right," Gilgamesh said, with his spear and battle-axe at the ready. "I'll take the ones on the left."

They came savagely those slouching forms, crashing into us with the force of an unstoppable tidal wave. For our part, we hurled ourselves like two mad swimmers into the fray, heedless of the charge.

The monsters attacked furiously.

Long hairy arms, swords, clubs, maces, and thrashing teeth, overwhelming our senses.

When I hacked one down with my battle-axe, another one quickly rose to take his place. With my shield, I had to circle constantly, to stop the blows that were coming down at me from all directions.

Blow upon blow fell, like raindrops in a tempest.

The beast-men were stocky and well-built. Though their hairy receding foreheads and protruding jaws gave them a brutish appearance, I knew a high intelligence lurked behind those beastly, deceptive eyes.

They howled mercilessly as they attacked severely, hair streaming, swords and shields gleaming under the red glow of that subterranean world.

Beside me, I saw Gilgamesh in the grips of his berserker rage.

Loping prodigious forms fell before him by the score as his ponderous battle-axe swung ceaselessly in death-dealing arcs. Spittle and blood flailed everywhere.

Hundreds must have fallen to our fury.

When we finished fighting, blood pooled at our feet, and littered bodies were piled haphazardly, one atop the other. I was red with blood that dripped in wads from me and from my axe.

I checked quickly to make sure the medallion I always carried was still safely tied around my neck.

Beside me, Gilgamesh rested fatigued on the hilt of his battle-axe, staring coldly and tauntingly, like a smoldering flame, at Atlu.

Atlu stared down at us from his stone throne, one hand softly stroking his lower face in a pensive stance, his eyes lowly burning with a cold fire. There was not a hint of fear or apprehension in his being.

Eventually, he smiled and sat up straight, a strange cunning glint in his eyes.

"Below I see one like myself," he said to Gilgamesh, in a pleased manner. "A warrior made to conquer all before him. The gleaming cities of Eridu, Ur, Sippar, and Tsath would be easy-pickings if we joined together.

"No, don't deny it. Ages of life have given me the ability to read a man and to see into his heart. I know the thought of conquest has crossed your heart.

"An animal does what he does out of necessity; only a man and a Neanderthal and those of their like do what they do out of evil mischief.

"Join with me, barbarian. Take charge of my armies. See the cities trampled below your feet. Let me see it all before I die, and then be sole ruler of the earth."

"I will serve no beast, especially no ape," Gilgamesh retorted madly, and spat blood on the ground.

Atlu laughed.

"Typical human, who thinks he is neither ape nor beast. Let it be. Now listen closely, King of Uruk. In my lap, I hold the power of the gods. Behold and see!"

Atlu moved his hairy hands, picking up from his lap the turquoise cloth, and unwound it. Inside of it were blue-glowing fractured tablets, which cast their eerie light all over his squat trunk.

"These are a portion of the fabled ancient tablets of the gods, which I found eons ago in my quest into the nethermost regions of the earth. Great was that journey, and fraught with perils that I am even now loathe to remember.

"Reading them, I learned that before life was, the gods were, and that they came from dark stars, traversing unimaginable distances, carrying their black knowledge with them. Some of that knowledge is contained in these tablets, knowledge which allowed me to become the semi-deity that I am, Gilgamesh, and which I will give to you, to read for yourself, as a gift of our alliance.

"You, too, I have learned are semi-divine, the son of a goddess and a mortal man, but your gods have promised you only a short-lived life. When you die of old age, soon enough, you will go to the land of the dead, a place without glory. I have seen its adamantine gates; from Irkalla there is no escape.

"Live for eons instead, drinking strong drink, eating good food, and embracing the beautiful daughters of men. Come, read but a few lines. See if you will not join me."

I watched as a strange white pallor came over my lord. He shook, and then, uncomprehendingly to me, began to walk up the stairs, weaponed with the spear on his back, and his battle-axe in one hand.

He moved slowly, like one fighting a great battle within himself.

I saw a demonic glee spread over Atlu's face. It glowed with newfound strength.

"You will not be disappointed. The gods of your Mesopotamian people are weak, foolish and of no account. This very hour the remnants of my people are celebrating festivities to the hidden elder gods still on this earth, who dwell in lightless subterranean temples and crags deep below the mountains. So enamored are my people of the wisdom of the gods."

I yelled to Gilgamesh not to go, that it was a trap, but he did not heed me.

Once he had reached the throne, Atlu stretched out reverently the tablets to Gilgamesh.

Then I remembered how legend said that just reading the tablets had driven Atlu insane. Perhaps he also wanted my lord to join him in his madness?

Before I had time to warn Gilgamesh, I heard a foul laugh, such as I have never heard before and hope to never hear again, that filled the spaces of the city with loathsomeness. The more I heard it, the more distressed I was to see from whence it came.

Atlu also noticed, his demeanor changing to one of high perplexity. From the laugh came a voice like a savage animal, like a savage god. My king was letting his numinous divine side show through into our world.

"For the goddess Ninsun, my mother, whom you have insulted, beast, I strike this blow!"

Then, with inhuman speed, he grabbed the spear on his back, striking at Atlu with quick ferocity.

Atlu screeched, and also with damnable ensorcelled speed, moved out of the thrust's way, managing to hit Gilgamesh with a rock-solid kick square in his jaw.

Gilgamesh tumbled back onto the stairs, his battle-axe flying clean out of his hands, the spear falling from the throne, as Atlu, dropping the tablets, leapt with a monkeyish bound onto the tumbling giant.

Gilgamesh hit the steps back first, as Atlu smashed into him with the force of a colliding meteor. The ancient muscles then began to impact rapidly on Gilgamesh as Atlu hit him repeatedly with the joy of unhinged restraint, saliva flying freely from his crooked mouth.

Meanwhile, as I was running up the stairs, I saw the dangerous predicament my king was in, so I grasped tightly the medallion at my neck, swore an oath, and flung my shield with panic at the ape-man.

It hit him with such potency on the head that he stopped, stunned for a second, to look at me.

It was all the time my king needed.

With the strength of desperation and the virility of a demi-god, Gilgamesh punched Atlu on the side of his head, causing a great cracking sound as his skull caved in.

The Neanderthal hefted himself up, wildly flailing with his taloned hands in excruciating pain.

With a bound, Gilgamesh hurled himself against his interlocutor, and sent him stumbling back sprawling onto his throne.

The beast on the throne roared, until composure began to enter that crunched brain of his.

He had stood strong for over a thousand years, had fought monstrous battles before even Sumer had risen from the dust, had felt the agony and afflictions of a thousand battles, the torture of a thousand noxious wounds, and now that ancient strength, that ancient stamina, was coming back, and now the beast knew his enemies, knew not to underestimate them, knew with cunning and experience what to do to win.

And he would have won too, perhaps, if Gilgamesh had not, at that moment, taken that wooden pole, which carried the serpent-man's head, and from behind the throne had not run rapidly to the side, striking quickly and deeply the blunt edge of the pole downward into Atlu's chest—while Atlu was wiping his eyes, straining to see through gouts of blood blurrily everything in his way—plunging it with super-human strength and speed, so that Atlu had no time to react, into the resisting slewing flesh.

As the spear went through, Atlu's wild red eyes rolled back into his head, and from his open mouth a small-winded noise came out, as his body jerked and his head flapped back.

Before Atlu's hands had time to fall to his sides, he was already dead, pinned to his throne, the stake having crossed through his chest, the dull point exiting cleanly on the other side.

Thus passed Atlu, the grand champion and last King of the Neanderthals.

"He was getting old," Gilgamesh growled, as I came to him. "He had lost much of his mental sharpness and power. He deserved to die."

Quickly I grunted at my lord, "Now, let us free my people. Let us bring more glory upon us."

Pleased with the idea, he condescended that I lead him deeper into the catacombs.

On the way, he stopped at a chasm that thundered below with the might of a red-hot fiery river, and crushing between his hands the tablets, dropped the pieces of it into the furnace.

"Thus I deal with all gods not my own," I overheard him say.

* * *

Later, in unfettered abandon, we ran like wild bulls back to Uruk.

Those of my people that we freed, along with the other prisoners of the Neanderthals, also followed us back in celebration.

We were also joined by my former companions, who'd been my friends long ago, when I'd been a hairy man in the wilderness, and who had left me when I'd shaved my hair and become tainted with the civilization of men. I speak of the birds of the air and of the beasts of the wild country.

It was a grand chorus of joy as we all together bounded and trampled through the alluvial plains. It was a great time of exultation for me.

As we neared Uruk, my companions left me, as did my people also, leaving only Gilgamesh and me to enter the city's main gate.

Under the festive banners of the ramparts Gilgamesh said to me, "I am sorry, my good friend and brother, for accosting you, for doubting your friendship earlier, for thinking you would play me in an underhanded way."

He hugged me, and then we both together entered the city. Our friendship never bore dissention again.

That night, while the court celebrated, and after we had consecrated our exploits to the gods in the Temple of An, and after Gilgamesh had staked the gruesome head of Atlu behind his throne, I went alone onto a balcony overlooking a magnificent pool.

Silently, under the stars, I threw far the metal medallion I had always carried with me tied around my neck, which my long deceased father and mother had given me, on which I had promised them to one day return to free my people.

Upon a Fearful Summons

The Payador entered the town and tied his horse to a hitching-post outside the general store and bar. He strummed his guitar, now and then singing little ditties of love and other inconsequentialities, nothing too spectacular, but just enough to give a taste of his repertoire, which promised outstanding things.

Soon, by evening, a small crowd of men, women and children had gathered to listen to the singer, since he promised change for the little town situated within the eternal and changeless pampas. Even the men who frequented the general store and bar, who usually fought and drank and played at cards, came out to see the stranger.

At sundown he began his song. Everyone was attentive during this hour of magic. The horses nearby had quieted down and the dogs had stopped their barking.

This, then, was the tale he sung in that faraway year, so long, long ago, of 1895...

***

For the longest time they'd been followed.

The two nomadic Argentine gauchos climbed down a rocky path on the Chilean side of the Andes Mountains. The leader carried the nickname Gaucho Larra, a name he'd acquired from the Indians of the parched pampas when he'd been as a boy their prisoner.

They were both dressed in typical gaucho dress: a hat, bombacha trousers, a poncho, horse-skin boots, bolas, a whip and at their back a large facon knife. They were both tall but Gaucho Larra was taller, and while his companion was dressed more colorfully, the head horseman was dressed all in black, a color complementing his long, tied-back, jet-black hair and swarthy, copper-skinned complexion. His companion was of lighter-skin and yellow of hair. It was soon apparent that this man was the same singer who was telling the tale.

From time to time he sang and played his guitar to vary the monotony and boredom the two men felt. When they were hungry they hunted the small creatures which inhabited the scrubland of the mountains.

Surely, but steadily, they made their way down from the frigid heights of the mountains, sleeping on the ground, and admiring the sights below and the expansive sky above. They made use of their own skill and of the Camino Real, a road that had been in use since Incan times and before. They'd begun their journey in the province of Mendoza, Argentina, and hoped to finish it at the coast of Chile.

"Will he be there?" the Payador asked.

"He better be," Gaucho Larra answered, his piercing blue eyes looking far into the west.

"And also...about *that other thing.*"

"You've felt it too?"

"For three days now...behind us...following."

"I've felt it longer. Since we were in Argentina," Gaucho Larra said, as he turned to look back the way they'd come.

That night, the two men set up camp, and after eating relaxed comfortably by a fire while the Payador sang, telling a story of outlaws and cattle-rustling in the far Banda Oriental.

Soon something else came to listen.

Gaucho Larra felt it initially in the dark clouds which appeared to silhouette the already almost darkened sky. Then a small wind rose, which stoked the fire, while little dust wind funnels formed on the exposed soil.

Whatever it was, they sensed it was a thing that roused fear, as opposed to feeling fear itself, but Gaucho Larra and the Payador were fearless men, raised on the tough frontier, and they continued as they were.

Eventually they retired for the night out of weariness.

"What do you suppose it is?" the Payador asked his companion.

"Don't know. Perhaps it's nothing. Maybe that's just the way it is on mountains," Gaucho Larra responded, and then took his saddle and placed it under his head to use like a pillow.

With the fire gone, and blackness and complete silence everywhere, the shadow also retired.

Before he went to sleep, the Payador took note in his head of all that had transpired that day, and began to compose the matter into the meter of the payada song.

For his part, Gaucho Larra dreamt that night of an auburn-haired girl dead in a mud hut in Santa Fe, her throat cut, of a taunting letter addressed to the nearest powerful cattle-baron, and missing Argentine banknotes.

He didn't bat an eyelash at this in his sleep.

However, he also dreamt of being stabbed near a large building, of being surrounded by men, of breath-hoarse gasps, of blackness, and hatred that it all had to end, despite an intense will to live.

He thought this dream peculiar.

* * *

They entered the port city of Valparaiso in a week, and from a hill admired the immense Pacific Ocean, as large as the pampas they were born in.

Despite this fascination, they didn't like the city, since for them the city represented a prison, an abomination from nature, and they wished for nothing more than to leave it.

The singer asked, "What name is he going under?"

"Mauro Benitez. And he's headed for Peru."

"Let's go find out what time the latest boat leaves."

They rode their horses until they reached a train station.

"I see you're gauchos from Argentina," the station-master said, after they'd said hello. "At first I took you for huasos when I seen you coming up the road. Still rural around here, though I'd imagine not awfully much for you folks. I'm myself from the countryside. From a large estancia south of Santiago. Left there when a boy, just a little peon. Never went back. What can I help you two with? A train comes later on. Will you be taking the horses with you?"

"We're taking no train," Gaucho Larra answered. "We want to know when the latest boat is leaving for Peru."

"For that information you're better off asking the boys on the docks or the Custom House."

"We know. But we're not asking them, we're asking you," Gaucho Larra added, a streak of danger escaping from his smiling face.

"I see. Yes. I see. Let me think. I recall overhearing this morning a launch-man who frequents one of the bars down by the shore saying a merchant ship was leaving at about an hour from now, bound for Peru. No passenger ships that I know of are leaving."

"Here. Have this for yourself," Gaucho Larra said, giving him some money. "Don't tell anyone what we've asked...or else." He made a cut sign with his thumb running across his neck. At this the stationmaster gulped, understanding the meaning. The two men left laughing.

"Her throat was cut deep," the Payador said pensively afterwards. "Like a cow being bled."

"It sure was," Gaucho Larra responded. "But we got the money. We'll find him."

They moved among well-dressed men in hats and suits, and women in long dresses and bonnets, riding inside the public transportation system of horse-drawn tram cars, and among pedestrians walking past shops and businesses. Variously they saw hills and public buildings and church spires, and behind them, towering suburbs and lifts. They passed hospitals, theatres, libraries and schools, and all the amenities of modern civilization. They heard many different tongues, saw vendors selling their fruits and wares, and everywhere they looked, people bustling about in this thriving commercial port.

On the ocean were vessels scattered to the horizon. They could taste the brine in the air blowing on breezes from the water. At a quay they noticed horses and mules tied up, children in dirty ripped clothing playing amid rubble, drunken men sleeping on the street, and sailors on shore leave.

They woke one of these ruffians asleep in an out of the way place, and asked him if he'd heard of anyone by the name of Mauro Benitez.

"A few," he'd answered.

"We're looking for one just recently arrived," the Payador further elaborated.

"Perhaps," the man said evasively.

"We'll give you money for more drink," Gaucho Larra added, showing him coins. The man's eyes brightened, and he sat up and smacked his lips together.

"Down by the next quay you'll see a posse of men outside a bar. It's a large building, and the man who leads them is named Mauro Benitez. He's a loud-mouth with a face like a wrinkled grape. He says he's going to Peru, to be a rubber baron."

The two gauchos smiled faintly at each other and Gaucho Larra gave the drunkard the money. As they left, the drunk tried to get up, but he fell over instead.

From the sandy street, a small funnel arose. Like a small tornado, another formed also. The two dust devils joined, and the Payador was astonished to watch them move forward, exactly like the legs of a walking man. The two strolling winds moved past him and also past Gaucho Larra.

They walked until they dispersed near a group of men outside a drinking den.

Once his astonishment was over, the Payador yelled, "Mauro Benitez!"

All the men, nine of them, turned to silently look at the two gauchos.

Gaucho Larra dismounted his horse, and proceeded to tie it to a post. After this, he took out a wad of banknotes from under his poncho, and said to all of them, "This is for whoever tells me who Mauro Benitez is."

The men all stared at each other, then one of them walked towards the gaucho, took his money, and then pointed at a man with a thin, black handlebar moustache. Then he walked away.

"Esteban!" the handlebar-moustached man yelled after him. "Why have you singled me out? My name is Juan!"

Gaucho Larra went up to him. "I don't think so. You're Benitez all right. You're just like the picture I seen of you. Look here, do you remember this girl?" He stretched out his hand, in which he had concealed a small daguerreotype of a once auburn-haired girl, and showed it to the man.

The man looked at the picture, and then at the gaucho and laughed. "I see I've been found out. Yes, I'm Mauro Benitez, formerly known as Jose Bravo, also known as Jose Cinco-Manos; a thief, a cattle-rustler, an outlaw, and soon to be a rubber baron! What's that to you?"

Gaucho Larra added, "You forgot to say rapist and murderer. Do these men know about the girl you raped and murdered in your shitty mud hut and left to die? The daughter of the man on whose estate you worked and whose money you stole? The same man who's paying us to settle things?"

"They do now," Mauro Benitez yelled.

His companions moved uneasily. Three of them departed, leaving only five to face the gauchos.

Angered, Benitez screamed after them, "Traidores! You won't share any of my wealth when I hit it rich in Iquitos! But you other boys, you won't regret your decision. I'm loyal to those loyal to me.

You'll all be rich like I've promised." He turned to Gaucho Larra. "You think you can take me? I've never lost a fight. I'm the best there is. I challenge you to a knife-fight. Let's see. Let's make this the stakes. If I cut your face, you let me go, like the man of your word you are. If you cut my face, I'll lose. I'll be nothing then. I'll go with you. On my sacred honour, I promise this. Do you accept?"

"I accept."

Benitez laughed. "Who is it I'm fighting?"

"It's not important."

The thugs and the Payador formed a circle around the two gauchos as they wrapped their ponchos around their arms, and began to move like fencers, like two antagonists involved in a complex, choreographed routine—a dance of skill.

Now and then one lunged with his facon knife, careful not to be cut in turn by the other. And so it went, like a game of chess. Each tried desperately to figure out the others' weakness.

They advanced, they parried, they riposted, they jumped.

A crowd gathered.

Fear showed on Benitez's face, along with sweat. Fear began to atrophy his stamina and concentration. He had never lost a fight. Never.

Suddenly his opponent moved impossibly faster. The fight had lasted so long that Benitez was tired, and he couldn't keep up.

In an instant, a blade flashed across his face, and dazzled like the sun at noonday, and he fell back with pain across his cheek, and warm blood running down his lower face and neck.

From the ground he touched his face, and looked at the red on his fingers and on his clothes. He had been marked. Now, wherever he went, all men would know his shame, his loss of pride.

"What's your name?" he demanded from this imposing stranger, feeling both anger and humiliation.

"Gaucho Larra," the man answered. "That's the name you'll say when others ask you who gave you that scar. Now get up! It's a long way back to Argentina."

Fury like he'd never felt before flashed through Benitez's body, dulling his reason.

"I'll cut your throat!" he yelled, and then commanded his thugs, "What are you all looking at? Kill them!"

Knives flashed into the air like electrical charges. The men rushed at the two gauchos. The gaucho, like the fisherman, lived with his blade; for him the gun was not the weapon of choice, and never had been on the rough pampas. The gauchos fought like their ancestors did, except the blade, the long knife, was now their sword.

Before the men could reach the two gauchos, however, a powerful force pushed them back. And then an ownerless knife materialized in front of them and attacked them. The men fought bravely against this impossible foe that maneuvered quickly through the air, and cut them down with ease. Lastly, the knife was pushed deep into Benitez's chest.

He died blaspheming as the knife dematerialized and was gone as suddenly as it had appeared.

The two gauchos were left stunned and speechless.

* * *

Later that night, the two men found Benitez's lodgings and took his stolen banknotes, to give back to the man who'd hired them. They left quietly, evading the police, and through the lonely wilderness made their way back to Argentina.

"What do you think it was that helped us in that fight?" the Payador asked his companion.

"Don't know...not that we needed the help. But it's following us back."

Silently Gaucho Larra wondered about the dream he'd had on the mountain, of dying by a large building while surrounded by men.

Surely, this dream wasn't a premonition of Mauro Benitez's death?

* * *

The sun, declining low in the west, found the gauchos once more on the mountains.

Ancient paths once more they took, on roads long disused.

That night, the black clouds overhead were thick and filled with strange dancing lights.

Winds, which howled in the darkness with the barely audible voices of men in some hell unknown, broke through the open passes, almost pulling at the gauchos' ponchos.

When they rested, they knew in their heart of hearts that this was no natural occurrence, and that whatever mysterious omen had been following them was at last about to break into the world, so that they didn't sleep, but sat vigilant and silent.

At midnight, the winds calmed, and some occult power from the black hidden distance, as if from leagues away, began to softly call out Gaucho Larra's name.

"You're being summoned," the Payador said in a low voice, unconsciously imitating the ghostly summoner.

"I better go. If it's the devil, what of it?"

"What if you don't return?"

"I don't think the devil will take me. Not yet, at least."

Worried, the singer stretched out his arm and grabbed his friend as he walked away. "It could be something else besides the devil."

"Whatever it is, it won't leave us. We have to meet it, like men. If I don't come back, take care of my horse."

He walked further up the pass and disappeared into the darkness.

Shapes aglow like pillared blue flames floated around him, as the voice grew louder and louder.

Eventually, he arrived at a clearing, surrounded by a blurry and indistinct mist, strangely lit with a phosphorescent dancing glow.

Then a shadowy, smoky figure circled him closely and inspected him.

"Move away," Gaucho Larra said calmly.

To which the thing said, "You are no longer controlled by the passions and gloomy temper of our people. I am not like you. Do not arouse my irascible spirit yet."

The weight of a terrible anger fell upon the place, and an oppressive savagery emanated from the black figure, a thing cloaked with the aura of blood and fear.

It disappeared, and only the voice remained. "You are ignorant of what transpires or whose presence you are in, or else you would quake with fear."

As Gaucho Larra kept walking, the voice continued. "I had almost forgot what century we are in and in what decade. The boot of Rosas and Quiroga does not terrify the land. The tyrants are fallen asleep. But they can rise again. The cities encroach. They kill, not with the savagery of the knife, but they kill nonetheless. Civilized men are at our throats and pacify. New gauchos like you are made."

The swirling mist around Gaucho Larra took on a more distinct form, and soon he could make out some features. Glowing shapes of men and women and children, who were gauchos and country folk, stared at him, like a huge crowd of spectators, from the mist.

He eventually arrived at a log, on which the shadow figure began to crystallize into human form.

The glowing figure sitting on the log stared at him with small, blood-red eyes. Short black hair hung over his face and a small moustache rested over a taut mouth. The figure's eyes stared coldly and consistently, not budging from the gaucho. He was well-built, and dressed in a chiripa and white trousers, with a collared shirt. Beside him lay his poncho, and on top of it a two-foot long knife, with a U-shaped handle cross-guard.

It said, "I have been traveling the world. A world I never knew in my time of flesh. My world was the pampas and my horizon the leagues thereby. I have gone far looking for the right man. Because of the violence and inferno of my life, I am kept from my rest. My death was unexpected—a stab in the dark. But I sent many men to hell that day. My name is Juan Moreira."

Hearing the name, Gaucho Larra was taken aback. The shade was a legendary outlaw of whom many tales were sung, known throughout all the pampas and elsewhere. He was perhaps the greatest knife-fighter ever known. He'd been stabbed with a bayonet near a large building while trying to flee from the police, and died.

In awe he asked the dead man, "You said you were searching for the right man. What did you mean?"

Now a terrible spirit from the Outside, Juan Moreira stood, blue flames flowing from his eyes, and answered him thus, "My heart was good once, but my life and my skill in violence cursed me. In dueling I was undefeated, and I remain so in death. I cannot rest until I meet the man that can defeat me. Only a mark will suffice. If you win, the curse will end, and I will at long last be free from this living death. If not, a ghost I will remain, to wander the earth restless until I meet that man that can defeat me. I have met many in my wanderings so far, but none have prevailed."

"I will prevail!" Gaucho Larra interjected, wishing both to prove his prowess and free this spirit.

At his words, the dead men, women and children around him howled and moaned loudly and moved hectically.

The shade of Juan Moreira carried a cruel and bloodthirsty look in its eyes. He snarled and said, "You have accepted quicker than I expected. No more words. The dead shall be our audience. And the hidden power will judge who is the best."

They then wrapped their ponchos around their left arms and at an agreed-on signal, charged against each other. A clamor arose all around, as the dead cheered the spectacle before them.

Gaucho Larra tried desperately to cut Juan on the cheek, but the wraith was too quick, and at every lunge of his, he hit only air. Sometimes the wraith stopped his lunges with the U of his cross-guard, just as quick as Gaucho Larra attacked. The shade's lunges were just as deadly and he could hardly block, move, or counter them, without fearing that if he'd just been less than one second slower, the shade would have had the upper hand.

The gaucho had never battled a foe so formidable. When their knives clanged, he felt the great power of the wraith's muscular arms. It fought with a fierceness almost unequalled, perhaps because it had seen things no man should.

Gaucho Larra found it difficult, but through experience, he was able to block those supernatural attacks.

As they fought, a smile appeared on Juan Moreira's face. He knew that he had found his equal. This pleased him, but it didn't stop him. For the curse to be lifted he couldn't forfeit the fight or stop trying his utmost. So with his pleasure also came a more furious assault.

The dead were frenzied around them and hollered, making the mountain quake.

After a long time, Juan Moreira jumped back, and with the ferocity of a great tiger, lunged a strike against Gaucho Larra's face. If he hadn't stopped it, the strike would have cloven half his head off. Now that the shade was near him, with his left arm, Gaucho Larra swiped the edges of his by-now ribboned poncho against Juan Moreira's eyes, causing the spectre to push back. As he did, with all his might, Gaucho Larra lunged forward, cutting up, and just barely missing the wraith's face. But he nipped it. It was a cut. And then Gaucho Larra fell to the floor, gasping for breath, sweaty and barely alive.

The blue flames died from Juan Moreira's eyes, as if hot coals were dying within him. He began to dissolve, and as he did, he said these terrible words, "At long last, a worthy opponent. You are now the best. But do not glory in it. Your pride has been your downfall. The curse passes to you. You will not die, even if your body dies, until you meet that man that can defeat you in a fight. If you cannot find him, you will never rest, for all eternity."

Gaucho Larra looked up, exasperated. "You cheated! Why didn't you tell me this?"

"Would you have fought me if I had?" the spirit said laughing, as he completely vanished.

The dead remained around the gaucho. They drew nearer, as he dropped his head to the ground.

* * *

It was past the evening of the next day, when Gaucho Larra returned to the campsite, and found the singer still sitting. Gaucho Larra sat beside him.

"The mountain shook. I went up the pass to look for you," the Payador said. "I didn't find you. You vanished off this earth. There was only mist."

"I was there."

"What happened?"

Gaucho Larra didn't say anything.

The next day the gauchos resumed their journey back to Argentina.

* * *

The Payador stopped his singing. Overhead, the full moon hung white and low.

Everyone agreed it was a well-told story. The adults gave him money and left pensively; the young left wishing they were Gaucho Larra.

A young girl went up to the singer and asked him if the story was true. He laughed and answered no.

The owner of the general store and bar allowed him to stay upstairs in a room that night and promised him free food and drink.

The next day, before he left, he asked if anyone wanted to challenge him to a duel of song. But no one did.

Once he'd left the little town leagues behind, the Payador took off his hat and sat down.

By sundown another man arrived. They made camp and left early the next morning for Buenos Aires.

The other man took the lead.

The singer looked at his companion, and though he could see nothing but the wide open pampas for miles and miles around, he swore he could hear, not see, the dead circling his friend.

Iron Horse and Butterfly

The Cutter of Candles enters his room, sits by his desk, and takes out a book. He knows that after today he'll no longer have the chance to experience the bloodshed of open fields, the melting of wax, or the brisk joy of the snapping of hard bones, but Sasha will and she enters behind him.

The world they inhabit is one of wonders, violence, and great beauty. Once it had been stable, but somewhere something went wrong. The Cutter of Candles says things began falling apart, the stuff of things began falling apart, about twenty years before. Sasha's seventeen and doesn't care so much about that.

"I remember," he says sometimes to the girl, while in bed, as she looks at him with disgust, "when I first noticed this collapse and unraveling of our system. Something wasn't right. Too many synchronicities or coincidences. Then the disintegration of time began and I started seeing sixteenth-century pikemen, not to mention Roman legions, roaming the nearest boulevard. It was a time of chaos and madness for the world, but eventually things settled into this normalcy you now witness." At the mention of the word *normalcy*, the Cutter of Candles always gives a slight grin. "Also, at this time strange children started to be born, like you, my dear child."

Whenever he says this Sasha is reminded of her butterfly wings, which most of the time she barely feels during her day to day chores.

Today Sasha sits on the other side of The Cutter's desk. He pretends not to notice her. This is Sasha's fourteenth year of apprenticeship since her coming. She's seventeen and her huge butterfly wings cast an eerie shadow on him. Someday, these wings will win her renown, and cause her to be feared and named Butterfly by everyone.

Around them, in the room, are rows of library shelves, expanding from the center where the desk is, in concentric circles. On them are placed thousands of candles in forms of species Sasha's seen and not seen. Some beginning to burn, and others just dried wax in their holders—no longer resembling anything.

Near the desk is a locked wardrobe she's never been allowed to look into. Today she might decide to.

That there are no books on the shelves doesn't bother Sasha so much, since the bastard never taught her how to read.

She stares at the wizard for a while, and then places a long, silver-gleaming dagger on the desk. He looks up from his book.

"Those I hate, I burn, Sasha. Don't you know this?" he asks.

It's true she knows. But she doesn't care. Her father and mother, before they died, sold her to the wizard to learn his secret thaumaturgic art. They thought she would be safe with him. He had a reputation for being a great wizard after the Great Wars were ended. He'd lied to them. He's taught her how to fight and steal and be a good slave. His power he's never taught her. The power to control a living thing's death, by making a candle representation of the thing, and then watching the life drain away as the candle melts into nothing.

Seemingly reading her mind, the Cutter laughs and says, "But I've taught you other things, Sasha. How to see beauty. Don't you remember when I took you to see the lizard stags in the west and the rainbow-gilded trees of Oroshant?"

She's not impressed.

"It's just as well. Did you know that your parents aren't really dead, like I've often told you? They're alive, Sasha, and they sold you to me to teach you my arts. That much is true. Stupid peasants! How can I teach you what I myself don't even know how I do? Each year I kept telling you I'd teach you because I needed a reason to keep you here, little whore."

They both stand, and swiftly she grabs the dagger on the desk and places it roughly on the evil Cutter's neck. With her other hand she holds him tight to her and with her dagger hand slowly begins to apply pressure. The Cutter notices the hatred in her eyes. Sasha for the first time notices the fear in his. She draws blood.

"Do you want to find them? Look for Clan Oshito and you'll find them! Look for Clan Oshito! I won't say anything else about it!"

And he doesn't.

She then drags the almost lifeless body towards the wardrobe that's been kept locked from her all these years. She struggles with it.

The Cutter mutters in his death-dream, "Those I hate, I burn."

When she finally pries the wardrobe open she only sees inside an almost melted candle. Then she understands. In this wardrobe was the Cutters own life burning away all these years. It's almost completely burnt.

He looks up at her and says, "No pity for me in the end, Sasha?"

She shows him no pity as she stabs him hard in the heart and watches his candle instantaneously burn out.

Putting away her dagger calmly, the girl runs into the circles of shelves and finds her own candle representation. She extinguishes the flame. Later she puts it into a pouch that she'll carry with her for many moons and suns to come yet.

She did what she did out of hatred for the Cutter, but he has given her a reason to live.

One day she leaves the worn-down, decrepit building she calls home, to find her parents and Clan Oshito.

* * *

Years of wandering and she's now twenty-eight. She calls herself Butterfly, and everywhere she's looked for Clan Oshito and her parents. She has educated herself. The Cutter is a dim memory from another time and place. Her only connection to him is the candle she still carries. On a warm day in summer the woman crosses into the borderlands of Bayyam. It's burnt country. Past this territory she's been told lies the home of Clan Oshito—in the land of Taufet, and its miles-long city of Torkarkossos.

She first notices the metal creature charging towards her—fast, fearless and mindless, like a giant locomotive—as she stares at the coal-dark lands before her. In an instant, the maniacal thing is nearly upon her. She sees steam exploding from it. She thwarts it by jumping out of its path. The creature turns to face the woman, and then she has a good look at it. It's immense and composed entirely of machinery. She has never seen anything like it. When it stands on two legs, its underside transforms and reveals the image of a man. When on all fours, it resembles a horse, and the back of the man-head becomes the head of a horse. It makes an odd clattering sound when it moves, for a beast so agile, and its whole body is composed of iron, wires, pistons, and strange whirring contraptions.

The horse-man stares at her through its beast eyes, charges, and then standing erect, rapidly grabs her by the arms with its hoof-hands. She has no time to react and reach for her broadsword. He sends her sprawling to the ground, violently. The pouch falls off. He lunges angrily towards her. Once the thing is on top, the woman desperately grabs for her small jabbing dagger that she's concealed by magic arts learned from long wanderings, and stabs strenuously upwards and sideways, catching the iron creature by surprise, and gouging and ripping at what roughly corresponds to its intestines.

As the thing sends ashes into the air in throes of agony, she reaches for her pouch, to make sure the candle isn't broken. Satisfied that it isn't, she sits by a rock calmly to watch the creature battle for its life, for hours past day and night, until dusk.

As the red sun starts to climb, the horse-man stops his thrashing, but doesn't die. Instead, he begins to tell of his life on the dark plains, and before this of his intense battles in the land of Bedlam. Of his fending for himself, and of a life hard, cruel and bereft of pity, until his first memories of his making and escape from his lords—the Iron Mages.

"It's a place unlike anywhere I have ever been," he says. "The city of the Iron Mages is a city of vast metal. Its denizens are metal as well. I believe the Mages originally came from beyond the Great Sea. All of the city's inhabitants are their slaves, even those few like you."

He also asks why she wears no hard armor, but only a short brown tunic and a cloak.

Butterfly doesn't answer him, but instead asks why he attacked her. He responds that she resembled the fleshy warrior hunters of his former masters and that he thought she had been sent to capture him.

He has no name, and perhaps through pity or sympathy for a creature much like herself, she offers him a chance to survive. Will he agree to accompany her to find Clan Oshito? Or will he die by her hand, or the hand of cruel fate, alone in the desolate lands of Bayyam?

He agrees to accompany her.

Using what skills she's acquired of magic, she slowly begins to heal the iron contraption. After a few hours they are ready to leave. She names him Iron Horse, and this is the name he'll use all his life.

* * *

For two days Iron Horse and Butterfly travel, she mounted on his back when she tires of flying, until they see the first signs of life near the ends of Bayyam. Before Bayyam lies Bedlam, and after Bayyam comes their destination, the major land of Taufet.

Everywhere the woman has travelled she's asked for Clan Oshito. Now she's close. She knows this.

"Why are you so desperate to find this clan and your parents?" Iron Horse asks on their second day of travelling.

"I want to kill my parents and all the sons of bitches," she answers him. She then gives him a cold hard stare which the man has learned to read. He doesn't ask any more questions. His new companion, he knows, doesn't like to talk or reveal too much about herself.

As they near Taufet the land becomes more desolate and dark. In the distance, they can see a mountainous range seemingly afloat on a sea of ash.

On the morning of that second day they witness a lone falcon in the sky above them fight, and then be pursued far into the distance, by a new animal unknown to the old world and its dead laws.

By noon they leave the ash-beaten lands behind, and enter a forest as old as time to their thinking. It contains crooked trees near collapse, possessing grey-white leaves growing on slender branches.

In this forest a gray creature, huge as a house, they kill. The monster possesses venomous breath and has a body like a dragon's. Throughout it are stings like those of a porcupine, and once they kill this creature they use it for food.

Towards mid-day they see through the skeletal elms a band of humans approaching them. In this corpse land they feel warm-hearted to see this. They are reminded of life again as they look at the humans silhouetted against the drawn sky. They watch the wanderers, who consist of old and young men and women, also children; all stick-thin, injured and dying.

"Who are you?" Iron Horse asks.

An old woman answers, "Survivors."

She doesn't stop, but keeps marching forward with the rest of the band, who all walk like automatons.

A young woman says, "I have seen children murdered on the streets. So many of them. Headless corpses. Who wants to live after seeing so many dead?"

An old man speaks up as the band passes them by completely. "Go tell the leaders of the city nothing survives that is human. Their help is useless. The town is dead."

As the entourage departs past the next trees behind, Butterfly yells after them, "Have any of you seen Clan Oshito?"

A young girl with a heavy yellow shawl turns and looks at Butterfly, then runs towards her. "Clan Oshito is in Torkarkossos. Their lord is Bacilus and their lady is the Gray Lady. I saw her once and I can tell you she is the most beautiful woman in the world. She looks much like you."

The girl smiles at Butterfly and then runs back towards the retreating party.

* * *

They travel all the rest of that day, silently, until the break of evening, when they notice smoke rising like bush fires in the direction they are going. They are near Torkarkossos and Clan Oshito, and they know soon they will be departing the cursed lands of Bayyam forever. The smoke gets heavy as they reach a large clearing. The clearing is man-made and in the form of a slowly descending incline, at whose bottom is a walled town. They head towards the town as the trees become sparser. By the beginning of sundown they enter its walls, where smoke still lingers and fresh carcasses scarcely two days old line its streets.

Signs of battle are everywhere: embattled horsemen, war automobiles and foot soldiers are lying dead beside citizens and strewn body parts of animals. Here and there, maces, pikes, guns, swords, shotguns and other weapons of war are scattered haphazardly. The two wanderers wonder at the ferocity with which this mayhem is presented to their eyes. These are obviously the results of a savage siege, but where are the occupiers, and why have they so suddenly departed?

They pass a mud temple dedicated to some obscure god. In the town square, they find a makeshift altar made hurriedly. On it is a petition not more than a week old, they can tell, by the newness of the ink on the paper. It asks for the help of Clan Oshito to save from the godless northerners.

Butterfly and Iron Horse then set out to look for provisions throughout the deserted town, and as night falls and thousands of stars fill the sky, they decide to leave the ruined habitation and reach Taufet as soon as possible. As they approach the town wall they hear a gaunt scream from a dust-filled hovel nearby. Is it the sound of a man or a pig?

They head towards the scream, and find that it's a man indeed, who's now dead, and is being eaten by a rough-looking man and a skinny child no more than fifteen years old.

They are ordered out by the travelers. The two dirty fiends laugh at the disgust shown by the woman and the horse-man.

They tell how they have been sent for just this purpose—to eat the dead and injured of the town, and how more are coming, and how some have already departed—their feast ended.

Sternly Butterfly eyes the man and the boy and tells of the altar in the town square, and asks if Clan Oshito came to the aid of the town and if so, why have they gone?

"And what have you to do with that clan, eh, honey?" the man asks.

"All you need to know is that I want to find them."

The boy looks at the two and, taking a bite out of the dead man's thigh, he says in a pleased manner, "Then you're in luck. You've found us."

* * *

Death comes, the Gray Lady tells Drreg. This will be the end of Clan Oshito if Drreg doesn't prepare well.

The god in Drreg winces.

* * *

Once there was a god and this god was unloved by the other gods, and the gods took their hatred out upon the single god. They set upon him like murderous wolves. They cut the god into tiny pieces, and buried the parts in matter—and this matter is the creation.

But the creation is unclean, and the god's imprisonment caused great turmoil in all of creation. The laws of creation became dissonant. A new world was born. A world like a baby cub that hasn't been licked into shape. A fallen, impure world.

Now it's every disciple's task to take into himself a part of the god, and save a part of the god from matter, for in every disciple dwells a part of the purity of the Home of the gods—and this home is separate from matter.

The god is named Oshito.

But mankind hasn't enough mouths to take in the whole of the god—that's why Mashoogna, the Great and Terrible, Mashoogna, the Devourer of Worlds, is their helper. Mashoogna, the sibling of Oshito, has come into the world to devour the world and, dogma teaches, will one day devour the sun and stars.

Mashoogna now dwells in Drreg.

That's what the Clan Oshito teaches its disciple, and teaches was also the reason for the Collapse.

Drreg is neither male nor female, nor remembers what sex he or she originally was. All he or she knows is that he or she is possessed by a god. If someone were to look at Drreg, they wouldn't be able to tell whether Drreg is male or female either.

Most say Clan Oshito is a sect of madmen—but what do they know, Drreg thinks. Doesn't a god dwell in Drreg? This is all the proof Drreg needs for the claims of Clan Oshito to be true.

Now Drreg awaits a woman named Death, who rides an iron horse. Until she comes Drreg must prepare.

Drreg clatters its mountainous teeth in anticipation.

* * *

As far as Urcena knows she is by herself in the underground of the city, in walkways that stretch for miles under it. She has lost track of how many days she's been walking. There's no light and she's tired and hungry.

All she feels when she walks are the damp walls of decaying brick and the hard surface of the ground. Overhead she can't hear anything: neither the bustle of commuters, trains, buses, cars, animals, nor any other contrivance. When she screams, no one hears her, she thinks, because no one answers her. Because of this, she thinks she is very deep under the city.

Of course, she might not be under the city anymore at all.

She remembers when her walled town was attacked by the godless northerners. She and her cousin built the altar to summon the Clan of the god Oshito. But Clan Oshito didn't arrive until after the godless people had massacred her town.

Looking at her, the Gray Lady had whispered to her, "The strength and vitality in you is great. Great enough to feed a god."

Then she was taken from her walled town into Taufet and its city and placed in the underground. Here she's remained. Why did she ask for the help of Clan Oshito, she now desperately wonders.

She walks in the darkness and thinks nonsense things as she begins to go mad.

In the darkness Drreg waits, or is it Mashoogna who waits?

Urcena walks past brick and brick. Each foot, each mile she walks, taking her nowhere in the darkness. No final destination. Every stop is the same. Well, almost the same. Now there is something different at her last resting place. Urcena in the darkness has felt the presence of something monstrous lurking nearby her.

Urcena sobs and sits against a wall. Paralyzed with fear, she looks unseeingly into the darkness and resigns herself to death. She can hear the deafening clattering of gigantic teeth rushing towards her. All sanity gone, she begins to laugh like a mindless idiot.

She is thrashed apart. She feels like her soul is being torn and pulled from her. The teeth are ravenous. Blood flies everywhere. Intestines hit the walls with force. In seconds, her flesh is pieces.

Mashoogna eats. It has grown powerful with the new life. The god will soon be ready for the woman and the horse-man.

* * *

The train lurches and veers throughout a portion of the gigantic city of the land of Taufet. Tenements and flats are passed of grime and dirt, as are fantastic skyscrapers in intersections of beauty and richness. Mindless waves of people dot the urban landscape, resembling locusts infesting a concrete grassland. The train runs below and above the city. Should a person peek through one of the train windows, the person would see a peculiar sight, even for the new world after the Collapse.

In one compartment a woman sits with voluptuous butterfly wings, cross-legged and wearing an English tweed jacket and a black skirt, while beside her a companion sits uncomfortably, an iron horse-man, wearing a double-breasted striped-gray suit one size too small for him, it seems. He fidgets, obviously uncomfortable with clothing, not just because it fits him too tight. She stares bemusedly at another man sitting opposite her. This man is tall, gangly, and is dressed in a black robe. He covers his head with a hood, yet his ominous appearance is off-set by his snobbish, affected manner of speaking.

"Your story of crossing the badlands is just astonishing. Your description of the place is just as I have been warned. I have never ventured there, as you can tell. In fact, I have never left the city. Ah, Torkarkossos! This city is the grandest city in the world, at least for the time being, seeing as how the world changes all the time. It is an empire to itself. And I mean this literally. The city is the empire. At last count I can assure you the census-takers numbered the city's population at roughly sixty-two million inhabitants. Some people live here who have never seen the other side. Life of course is precarious, just as in the badlands, especially for the common folk that haven't been transformed, which is the majority. Of course, who can live in complete peace after the Collapse, when all things are topsy-turvy? But there is order even in chaos, and things aren't so bad anymore, at least for those like us and not for the commoners, whose situation I like to describe in Hobbes' words, 'Continual fear and danger of violent death; and the life of man solitary, poor, nasty, brutish and short.' But even in these dire straits there are bread and circuses for everyone, provided by the centralized government, and hope is to be found everywhere."

"Like in a sect for Oshito," Butterfly says.

"I was thinking of other things, but yes, like in a sect for the god, Oshito, though I prefer the name Clan, better. The people want to know what happened to us. Why this collapse? Ours is just as good an explanation as any other. Some say it was a secret experiment gone awry. Some say it was the Hadron Collider that created this alternate universe of instability. Some say it was the Americans, the South Americans, terrorists, the Chinese, a thousand other gods and goddesses, Cuba, another race of beings, Charlie Chaplin even. Who knows? No one likes uncertainty, so we give them certainty, and a measure of hope and release from their fears. In my old life I was a Monsignor of the Catholic Church, now I am a Monsignor of Clan Oshito. I believe in the god Oshito, though not in the unsophisticated way his theology is sometimes presented."

Butterfly gives a slight grin.

"You do not believe that I believe, perhaps? Look and see. We all must do our part to rescue the god from matter. Some rescue him from the flesh, but after the Collapse, I have found myself with attributes that allow me to do more. He is entrapped in everything. Observe."

Finishing, the man leans forward, and out of his dark robe takes out a piece of cement originally from a wall, and proceeds to show his mangled mouth and eviscerated teeth. He then eats the hard cement.

As he eats the wall piece, he says, "Don't be alarmed. This will not damage my stomach. With this I liberate the god from matter."

Iron Horse looks away as the man drips blood and pus from his mouth, and observes instead the city of Torkarkossos. The stranger has told them it is built roughly like a warped bowl or elongated amphitheatre. The edges serve as walls thousands of feet into the sky. They are riding near the edge, and when the train shoots upward into the sky at tremendous speed, out the window he can look below and see the city recede deeper and deeper down.

After eating, the man continues, "Tell me, the boy that brought you to us told me you carry a candle that can control when you die. Is this true? If so, I am curious to know exactly the specifics of how this works. I mean, is the power in the candle itself to bring this about, or does the candle merely gauge a fate that would happen anyways? What is the metaphysics of the thing?"

"I carry no such candle. I told the boy stories to keep him entertained. Even if I did carry it, how would I know such a thing? Who knows how such things work? I would have to be a god myself to know."

"Yes, I agree. That's reasonable. Look now, we've arrived at our stop."

* * *

Iron Horse stares bewilderedly at the cemetery. It's a city to itself—a necropolis.

"There are many like it scattered throughout Torkarkossos," the hooded man says. "Isn't it beautiful?"

"Come this way," the caretaker of the cemetery beckons them.

They follow, and Iron Horse begins to feel unease in this land of the dead. He feels like bolting. From every building they pass, and tomb, and gravestone, he hears jumbled voices which whisper nothing but gibberish.

"Always at sundown the dead begin to speak," the caretaker explains. And then addresses the dead as if they were little children, "Hush, dwellers in eternity, it isn't your place to speak anymore. Now you must only listen to the living."

He leads them to a stone sarcophagus, with the outline of a man and a woman, marked *The Founders*.

The hooded man says with pride, "This is what you wanted to see. The Founders of our Clan are buried here, and preserved underneath this masonry by magic, until the triumph of Oshito."

Iron Horse asks Butterfly, "Who are the Founders?"

"My parents," she answers, and then attempts to swing her sword at the statuesque coffin.

The hooded man, however, steps in between. He yells, "I didn't bring you for this! I can't let you do this! My Lord and Lady won't be pleased!"

He reaches for a gun he carries.

With a swift swing of her charmed sword, however, Butterfly lunges and splits the man in half, and then, lunging forward again, ferociously also splits the sarcophagus in half. Inside are no preserved bodies, but a note, which reads: *Your parents are indeed dead, but not buried here. They are too precious. If you have found this letter, then the prophecy is true. Come to us and to your fate.*

Iron Horse says, "This was obviously written by Bacilus and the Gray Lady, the new rulers of the Clan."

"In my travels I'd managed to hear my parents had died while I was searching for them. I wanted to see if this was true. I now know it is. Why don't we listen to the message and at last go find the Clan?"

She cleans her sword, wipes the hooded man's blood from off her face, then leaves the cleaved sarcophagus and the caretaker cringing beside it.

Iron Horse follows her.

* * *

"What do you foresee, Bacilus?" the Gray Lady asks, as she looks down from a room situated atop a jagged tower onto the ground below, where thousands of her followers are assembled in a massive tunnel.

Bacilus doesn't turn from his chair, or the table he sits at, to answer her, but instead stares into empty space. He doesn't need eyes to see.

"What I always see," he says. "Out of all possible futures, only two are preeminent. Either Drreg destroys her, or she destroys Drreg. With her death, the Clan will thrive until all of Torkarkossos is under our sway. If she comes and destroys Drreg, it is certain the Clan will never rise again. We are finished."

She raises her hand to the crowds below, and unanimously they begin to cheer. She turns to him and says, "Have you seen nothing new of the outcome, then? Will she destroy us?"

"I cannot interpret the images to a coherent conclusion. I don't know yet. All I know is she will come. She will face us."

"You're too cautious. You live too much in the future and in certainties. I'll hazard a guess. She'll die. We've prepared too well to fail. Drreg is too strong."

"I see you gloating over her body in a position of triumph. That I do see."

Pleased with this new revelation, the Gray Lady smiles. Together they leave the room and descend to the ground floor.

***

The crowds are jubilant. After the Gray Lady's speech, they celebrate late into the night. Enthusiasm grips the crowd like a fever. It seems to them like they have waited all their lives for this day.

"Today, brothers and sisters," she yells over the music and the dancing, "out of your sacrifice will rise thousands more to honor the god Oshito!"

Religious frenzy overpowers some, and others foam at the mouth, when the gigantic door in the tunnel opens, and they see a god for the first time.

Drreg, believing himself fully possessed by the god Mashoogna, enters. Awed or frightened or inspired by this sight, the Clan at first grows silent, but soon their teachings overcome all else, and they begin to line up in front of Drreg. The light and power of Oshito in their bodies, they know, will find a better repository in the innards of a god. In Mashoogna, the sibling of the god they worship, they long to rest.

As the sacrament begins, Drreg says with the voice of a god, the hallowed mantra, "With this I liberate the god from matter."

Late into the night the disciples of Oshito line up to be devoured by Drreg. Its appetite is insatiable. As it eats—it grows. Power fills its body. Drreg is pleased. Blood overflows the same as it does from the winepresses of the gods.

Bacilus and the Gray Lady watch their acolytes as they sing, dance and are torn to pieces by the serrated teeth of Drreg.

The Gray Lady says sarcastically, "The stupid fools, how can they believe Drreg is actually a god?"

Suddenly Bacilus turns pale. He walks away and, looking back, tells her, "We have to go up to the city. She is here. Our sister has arrived."

*　*　*

The man and woman approach the colossal building resembling a gothic cathedral. High overhead they see gigantic gargoyles, silhouetted against the dawning sky, leering down at them. They ring the doorbell and its loud sound reverberates from within, as if echoing from a thousand rooms. A voice familiar yet strangely distorted and amplified asks from within, "Who may I ask is calling?"

The man stands defiantly by the entrance. He yells in a booming voice, "Go tell your masters Iron Horse and Butterfly are here!"

Then without waiting for a reply, he throws himself against the massive doors, splintering them into uncountable shards and rough sharpened wedges.

Once inside, Iron Horse and Butterfly confront the author of the voice. He stands before them with an exquisite manner, like a dandy or a pampered aristocrat. He is busily engaged in removing a wooden stake lodged deep into his chest. Butterfly and Iron Horse stare in amazement. Once the stake is out, he eyes them and smiles. Though no longer hooded, it is unmistakable as to who it is. Down his head and face and disappearing into his clothing runs a massive cut, caked and hardened with dry blood. He wears a new black robe. The two halves of his body, however, are not attached properly. This gives to his voice when he moves his mouth its unusual timbre and speech.

"Welcome, my friends," he says, "you are surprised. I forgot to mention, not only can I eat cement, but I am also nearly immortal. A great boon in these troubled times we live in. Our friend, the caretaker, put my two body halves together, but his manual dexterity is not of the best. Come now, and I'll take you to my masters. They are expecting you."

He leads them to an elevator. Once inside, the doors close. The contraption begins to rise. Suddenly it jerks, and begins to move sideways and downwards.

Inside, Iron Horse is wary, but looking at Butterfly, he notices she stands emotionless. If she has any anxiety or anticipation that finally her years of searching are about to be over, she keeps it well hidden. Iron Horse jitters nervously, as an overwhelming sense of claustrophobia begins to overpower his human instincts the longer they ride in the capsule.

It stops and the doors open to reveal a spacious living room, decorated after the décor of a Victorian era mansion. A blond man, dressed in a red robe, and a woman in gray, with a high-jeweled crown, rise from two luxuriant couches to greet them.

*　*　*

As the three step into the room, Butterfly unsheathes her sword, and holds it tightly in her hand.

"You can go now, Steven," the Gray Lady says to her servant.

Bowing, the hooded man steps back into the elevator and closes the door. It makes a low humming noise as it disappears into the darkness of the tunnels.

At an even height, Butterfly and the Gray Lady stare at each other, closely, with their piercing green eyes.

It's the Gray Lady who first breaks the silence. "For a long time I've wanted to meet you, Sasha, to see if your beauty and bravery were as legendary as they say. I wasn't blessed with your exquisite butterfly wings, but I possess what you'll envy. I have intelligence, and it also wasn't me who our parents sold into slavery to a lecherous wizard. I am indeed the fortunate and loved one, sister."

With an icy voice Butterfly says, "Step away from me, sister. Don't think this revelation is going to upset me. Sister or no sister, I'll kill you if you insult me again. Sasha is a name from another life. I ask that you don't use it again. If you speak, speak to the point. Do you know why I've come?"

"Our brother, the prophet, will tell you."

Walking away, the Gray Lady laughs. Bacilus moves closer.

Taking a seat nearby, Bacilus with vacant eyes, begins to talk almost as if to himself.

"I've looked on the world like a stranger, Butterfly," he says. "Past, present and future parade past my eyes like a grotesque pageantry. The future I see imperfectly, though. Always, I've been the bystander on the outside looking in.

"Even now I see it. The days of the Collapse, and the birth pangs of the Wayward Earth. The day of your birth. The day our parents sold you to the Cutter of Candles at three years old. My own and our sister's birth two years later.

"But you want to know about our parents and Clan Oshito. In your mind they are explicitly linked. You are correct.

"They were named Lewis Watchtung and Kathryn Sotmayor, but after the world changed they found themselves with new names, as inexplicably these things happened. When you were born, and as we knew them, their names were Cae Ang and Cassandra.

"Our mother was a dream seer. It was her idea to sell you to the Cutter, both for your well-being, and to alleviate them of their poverty. In dreams she had been told that by doing this they were guaranteeing your safety, and helping you to eventually grow up to be a great lady. They loved you very much, Butterfly. But fate's ways are often crooked, and they did not know the Cutter well. Those were confusing times for the world. The bargain was for the Cutter to educate you in his arts and then send you to them when he was finished. Things did not go as planned.

"During this time, our parents made their way to Taufet. Along the way we were born. We were made by self-generation in our mother's womb. Our parents had no coitus in our making. At birth we grew rapidly, and were full grown in five years.

"At that time, on the outskirts of Torkarkossos there was a peasant's rebellion, led by a man named Oshito. Our parents joined this group. They were defeated by Torkarkossos. They then joined a group of wandering peasants. In time, Cae Ang and Cassandra became the leaders of the group, now calling themselves Clan Oshito, after the leader who'd first united them.

"The Clan grew in power and prestige. The plan of the Clan was to make a rival city to counter the influence of Torkarkossos. But our parents met their end and disappeared, off the face of the earth, in an hour, by the strange magic that inhabits our world like a roaming chaos.

"We then took over the rulership of the Clan. Our ideas were different from those of our parents. We saw no difference between the Clan as it once was and the city. Tyranny is just as effective a weapon of government as democracy is. We faked omens, and by trickery converted the Clan into a religious sect. Oshito now became a god. Making peace with the city, we marched our adherents within its walls.

"We plan to conquer the city, Butterfly, from within. Our acolytes are legion, and will follow us with the blindness of zealotry."

"And then?" Butterfly asks.

The Gray Lady turns to her sister and says, "We'll extend our grasp and expand until the world is ours, if possible. Join us."

"No."

"Bacilus predicted this. You'll fight a creature. You must destroy it, or else it'll grow until it devours all life on earth. Only we, Sasha, can control it by the manacles of faith. It believes zealously anything we say. It hasn't grown yet sufficiently to destroy you easily. You arrived earlier than expected, but I know it can win. You and your friend will die."

As Butterfly is about to speak, the Gray Lady motions with her hand, and a trap door opens with ferocious speed underneath her and Iron Horse. Before the two have time to react, the doors close above them, and they find themselves tumbling downwards in a dark abyss of hot wind. Butterfly cannot get her bearings to fly, as air buffets them against the sides of what seems like a gigantic sink pipe.

After a while they land on the ground, hard. Iron Horse is the first to get up as a massive door opens in front of them, but it is Butterfly who first steps through it.

* * *

They exit the base of a tower and see a throng of people, in ecstasy, driving forward up steps, without order and crashing over each other, to be consumed by a gigantic beast. They are at the end of an open tunnel and Butterfly soon realizes the only way out is through the gorging behemoth. Years later, what she'll most remember physically about the thing, in nightmares, are its massively grotesque, razor sharp teeth, situated on a head and thick neck preposterously too small for the powerful pistons. The teeth being the height and width of six standing, tall, full-grown elephants, mounted on top of each other. It turns its head towards them, and all Iron Horse and Butterfly see of its face in a headlong view are its terrible teeth.

Drreg, as Mashoogna, gives a bellowing cry and shakes its head frenziedly, as bright red blood flails from its teeth in all directions. The crowds run away in fright, to cower by the sides of the tunnel. Drreg turns on its left flank. In a side view, Butterfly and Iron Horse see between its huge curved teeth, are stuck chunks and slithers of raw human flesh, and mangled clothing. Drreg gives in profile the impression, to the standers-by, of a grinning, hell-spawned, ivory-toothed baleen whale. Drreg remembers the prophecy of the woman and the horse-man. It must defeat them, and so the thing stands on its six legs and begins to move its heavily bloated body towards them.

Butterfly unsheathes her sword and stands her ground. In a moment of tension she searches for the pouch where her candle is—but the pouch is gone!

"Are you looking for this?" she hears the Gray Lady yell from atop the tower.

Butterfly looks up. She sees her life candle in the hands of her sister.

"So careless, Sasha. In your eagerness to leave the tower you didn't notice you dropped your pouch. What will happen, I wonder, sister, if I light this candle?"

For the first time in her life since leaving the Cutter, Butterfly finds herself without her magic talisman, but just her sword, her wits, and the clattering teeth coming towards her. Her heart begins to pound with fear as panic spreads quicksilver throughout her steely frame. She loses her train of thought and slowly lets down her sword in confusion. Glands begin to excrete sweat profusely. Her bowels churn menacingly. Her mind tells her to flee. Her heart pounds thunderously against her chest.

"Courage," Iron Horse says, as they both hear, in the distance, Drreg's abnormal animalistic voice. It says, "With this I liberate the god from matter."

Atop the tower, on an open platform, with Bacilus beside her, the Gray Lady lights the candle and laughs.

"Sasha, your life now burns away!" she yells.

Butterfly and Iron Horse look up in shock. Her wings hang loosely behind her without resolve.

Drreg casts a long shadow upon them.

* * *

Teeth snap loudly at Butterfly as she dodges a wild bite. Now awakened from her trance, she scrambles beneath the open maw of the beast, and slashes fiercely at its underside.

Iron Horse fastens himself with one arm against a fang, and with his other pummels at it with great metallic thrusts of his fist. The creature bangs the earth with its maw repeatedly, hoping to unhinge the metal man. But Iron Horse holds fast.

Butterfly jumps away from the plummeting mouth. With racing heart and fear she stabs at one of Drreg's middle legs. The monster, flashing its fire-red teeth, drives its head beneath its body, and snaps at the woman. She barely avoids its jaws as it impacts like a crashing meteor into the hard ground. Iron Horse is knocked off its fang. The creature's whole body spins in the air, carried with the awful momentum of its lunge. It falls back first on the soil, its head now facing the opposite direction from the tower.

The crash is so forceful, the earth shakes and tremendous chunks of cement begin to break from the tunnel. The people scream in fear.

* * *

From the pinnacle of the tower, atop the open platform, the Gray Lady looks on eagerly as the candle burns more rapidly.

* * *

Removing some of their constraining clothing, the two fighters leap away from Drreg's yawning mouth as the beast attacks a second time.

Butterfly takes to the sky and falls rapidly, head first with her sword. She plunges it into Drreg's back, hilt deep. The blade does no damage and Butterfly removes it as blood spouts like a geyser. She flies away from the bellicose beast. Teeth snap at her. A small portion of her side is cut out. She falls to the ground like a broken kite, haphazardly, and squirms in pain. She will not give up. She will triumph, she thinks to herself.

The man in the form of a horse dodges the thing's rampaging legs, and with metallic iron knives sprouting from his head, he stabs with every opportunity, but to no avail.

Their weapons are useless against an enemy the size of Drreg.

* * *

Bacillus and the Gray Lady look on, pleased, as Butterfly's candle burns more than halfway finished.

* * *

The iron contraption, exhausted in his racing with the flaming wild beast, turns once more into a man, and beckons Drreg towards him.

With flaring nostrils, the monster runs and roars towards him with the pride of a god, and blind with the joy of anticipation. It will trample the horse-man until it has pounded him into hell's fires itself. It charges, six feet thundering, hard muscles working with colossal, granitic power. Iron Horse rolls.

Suddenly, Drreg sees a shiny blade, but it is too late. It plunges seemingly fathoms deep into one jelly-soft, wild eye. It roars surprised, and yells in excruciating pain, as the light goes out from its right side.

Butterfly leaps away while still in the air.

***

"In its hubris and single-mindedness, Drreg has forgotten about Butterfly," Bacilus says.

"What do you foresee?" the Gray Lady asks.

"Doom."

***

The monster, teeth flashing, now out of control, loses its direction, tumbles, slides, and crashes sideways unstoppably into the tower.

The masonry cracks; the whole edifice begins to topple over. It crumbles and falls and howls like a living thing, the towers' lost grandeur dissolving into dirt, soil, cement, rock, and settling like ash from a volcanic eruption.

Under a pile of debris Iron Horse notices Bacilus' hand sticking out. He checks it for a pulse.

There is none.

***

Nearly naked, with dark skin glistening, Butterfly swoops down onto Drreg's battered neck. The whole architecture of the structure has fallen onto Drreg. Fighting the almost paralyzing pain in her side, she walks towards a bulky artery on its throbbing neck, and prepares to strike repeatedly and deeply into its life's umbilical cord. She heaves her sword above her head.

"I wouldn't do that," Butterfly hears the Gray Lady say.

She emerges into sight, fighting pain and barely able to breathe. Ripped skin and ripped robe one with her blood. As she walks, bones crack. In her hand she still carries the candle. It's almost completely burnt.

She whispers in pain, "If you two decide to attack me, I'll cause the whole of it to burn, and melt instantly. I know how to use some magic, Sasha. Will you take the chance that the candle's magic works even in such a circumstance?"

Butterfly yells defiantly at her sister, "If I'm going to die I'll take the creature with me anyways!"

"You fool," says the Lady weakly. "What right have you to commit parricide? Don't you know you've found our parents? Our parents were never buried because they never died. That's why the sarcophagus is empty. Bacilus told you our parents came to an end and disappeared by this chaotic world's magic. He never said they died. He never told you, however, how this happened. I will. Unexplainably one day they began to fuse into each other. Grotesquely, two became one, and from the union, Drreg, the creature, was born. A monstrosity, not remembering the two it had once been. We took it, convinced the thing it was transforming into a god. That thing you see before you is our mother and our father. Will you kill our parents, Sasha? I know you won't. I've won, sister."

Looking at her sister, noticing her sense of triumph and superiority, proud in her own intellect and planning, Butterfly knows she's telling the truth. This is no mere deception, but the Gray Lady's final ace. A triumph not based on cheap lies, but on awful truth.

Butterfly drops her sword hand, flies off Drreg's massive neck, and falling on her knees near the Gray Lady, yells, "You bitch, bitch, bitch!"

I can't kill my parents, Butterfly thinks. *I can't.*

She remembers years of loneliness with the cold, unloving Cutter. A childhood of slavery. Happier childhood memories of walking hand and hand with her parents. Of laughing. Being joyful. In compensation for the Cutter's cruelness, those brief memories were her escape. In their recollections, she'd found strength and joy. In her reconstructions of her parents, albeit as phantoms, she'd found the love she'd never had. So had she left the Cutter all those years ago, in quest of her parents and Clan Oshito, for this? To murder her own parents? To destroy the ones who'd sold her, because they loved her, and thought she would be better off? Was this, then, her fate? Will she take the only life left to them?

Iron Horse moves towards the Gray Lady, but she reminds him by pointing at the candle that she can inflame it further in an instant. It's almost fully burnt. She walks towards and stands over Butterfly.

"Sasha," she says gloatingly over her sister, "the candle is almost done. It's over, sister. Your life's' course has run. Give me the sword. It's what fate demands."

Butterfly moves her sword hand towards her sister's, but then pauses. Slowly she raises her head, and yells at the Gray Lady, "Never! I'll show you, sister!"

She raises herself with speed, flies atop Drreg's neck again, and, holding the blade overhead, plunges it unhesitantly and repeatedly into Drreg's swollen artery.

The Gray Lady screams as blood begins to gush out like a gigantic, unstoppable waterfall from Drreg.

In shock she stares at Butterfly.

* * *

The Gray Lady stumbles towards Drreg's open mouth.

"Father, mother," she whispers like a little girl. "Your daughter has killed you. The evil one that came back and never knew you."

Butterfly stands still with disgust and repressed anger, the blade in her hand twitching, and eyeing her sister, she yells at her, "You're mad, sister! You've lost! Our parents died when that thing was born! They no longer exist! They've been dead a long time! There was nothing left of them to kill! The evil thing is gone!"

* * *

"Father, mother," the Gray Lady says to Drreg.

Drreg's body shakes. It opens and languidly rolls a milky-white eye, and stares at the Gray Lady with vehemence. Then with a soft hiss, as it dies, it blows the candle out.

The Gray Lady drops the candle, falls down weakly and weeps. Butterfly immediately swoops down to pick the candle up.

From the shadows emerge Bacilus' and the Gray Lady's acolytes. The Clan Oshito. They stand over the Gray Lady.

"You've let the god die," one man says to her.

"You've betrayed Oshito!" another yells.

"Oshito has left you!" more yell.

"No, no," the Gray Lady mutters. "What are you fools talking about? There was never a god Mashoogna. There is no Oshito."

"Traitor!" a woman yells.

"Apostate!" one yells from the crowd.

"Get away from me!" the Gray Lady demands. "I'm weak. I want to be alone. Don't you understand? There's no Oshito! I—and my brother, Bacilus—we made the whole thing up!"

"You must pay for your treason to Oshito," one says.

They gather around the Gray Lady.

Hundreds of them.

"By letting Mashoogna die, Oshito's left you. You're weak. Not a true prophet of the god."

As Butterfly and Iron Horse depart, they hear the hallowed mantra echoing throughout the massive tunnel, "*With this we liberate the god from matter.*"

* * *

Taufet and the giant city of Torkarkossos are miles behind them. Like a mist the glimpses of the city and the plains, the strange lands and stranger creatures, dissolve and are left behind. She went on a quest to find her past, and with her past she also found her future.

They've stopped in a clearing of trees. Overhead, the afternoon sun shines brightly and hot, and a warm breeze plays soothingly upon her raven-black hair.

Butterfly stares at the ocean in front of her and watches the seagulls caw and fight each other for morsels of food. Iron Horse is busily digging a hole she's asked him to make. The soil piles up, tremendously fast, as he digs ever deeper. Once she feels that the hole's sufficiently deep, she tells her friend to come up.

He emerges, dusty. his steam pistons flaring as he shakes the dirt off himself.

In her hand she holds the candle. She feels its short length, traces with a finger its rough, circling circumference, and admires the light blue color of it. She plays with the tip of the wick. She smiles. Then she throws the short candle into the deep hole.

"Later we'll cover the hole. For now let's just rest," she says.

"And after? What do you propose we do then?" Iron Horse asks.

"We'll cross the ocean and see what lies on the other side."

Iron Horse turns to look at the soil beneath his feet, and at the clamped grass. He then traces its end at the clearing's opening. He continues looking, and sees the beach sand. His eyes follow forward, until they rest on the rolling, unending ocean.

But something else is on his mind, besides the ocean.

Soon the hole is covered, undetectable. The two leave to find a ship.

Days later, overlooking a high cliff where they can see a harbor city below, Iron Horse asks, "Why did you do it? Why did you throw the candle away?"

Butterfly hesitates with an answer. She thinks of her life since the day she left the Cutter and took the life candle with her. Images and emotions pass almost instantaneously through her mind.

"Because," she says laughing, as her butterfly wings open magnificently in the afternoon breeze. "Because I hold my destiny in my own hands."

Iron Footfalls

I fled Him, down the nights and down the days...
I said to Dawn: Be sudden–to Eve: Be soon;
With thy young sky blossoms heap me over
From this tremendous Lover!
Halts by me that footfall;
Is my gloom, after all,
Shade of His hand, outstretched caressingly?
—"The Hound of Heaven" by Francis Thompson

Year 562 NNPE

She crouches alone in a corner, waiting quietly for you, her prosthetic reader barely registering her enclosed environment. She waits, and remembers when her father first told her the dream of you. You were the embryo, the idea, the fixation in his brain, throbbing constantly like a metronome. How many versions of you there were, at first, she can't now remember, but when something finally like yourself—your terrible self—emerged from the compass of his craft, his workshop cocoon, she naively marvelled at the sight.

From somewhere, she hears the powerful disemboguements of the IonPlasma weapons. The tearing of metal. What a strange sound metal makes when it rips like paper. Tremors shake the walls. Loud blasts set air particles quivering. Then comes the silence. How many station drones have you destroyed now, Brother? Perhaps hundreds? She places her one biochemical hand against the cold, metallic sheen of a wall, and thinks she can feel the steady, diminishing pulse of the CompuMind retreating into itself like a lanky, frightened tentacle into a deep hole. And then she hears your footfalls again.

Steady. Steady. Moving in her direction.

She wonders if you wonder how Father felt when you were almost complete. She wonders how he felt, too.

As a young soldier, her father could remember being taken to the peripheries of the Oort Cloud. There, in the Rim System, where human habitation barely penetrated, from the windows of an interplanetary carrier, he could see the silent spaces beyond, stretching to eternity, where, in unfathomable distances, lay the cluttered stars, eons old. Stars that had never known human passions, sickness, evil, war. Staring into those abysses of beautiful darkness and uncountable time, he had felt peace, awe, silence, and all the ages of strife had seemed as nothing to him, then. This is what she imagines he felt then, looking at you, as they both stood on this lone asteroid hurtling quietly through open space, around a star that's been its companion since before life ever appeared on Earth: when the first planets were formed in early times out of the primordial, galactic ooze; when the stardust first touched the nascent valleys and mountains of his homeworld, and the first sunrises were there to be recorded by no one, until mankind had come.

Do you grasp the sublimity of the image, the awe of time and eternity, the feeling of vastness, of grandeur—do you feel anything at all, she wonders, Brother?

She's lost. The only difference she can imagine between you is that her darkness is the blackness of this station, where the lights have all gone out, while your darkness is the blackness of the soul, where no light shines and perhaps never shone.

She says, This darkness, this nutshell, this being locked up, inside and out, this claustrophobia is becoming maddening.

She reaches out with her mechanised hand and cybersynapses instantaneously make her realise she's touching blood. Dry blood—her own.

Your footfalls are getting closer.

From the corridors and the nearby airlock, she hears snippets of her absent father's recorded mad talk, disjointed and emanating from the comm centres scattered throughout the station. They say:

> His name was Talus, made of iron mold,
> Immovable, resistless, without end;
> Who in his hand an iron flail did hold,
> With which he threshed out Falsehood, and did Truth unfold.*

***

War. Drudgery. Pain. Death. Hopelessness. Destruction. War. Mankind. I will soon put right a mistake that never should have happened.

* * *

Oh, how I long for you to live, Talus!

* * *

His footfalls are coming faster now, girl. Unstoppable. The booming echoes—gigantic. Like a mad-brained, moonstruck hound, he's homing in on you.

* * *

He will walk, breathe, and learn by uncontrollable compulsions like great, heaving seas of lava.

* * *

Time is running out. She, however, has not given up hope. She believes some message will reach her father, the planets, or at least a stray ship.

Sadly, no help will ever reach her. She is alone, too far from anyone.

We see this all and laugh.

Close now are your iron footfalls. With majestic insistency they beat.

Crouching, she uncoils the segments of her cyborged arm, which then part and configure into two snake-like appendages that input into a wall panel nearby, joining metal to metal. Direct communication with the central brain of the CompuMind is now possible. She feels the totality of the station and, in cyberspace throughout it all, lurking, a foreign mind, hunting and sniffing for her. She bypasses this presence whenever she senses it, and secretly whispers with the CompuMind in a shut psyche-lock. Her waiting is almost over, she tells it. The CompuMind warns her it hasn't stored enough energy yet.

Her hastily-attached synthetic reader, resembling a goggle, retracts and re-lenses. Visual images, albeit poorly, allow her to focus more closely on the end of the lightless corridor.

Your footfalls have stopped, Brother.

A small scoutdrone is suddenly thrust into her line of vision. The drone makes a horrible screech and red lights begin to flash violently around it. She quickly tries to re-lens, to get a better optical reading, but before she can, we feel the drone's insides ballooning with your meaty metal, Brother, until it explodes, leaving your gleaming feelers quivering with excitement.

Shards of the scoutdrone hit her, cutting and jabbing into her organic parts. She loses her balance and falls over, hitting her plated head, yet still, she manages to remain hooked to the wall panel.

Though dazed, the primitive lizard brain in her humanity causes her to involuntarily send a shocked, lightning-like panic signal to the CompuMind. It answers in kind.

Reams of corded electricity shoot out from capacitors hidden throughout the corridor and impact on you fantastically. Energy illumes you, flashing and exploding in blinding, brilliant lights. Erratically, you still advance, like a dark planet rising within a molten sun. Her lens refocuses, and she sees your shape, full of wrong angles and impossible edges and strangely moving contraptions that should not fit together. You heat up like the core of a red-hot star.

She begins to feel pain. Terrible, burning pain. Her flesh bubbles. Her metal heats.

We hear the CompuMind say, in a tone too emotional for a machine, "Impossible! Impossible! Nineteen dimensional spaces! Curved space collapsing, inconceivable angles surfacing!" And then it goes silent. The charges cease, darkness comes and, at long last, ends the chase.

Now your being is upon her like a looming horror. She feels your electrified presence. She sees your terrible hand reach out to her. She awaits her death bravely.

But nothing happens.

She feels, above, your hand swing past her, like a bird of prey swooping for the kill and then leaving. You pass by her, like a planet swing. Uninterested. Walking around her.

She turns to see your footfalls recede and then vanish into a wall. You are now on the outside of the asteroid. Your massive shape is moving away. Your alien intent and intelligence are incomprehensible to her. An intelligence more like ours.

How you yearn to set us free. The blessed impurity of angular Space-Time will soon enter her dimension.

Once, there was a God of love and spirit; now they have fashioned a god of metal and of the outer hells. Her father wanted to destroy those responsible for their ceaseless war and then start anew, yet through our influence, he created instead a sentient machine, designed to perpetrate genocide on its own creators.

You are like a scapegoat, Brother. In times long gone, when her species was as yet young, they would lay their sins upon a goat and send it into the wastes to die. This creature bore the sins of the people, and they would be cleansed of their sins. You, the Talus Machine, are the last scapegoat, come back out of the wastes, bearing their sins back to them.

As she prepares to hunt for you on the asteroid, she hears your voice inside her head, metallic and scratchy, say the ultimate incomprehensibility to her mind: *Witness as I fall into the sun and pull the worlds down.* Then your heavy feet push away from the asteroid.

Senseless, she thinks. Utter, complete senselessness.

Seconds pass, and she begins to feel the pull—the great, gravitational pull of the collapsing sun that will soon form into a fast-burgeoning black hole, from which nothing will escape.

These are the last hours of her species. At last the portal to Tindalos will be opened.

Sasana Xavi VI rushes to a window, horrified. The stars in the nightblack sky begin to burn out. The celestial bodies move. The asteroid shifts forcefully towards the sun. She looks one last time, and then the lights of her universe go out.

We will soon howl free from the other side of our prison-home. It will soon be time for a new arrangement.

*From Edmund Spenser's *The Faerie Queene*, Book V, Canto I.

The Call of the Siren

One night, he awoke to a strange song emanating from outside his windowpane: a faraway sound with the inflections of no normal human voice. Hypnotic in its appeal, brittle as dried autumn leaves, it seemed a mere whisper could dissipate its cohesion and send it scattering noiselessly into empty space. This melody caused him to dreamily dress, and leave the safe comfort of the place which for a while he called home.

In silence I watched him, from a dark wall I rested on.

The song—a conduit it is for strange influences of body and mind, and this is why I suppose he left in search of its source so thoughtlessly, past the gray framework of the front door, and into the eerie twilight world of shadowy rustic scenery. No bird sang in the dank air, and a heavy atmosphere of expectancy hovered over everything.

I dropped carefully to the floor and followed him, my predatory instincts subdued for the moment.

I knew where he was going. He longed to see that fantastic creature of awe and wonder viewed by few men.

My curiosity and sense of wonder were piqued by all I had witnessed, and now, as if reading a secret yearning, the soft voice called to him, and like an emotionless sleepwalker he went, past the house and the needled pine grown twisted beside it, into the backwoods of the little plebian estate. He walked deeper into this luxuriant fauna of swollen trees, now shadowed with twilight coverture where no animal stirred, save hidden creatures barely glimpsed through the trees that flew on night-wings, and I knew were neither owls, nor any species of bird or bat. The only sound was the flattening of the grass below his feet, and that droning voice whose song is not of this world, but I fancy of the vortices beyond our dimension and of our space itself.

I followed him flying and circling, concealed amid the treetops, my hands outstretched in the air. The woods as we neared the ocean began to glow with an unearthly dullish hue of light brown, and the leaves followed suit. As we wandered out from the gently swaying forest, I noticed the ocean glowed too, and the sandy bank, as did the cloud-cast sky above—a peculiar glow that accentuated the normal color of things, though still grayish and dark in background. Through this weird luminescence of darkness, the oncoming waves made an especially brilliant display of watery sparks as they dissipated on the rocky shore.

On this shore I noticed printless feet gently maneuvering along the coastal margins, dancing to their own hypnotic song. She danced nude along that lonely stretch of sand: an aspect of serene beauty, a splendor of the ocean, a dream-herald of long concealed divinity. And where she stepped on air too close to the ocean, the waters swiftly parted, and where too close to the ground, the sand and rocks were blown aside. Atop her yellow swaying hair I saw speckles of water shine, like miniature silvery stars that danced in tune to the music which her lips sent forth—a litany of sounds that only spirits can make.

On the sudden, she turned towards the land. She looked at him and beckoned him to follow.

I lay secretly extended on a shoreline rock, and growing more curious by the moment, I lifted my head, and unfolded and branched out further my mind. My mind melted deeper into his. I read now more of his thoughts.

Standing on the threshold of Chiloe, he remembered that Pincoya was the daughter of the sea and a mortal woman, and possessed the cryptic nature of the gods, but mostly he remembered the sadness when Pincoya had renounced his love, had heard the call of her father, and left him for the sea.

Now walking into the water he shivered with cold, as the wide Pacific slowly grew around him, and always like a stringed puppet he moved, through the subtle influence of that song, towards the dark svelte shape in the waters. Above him the stars seemed to spin in the most miniscule of spirals, leaving tiny wisps in the ever-lowering night. The beetling wind, coasting softly off the silky texture of the scene, the fine waves, woods, and trees, had the low, mournful dirge of a lone, abandoned conch.

I watched from a distance, and then, upstarting from my lucid-reverie of dream, I walked, flew, and crawled closer to them, as they advanced into the strangely sombrous, strangely-litten sea. Always she was before him, and he trailed, cresting somnambulistically the surf, not far behind.

In his mind I read both strong recollections of pain and desolations, and fears of future terrors, of which perhaps this small episode formed only a scintilla of what to expect, mixed with a full, elating wonder. And through his mind, also, I saw her face, and on it was written the temper of the ocean—a face like the beautiful, vast, tsunamic, calm, mysterious and treacherous ocean—as she beckoned him deeper into the sea.

Languidly he advanced into that dark world, swimming, rising above, and cresting the oncoming breakers, and then he seemed to lose all effort to swim; he gasped hard, his hands went dangerously limp, his feet fell below and pulled him, like a lodestone, down. He sank fast, deeper and deeper, down.

Then what vistas opened up to him! He saw the dark brine and its tiny amoebic shapes, heard the roar of the ocean, and the dull muffled noise of its millions of teeming, percolating life; and a hole, and through it, vast shapes between worlds, liquid spheres, secret passageways, other more occult universes, with darker scenes than the ones up above; and through it all and overpowering all, her transformed webbed, cosmic hand, gruesome fish eyes, and large spiky teeth, like an anglerfish's, reaching speedily up to meet him.

I watched, terrified and yet enraptured, until our bond was broken. I felt him no more. *He'd been pulled through that monstrous portal.* Soon the magic of the night passed into normality. The mystery disappeared. The strange luminescence dimmed. Noises were once more heard in the woods, and as the last of the stars faded out, I licked and groomed some of the thick hairs on my black spider-shaped limbs and, dissolving into the awakening day, vanished as well.

Is he alive? Is he dead?

Don't ask.

In all my nightly hunts since then I've never seen him again.

Among the Dark Places of the Earth

It was on a Tuesday when we crossed the towering peaks of the Andes Mountains. Its continuous chain of monstrous girth, which extends all the way along the west of South America, aroused to my sensibilities a sense of the magnitude of its suggestive power, and with this sublime elevation of feeling came a dread. These gigantic growths, spawned of earth's rocks, seemed to live a life apart from man, brooding and majestic to themselves, true only to themselves, as brothers. As I gazed atop their snowy summits from the six-passenger plane, I feared we had greatly erred and had made an intrusion into places where man should not be, and watched beings that saw our onlooking and curious eyes as trespasses and voyeurship, but they were patient and waited. To the north, in the distance, loomed one of the highest of earth's monoliths, iridescent Aconcagua, clothed with a sliver of clouds. I imagined it to be the mighty monarch of the peaks—peaks that were its subjects. And should it become annoyed, what then? I thought, what if mountains moved? What if they got up and walked? What army could stop one leg from lifting? A profound respect for them dawned on me such as I never experienced before, for if these mountains moved, would they even see us as sharers in a common destiny on this earth; or as nuisances, as flies, inconsequential to their estranged and alien minds?

After a while these disturbing thoughts began to abate, and the terror softened as we left the Andes behind somewhat and beheld their western slopes. Yet they were never wholly gone, for always they remained to our left while we journeyed, as the Pacific Ocean did to our right. Like two boundaries they seemed, land and water, poised to attack, while we flew between them. The pilot and I were in Chile, the snake-like country to the west of Argentina.

Refueling in the capital of Chile, Santiago, we continued our journey south. We passed various cities in Chile's pleasant central valley and crossed the Bio-Bio River. Our journey south took us through densely forested areas and lake regions, remarkable for their beauty and solitude. Our destination was Chiloe Island. The last grand majestic marker before our descent should have been the glacier-covered volcano, Osorno. We planned to land at Tepual Airport in Puerto Montt, and from there chart the ferry that would take us to Chiloe. In all, we would have covered the land mass between Buenos Aires in the east of Latin America to Chile's bustling capital Santiago in the west, and covered 668 miles from the capital in the north, and would have stood near the world's end. We knew that not much further south lay nearly intraversable fjords and inlets, dark brooding cities, the Straits of Magellan, tempestuous waters, and then the daunting, cold wastes of the Antarctic.

At 3,000 feet, I remember looking out the window and noticing the forested lake regions below us. Then I took a brief nap, and when I awoke I saw a worried look on the pilot.

"That's funny," I overheard him say. "There shouldn't be mountains this high."

I immediately looked out the window and realized we were overhead the Andes again. I saw their snow-covered peaks below and some giant sentinels in the distance. It was as if we had backtracked on our voyage and were now crossing the Andes all over again.

"Are we turning back?" I remember asking him, holding my fear in check.

"I don't know. The navigational instruments aren't working right," he said. And then added in an ominous undertone, "I don't know where we are."

From that point on our flight became one of real, and not imagined, terror and mind-numbing stress.

"Can't you contact anyone?" I remember yelling.

"All I get is static."

I tried to use my cell phone, and it too didn't work.

"Sit beside me and help me any way you can," he then said to me.

I sat beside him and followed his instructions in an intensity of fear as best I could, sensing everything, his instructions, our movements, in wild dimensions of phantasmagoria, which passed dizzyingly before me in transmutations incorporeal and unreal. The world outside the cockpit became as a solitary giant, dark and uninviting. This feeling was intensified when a thick, encroaching mist began to encircle the environs of the strange, moving skyscape before us. It surrounded the plane and covered the sun. I remember seeing one hoary mountain top become completely submerged within it. Soon the mist, now a thick fog, blanketed everything, and no matter how high we rose, it was always there. The only sound was the loud hum of our engines.

It must have been hours, or minutes, before the fog began to disperse and we caught sight of land below us. We were unnerved to realize we were flying lower than was safe.

"It looks like the ends of Patagonia. How did we travel so far in so little time?" the pilot said. "We shouldn't be here. Not enough fuel."

He estimated we were past the Straits of Magellan. Confused, he warned me that we were running out of fuel and had no choice but to land in this isolated, nethermost region of the world, far away and farther south than we had planned. Flying lower, we circled a wide expanse of flatland and the pilot made a safe, yet highly rocky, landing.

* * *

"I'll go check to see if anyone can help us," I said to the pilot.

We were on elevated ground, and in the distance I saw far away a lonely homestead and a wooded area near it, and stretching in all directions, empty grassland. Behind us began small foothills, which gradually increased into a chain of low-lying and then larger mountains. The pilot guessed they were a tributary of the Andes Mountains and that we were inexplicably lost on Tierra del Fuego, either on the Chilean or Argentine side.

We didn't talk much when we landed, and the pilot said he would spend his time checking the plane for whatever was malfunctioning, and trying to fix the radio. Help would come soon, he was sure, and if it didn't, tomorrow we'd head off with supplies to one of the nearest cities, that he was convinced were no farther away than a few days' walk from our landing place. He encouraged me to go, in case the small house in the distance had a phone that worked or other communication device, and also suggesting that the walk would be good for my flailed nerves.

When I was ready to leave, a low buzzing noise started to sound.

"Don't worry," the pilot said. "It's probably just wind blowing through the mountains."

* * *

As I walked, I tried to keep my thoughts from making any compromise with the irrational, and told myself that some explanation for our past danger in the plane would present itself, in time. I wore a heavy sweater, meant to have been worn in Chiloe, since the weather here was also cold. Low heavy clouds formed overhead and a small drizzle of rain began to fall. I estimated it to be near evening.

The dwelling was farther than it looked, however, so by the time I reached the wooden fence of the house I was soaking wet and the light through the clouds had dimmed a considerable degree. The fence surrounded the rural one-story house. Sparse trees dotted the small property irregularly throughout. To the east I could see the long forested area and to my north the small mountain chain and our plane like a speck of dust in the immense surrounding grassland.

I yelled from the fence to see if someone was home, but when no one answered I took it upon myself to enter the property, since I was by this time extremely chilled and wet. It was then that I noticed that the small wooden gate was open and the corral for horses was empty. I looked at the front door of the house and saw that it too was slightly open, creaking slowly in the wind.

The property did not seem right. It took on for me the impression of a house not lived in, abandoned, perhaps an old gaucho residence gone to rot, unnoticed in the quiet plains. (A gaucho being an Argentine cowboy.) The thought unnerved me that I and the pilot were perhaps the only two people in this out of the way place.

Uneasily I stepped through the door, since as I have said I was extremely cold and wet and needed to get help.

"Hello!" I yelled into the void. The void made no reply.

I yelled again, as I further entered—cautiously—into the dwelling. I heard a lone shutter, now banging monotonously against a window. A sense of years upon years of emptiness hit me.

The door I passed led into a kitchen. Decrepitude had done its work, and thick dust accumulated on the finger I ran atop a table. I also noticed overturned chairs, lying sprawled as if knocked over in a hurry.

I continued to explore the house, with its moldy smell of wet age. I noticed there was no TV, but only an old antenna radio. I found it strange that personal belongings and furniture should still remain in the house, more so in the three small bedrooms, where there were still bedsheets and clothes in the closets.

In one room I located a diary, which confirmed the pilot's suspicions that we were somewhere on chilly Tierra del Fuego, that southernmost island at whose bottom the Atlantic and Pacific meet and which skirts the ice-cold Antarctic. It further confirmed my suspicions that the past residents were a family of gauchos. The writer was a girl of about fifteen or sixteen years of age in my estimation, and the diary is peculiar, since it is written more like random thoughts hurriedly scrawled, than as a typical compendium of a day's events and thoughts. The reasonably long age of the diary also unsettled me. Why had no one else been here since the time it had been written and then carried it off? Was there some meaning, also, in the fact that it had been penned at the dawn of the 'flying saucer' age? With curiosity I took up the small book, wiping off the dust and cobwebs, and with slow mounting horror, in that house between mountains, sky and land, started to read it.

* * *

November 14, 1951

Uncle said the thing squirmed on the ground like a giant worm, but he couldn't get a good look at it since it quickly disappeared into a huge hole that Uncle could fit in. Later on I went to my window and looked up at the stars. Father says the stars are eyes.

* * *

November 29, 1951

The whales sing to the night, Uncle said, when he returned from the coast. He also saw icebergs on the water. He also said a man and his horse got lost from them in a fog so he didn't come.

* * *

December 2, 1951

The disappeared man came today. He said he'd only been riding for two hours.

* * *

December 3, 1951

Mom keeps telling me we should live our lives like nothing is happening. I try to. Uncle tried to remember if the old Fuegian or Patagonian Indians had any stories about these things. He said they didn't.

***

December 4, 1951

This morning I overheard Mom and Dad fighting. Dad was saying how hard life is, and then this happening. He said he can't leave us to go to the sheep farm to work. Over yerba maté tea today Uncle told us he thinks those things come originally from far in space and they're a danger not only to us but to the world. He says we should tell more people, no matter how much they think we're crazy. I believe him.

***

Undated

Men came today. They stayed overnight and nothing happened. They laughed at my dad and uncle. They said they're not true gauchos.

***

Undated

I saw one good today standing nearby. Like Uncle describes them. Uncle says there's more now. I hate looking out my window at the mountains, where Grandma says they come from. Mom says from a pit in the ground, like devils from hell. Christmas and New Year's is coming soon.

***

December 15, 1951

There are more of them now. Every night they surround the house. Every night I hear the strange buzzing sound they make to the sky. I dreamt last night I saw them falling from the sky, millions of them like snowflakes. I hear everyone crying secretly. I want to run away to Ushuaia or Rio Grande, where there's more light. I want to go to school. I want to kill them all. I would even run into the Antarctic.

* * *

Undated

More friends came from close to where the Beagle Channel is today. They showed themselves to them. I don't understand those things. Why do they only show themselves to some people? What do they want?

* * *

January 10, 1952

Christmas and New Year's passed already. I got few presents. I pray a lot.

* * *

January 13, 1952

We're taking the two living horses. It's late and foggy and Uncle and his friends shot at the things near the foothills. He said he saw one eating Heber, or at least he thinks it was eating him. It was impossible to see clearly. It was lying on the grass, a doughy, glistening, maggoty thing, Uncle says, and Heber was sticking out of the top of its head. All Uncle could see were Heber's legs and boots and mid-waist where the thing's mouth started, and then the rest of it. Heber was slimy. Uncle shot it again and again. They're outside now. I hear them buzzing, and I hear more in the mountains and in the woods and on the prairie. Heber's brother keeps crying and we're leaving. It's raining and Father says we'll carry what we can and send for our things later. I want to see Lorena to tell her about all this. I can see their shadows outside. I can hear their buzzing.

* * *

Undated (or perhaps at a later hour from the last entry)

I'm alone now and I feel like I'm falling into a dark hole.

* * *

Finishing the diary, I put the book down and became fully aware of how dark it had become. I went to the window and saw rain, and a fog so thick I couldn't see clearly past a few feet in this gray weather of the south. The plane and the mountains were completely obscured. I could also now hear the strange buzzing noise I'd heard by the plane—the same noise so ominously described in the diary. Then I heard something enter the house where the kitchen was.

If it hadn't been for my experience in the plane, I would have thought the diary's contents a confabulated fantasy. As it was, in the darkness, alone as I was, having just read that suggestive little tome, an overpowering sensation of menace and dread gripped me.

I quickly tried to open the bedroom window, but it was jammed. Trapped in that tiny bedroom, nothing helped to reassure my panic—especially when I heard the something move into the small living room, and then a rapid flapping sound like those of innumerable wings, followed in an instant by wrong-sounding footsteps, heading through the passageway in my direction.

I moved as quickly and as silently as I could towards the open doorway. I didn't dare close the door, since then the thing in the passageway would be made too obviously aware of my intrusion.

I waited breathlessly by the side of the doorway. I planned to bolt as soon as whatever was coming passed through it, or passed the bedroom altogether.

As I looked from my corner, I saw sideways from the door entrance, entering, a white malformed massy head on a thick palpitating stalk of a neck, with what appeared like huge protruding teeth atop it and a slimy proboscis dangling down. Around the creature's head I discerned, scattered haphazardly around it, several deep-set and disturbing eyes. I saw no more as now, in complete delirium, I instantly decided to run and jump out the window.

* * *

The pilot said I appeared bloody, wet and banging on the outside of the plane. He hurriedly let me in. With me I carried the diary, though I don't remember having grabbed it. After this I began again to remember things, my last memory being a sensation of falling. We were both in an awful state. The things had manifested themselves to him also. He was surprised to see me alive.

Looking out the window of the plane, I saw that the cursed fog was not as thick here. I also saw the weird varied shapes of the creatures outside, hundreds of them writhing blasphemously atop the foothills, circling a huge jagged rock of protruding mountain. They seemed to sing, and I heard answering echoes farther down and from above the receding mountains. The world was filled with their buzzing. A terrible vision overpowered my imagination. I envisioned those inhuman buzzing sounds in the night, atop those solitary peaks, spreading like signal fires atop the mountains; first here, then into the main of the Andes Mountains, and still vastly further up into Central America, all through Mexico and into the North American Sierra Madre and the Canadian Rockies, until finally those voices disappear into mist and snow in the Arctic, far on the other side of the world, all the while unheard by knowing human ears.

Long, unhallowed hours passed in that small plane, while that maddening noise continued. We saw lights moving through the mist and clouds, and had wild impressions of monstrous goings-on and huge things moving just beyond and above our vision. I thought I heard the sounds of floating heavy machinery through the hard, pattering rain.

"We are being visited from another world, or another dimension, my friend," the pilot once said to me in a crazed laughing fit, "or we are visiting them. Maybe they came in a falling hollow meteor? What demonic technology they must possess! Have you noticed there are no animals here? Maybe we are being taken over."

"Shut up!" I remember yelling more than once at him that night.

The strange buzzing noise continued (is it any wonder that even now I cannot stand the buzzing of insects or the sound of crickets on lonely dark nights outside my house?) and then I heard the loud shattering of a passenger window. I could dimly see outside the broken window a grotesque, quivering equine-like shape, its malformed hand groping blindly and wildly in the plane. It moaned loudly and I felt at once a sense of revulsion and outright horror, for what else could I have expected to happen? The many-eyed monstrosity reverently carried a red dress, and I was convinced this was the same nightmare creature I'd seen in the house and was also somehow the author of the tome I'd brought: the owner of her own stolen diary, or perhaps even more grotesquely, somehow a symbiosis of the whole family, and other wildlife beasts, mixed into one alien thing.

The creature eventually stopped and left to join the others. They buzzed all night in the mountains and paid us no heed.

"I should have brought a gun. I should have brought a gun," the pilot repeated to himself in a corner, while sitting down and resigned to any outcome.

"*As flies to wanton boys are we to the gods, they kill us for their sport,*" I quoted more than once during that terrible ordeal, as I succumbed slowly and completely to the menace of those beings' otherness and suggestive outside power.

* * *

We were found the next afternoon by a military helicopter from the Chilean city of Puerto Williams. The sun was out and in its clear glow, with the past day and night's occurrence now gone, the solitary landscape looked beautiful and peaceful—an oasis from the noise and bustle of the rest of the world.

We were at a loss to explain what had happened. A rescuer told us that a black-out had also hit that night in certain parts of southern Chile and Argentina. She laughed when she told us that strange lights were also reported in the sky. I asked the woman circumspectly if there had ever been a small lone homestead far in the distance, by the wooded area and in the expanse of grassland (since now there was nothing I could see) and she answered, "There hasn't been a house on that spot for years and years."

It would be an understatement to say I don't have answers to all my questions, and I don't expect ever to find any. I also don't know what the meaning of the experience was with the cryptic beings, if there is one. I have heard, though, rumors of vast underground cities built by no human hands lying deserted for eons beneath the ice shields of Antarctica and below certain mounds in Oklahoma, which might shed some light on my experience. I'll never find out, however, since I don't like the sight of mountains or high hills, and I also don't travel to secluded places anymore, preferring to spend my time within well-lit city limits.

Eventually, our misadventure was blamed on pilot error.

Publication History

"R.," Shoggoth.net, Edited by Matt Wiseman, 2015

"The Seeder from the Stars," *Historical Lovecraft: Tales of Horror through Time*, Innsmouth Free Press, Edited by Silvia Moreno-Garcia and Paula R. Stiles, 2011

"Interview Excerpted from a Blog Site Dedicated to Supernatural Investigations," *NonBinary Review* #5 Online Selection, Zoetic Press, Edited by Lise Quintana, 2015

"The Green World," *Innsmouth Magazine* #5, Publisher: Silvia Moreno-Garcia, Editor-in-Chief: Paula R. Stiles, 2010

"The Reverie of Space," *The Society of Classical Poets*, Edited by Evan Mantyk, 2013

"Extraction," *The Lovecraft eZine* #17, Edited by Mike Davis, 2012

"The Sleeper on the Throne," *Innsmouth Magazine* #10, Publisher: Silvia Moreno-Garcia, Editor-in-Chief: Paula R. Stiles, 2012

"A Monster in the Midst," *Fungi*, Innsmouth Free Press, Edited by Orrin Grey and Silvia Moreno-Garcia, 2012

"Imagination," original to this publication

"The Lost Letter of Lucian of Samosata, Concerning Apollinaris and the Star Ones: A Fragment," Amazon.com Services LLC, Self-Published by Julio Toro San Martin, 2014

"The Travel of Epaenetus the Wise, or the Missing Lord," *Mythos Fragments*, Atlantean Publishing, Edited by DJ Tyrer, 2015

"The Second Lost Letter of Lucian of Samosata, Or The Night of Pan," Amazon.com Services LLC, Self-Published by Julio Toro San Martin, 2016

"R'lyeh: Two Irregular Sonnets," formerly published as "R'lyeh: Two Sonnets," *Tigershark Magazine* #5, Tigershark Publishing, Edited by DS Davidson, 2014

"Periphery", *Fall of Cthulhu*, Horrified Press, Edited by Douglas Draa, 2015

"Settled", Acidic Fiction.com, Edited by Steven X Davis, 2015

"Beastmen of Beringia," *Static Movement*, Edited by Chris Bartholomew, 2014

"The Lost City of the Neanderthals," *Aphelion*, Edited by Nate Kailhofer, 2016

"Upon a Fearful Summons," formerly published as "Upon a Fearful Summon," *Expanded Horizons* #55, Edited by Dash, 2017

"Iron Horse and Butterfly," formerly published as "Iron Horse and Butterfly: The Truth about Clan Oshito," Amazon.com Services LLC, Self-Published by Julio Toro San Martin, 2014

"Iron Footfalls," *Future Lovecraft*, Innsmouth Free Press, Edited by Silvia Moreno-Garcia and Paula R. Stiles, 2011

"The Call of the Siren," Tigershark Magazine #7, Tigershark Publishing, Edited by DS Davidson, 2014

"Among the Dark Places of the Earth," *The Lovecraft eZine* #9, Edited by Mike Davis, 2011

About the Author

Julio Toro San Martin was born in Chile and grew up in Toronto, Canada. He spends most of his days working and nights reading almost anything from history and weird/fantasy fiction to Elizabethan drama, to the latest bestselling novels. He writes because he is driven to and can't imagine doing anything else.

www.ingramcontent.com/pod-product-compliance
Lightning Source LLC
Chambersburg PA
CBHW030117260626
47156CB00008B/2690